F_{THE}EUD

NOVELS BY THOMAS BERGER

THE FEUD

a novel by ————————

THOMAS BERGER

A DELTA BOOK/SEYMOUR LAWRENCE

TO MICK MOONEY

CHAPTER

1

One Saturday morning in the middle of October, Dolf Beeler, a burly, beer-bellied foreman at the plant in Millville, but who lived in the neighboring town of Hornbeck, came over to Bud's Hardware in Millville to buy paint remover and steel wool for the purpose of stripping a supposedly solid-walnut dresser to the wood that underlay the many coats of varnish. Years before, in an expansive moment after a good meal, Dolf had promised his wife he would begin this job the following evening. It was typical of him not to have acted quickly on his promise, though it was also characteristic that he did not forget or dismiss it and that he acted on it eventually, for he was a good husband and a nice man, and therefore his wife—called "Bobby," from "Roberta"—did not pester him about this or anything else.

"Paint remover," said the skinny high-school-aged boy back of the hardware-store counter. "Did you want a quart or a pint of that?"

Dolf chewed awhile on his unlit stogie. He had never

stripped a piece of furniture before and therefore had no sense of how much fluid would be required. A certain pride kept him from asking the pimply-faced kid before him. He would have preferred to be waited on by the grown man farther along the counter, who was presumably Bud, the owner, but the latter was engaged in conversation with a thin, white-faced man whom Dolf heard him address as "Reverend."

Though he had worked in this town for years, and lived in Hornbeck only a mile from the Millville line, Dolf's acquaintance with many of its essential personages was slight. He knew none of its clergymen, police officers, doctors, lawyers, and no teachers except a substitute practitioner in the grade school, who was married to a man who worked under him at the plant. Dolf had come to Millville's hardware store today because the one in Hornbeck was closed, owing to the recent suicide of its owner, George Wiedemeyer, for reasons as yet unexplained.

"Lemme look at the cans," Dolf told the boy. "I know what a pint and quart is, but I can get an idea if . . ."

"Sure thing," answered the lad, who had a quick, bright manner that Dolf never really liked to see in a young person: it seemed too fresh. "But I'll have to ask you to get rid of that cigar."

Dolf had removed the stogie from his teeth while pondering on the needed quantity of the paint remover. He put the butt back now and said, through it, "It ain't lighted."

"Well," said the boy, "I grant it don't look like smoke is coming from it, but you know—"

"You just let me worry about that," growled Dolf, who had not lived half a century to be criticized by some kid with pimples. "You just do your job and show me that paint remover."

Now the boy was stung. "We got danger of fire back there. It ain't my own idea—"

"What's trouble here?" asked the man who had been talking with the preacher but had now said good-bye to him and come up the counter opposite Dolf's position.

"I need some paint remover," Dolf said disagreeably. "If you people don't want to sell it to me, I'll take my business elsewhere."

The hardware man, who was bald in the middle of his head and wore a suit coat, a sweater vest, and a black bow tie, spoke reproachfully to the lad. "Well, why don't you take care of this genmun, Junior? We got all the paint remover in the world out back."

"Sure," Junior answered. "But I don't think he should be smoking a cigar back there."

"Oh." The bald-headed man nibbled his upper lip. "I guess I'd have to say the boy is right," he told Dolf, though looking at the counter top. "There's strict no smoking due to the insurance."

Dolf breathed strenuously in and out, past the stogie, which anyone could see was dead. He was not given to excess speech.

The boy suddenly looked worried. "He says it's out, though, Dad. So he ain't really smoking."

Dolf turned his weighty head and smirked in chagrin at no one, though the preacher had halted near the door to observe the argument from afar.

The hardware man, who Dolf believed was probably Bud, the owner, said to his son, in some exasperation, "Well, then, Junior, I don't know why you're making a fuss."

Dolf spoke then. "Because he's too fresh."

Bud (if it was he) flinched a little but made no rejoinder—which showed business sense.

The boy however decided to take it as an insult. "Oh, yeah?" he said. "Well, you just—"

His father slapped his face at this point. "Don't you ever answer back," said Bud, in a voice that was earnest but strangely calm.

Even Dolf thought that a little too strong. By now he was beginning to regret having chosen this day, after two years, for the stripping of Bobby's old dresser, which might not even be solid walnut, and when Bud went on to demand that his son apologize, Dolf stepped away from the counter.

"No," said he. "That's all right. Forget it."

"No sirree!" cried Bud, his bow tie bobbing at his Adam's apple. "We ain't going to lose customers through bad manners, I'll guarantee you that." He stared sternly at his son, whose face was flushed where it had been hit, whose eyes had got smaller with sullenness.

The minister had come back from the door. He wore a dark suit and a felt hat. He peered at Dolf for a while and then said, "You oughta get rid of your butts before you enter an establishment. Then there won't be any trouble about them, lighted or not."

This was too much. Dolf believed all preachers were loafers, and he didn't go to church even in Hornbeck, though his wife did. He said now, "You stick your nose into things that don't concern you, and you get it broke off."

"Oho," the minister said ominously. "You better be careful who you're talking to."

"Oh the hell with you!" Dolf said, and started to leave the place, but the preacher, though considerably smaller, took a spread-legged stance, blocking the route to the door.

"You bum you," he said levelly. "We got a vagrancy law in this town."

Bud now tried to call things back to reason. "He don't mean no harm, I'm sure, Reverton. Mister, I'll just go get that paint remover for you." However, he made no actual physical move.

So the man wasn't even a preacher. "Well, *Reverton*, if that's your goddam name," said Dolf. "You just get yourself out of my goddam way or you're gonna have my goddam foot in your ass."

Bud cried in outrage, "You can't use foul language in my store!"

Reverton swept back the tail of his suit coat and pulled a revolver from a holster that hung there. "You sumbitch," he said to Dolf. "You just back up against that there counter, you shit-heel bum. I know how to handle your kind."

Dolf could not believe in the reality of this sequence of events. You went to buy paint remover and you had a gun pulled on you? He now tried to be reasonable.

"See," he said to Reverton, "I never came over here to fight or anything." This was what he tried to say, but having a gun pointed at him seemed to freeze the words in his throat. What he heard emerge was at least to himself an incomprehensible mumble.

Reverton appeared to be enraged. "You dirty sumbitch," he said through clenched teeth, and he thumbed back the hammer of his pistol, with a sickening sound.

Dolf fell to his knees on the wooden floor, his hands crossed over his protuberant belly. But then he lifted them in supplication. He pleaded, "Oh, God, don't kill me," and sobbed, and blubbered, and degraded himself so thoroughly that later on he could not remember it without wanting to vomit.

Yet Reverton was not appeased. "Get up off'n this floor,"

he said. "You bum, you think you can make fun of me in front of my relatives? *Kill* you? I'll make you eat them words! Stick out your hands." From under his coat, in the back, he produced a pair of handcuffs.

What did this mean? Dolf struggled to get to his feet. He extended his wrists. "Are you some kind of cop?"

Reverton snapped the cuffs on him. "What do you think, brother?" He sneered into Dolf's face.

"How come you ain't in uniform?"

"When the day comes I got to explain anything to the likes of you," said Reverton, and never finished the statement.

Dolf now almost wailed. "Look here, officer. I'm a foreman down at the plant, right here in Millville. I live right over in Hornbeck. Everybody knows me over there—Dolf Beeler? And anybody down work can vouch for me come Monday. They're closed up down there today, except the watchman, he's an old-timer, Jim Watney? Listen, I'm O.K. I ain't no troublemaker. I'm a second cousin by marriage of the mayor over there, you know, Hornbeck? Horace Hemple? You might know him."

Reverton was looking at him expressionlessly. After fastening the handcuffs, he had put his pistol in its holster. Finally he spoke laconically. "Anybody could make them claims."

Bud came around from behind the counter. He said, "I figure he's telling the truth, Rev. All that stuff could be checked too easy to lie. Just let me get that paint remover. He don't mean no harm. I can see that."

Reverton went into the lower right pocket of his black vest and brought out a little brass key. He held it up, displayed it to Dolf between thumb and forefinger. He narrowed his eyes, which were normally close together, and showed the tips of his wolfish teeth.

"Welllll . . ." He was making the most of the moment. "I might take a better view of it if you was to apologize."

Dolf was forced to gesture with both hands, as if praying. He was not sure of what he was supposed to atone for, but he said, "O.K., I'm sorry if I caused you any trouble."

Reverton shrugged and unlocked the handcuffs. "You just keep your nose clean from now on."

Dolf nodded dumbly, rubbing his wrists. He could not understand what had happened to him, how on a normal Saturday morning he could have had such a terrible experience. On the one hand he couldn't wait to get home and tell Bobby about it, while on the other he was not sure he could endure the shame of doing so. Luckily nobody he knew had witnessed the scene.

Bud said, "I'll just step back to the storeroom and get the paint remover. I figure you'll want at least a half gallon." Dolf remembered later that the little skunk had made that a statement and not a question.

Reverton bade good-bye to Bud and Junior. He left the store without looking at Dolf. When Bud had gone through a door in the back, Dolf asked the kid, "I guess that cop was off duty?"

Junior said, "He's a railroad detective, is what he is."

"He's not a town cop?"

"He's what you call a railroad dick," said Junior. "He's up in the yard, in Hamburg. He rousts a lot of hoboes up there."

"What's he doing down here?"

"He's my dad's cousin, see."

Dolf went to the door of the storeroom. Bud was just coming out with a half-gallon can in his grasp.

"I just want you to tell your little bastard of a cousin," said Dolf, "who ain't even a real cop, that I'm going to get him." He put his index finger, like a weapon, in Bud's face. "I'm going to get him. He won't know when nor how, but I'm gonna get him."

Bud changed color. He lowered the can to the floor and said, "That was quite a misunderstanding. Thing is, Rev deals with the type of person you got to be mean with or they'll walk all over you. He don't understand respectable customers. He thinks everybody he don't know is a tramp. He's got a hair-trigger temper and goes off half-cocked. He means well, but he goes too far sometimes." He sank his hands into his pants pockets and kicked at some imaginary objects on the floor to the left of the can. "Tell you what I'm willing to do, so there won't be any hard feelings. I'll give you a price on this here paint remover. I'll shave the profit." He smiled expectantly at Dolf.

"You go shave your ass and walk backwards," said Dolf. "You'll be prettier."

He turned and strode ponderously to the front door, tore it open, stepped out, and slammed it behind him. The glass vibrated violently but did not shatter. On the sidewalk he scanned both sides of the street for Reverton—planning, if he spotted him, to sneak up and put a hand across his throat from behind, lift him off his feet while going after his gun with the other hand. From there on the details were not filled in, though he had no intent to shoot him: maybe take the shells from the pistol, then smash it on the cement pavement, and probably kick Reverton's ass publicly, with the heavy work shoes he wore even on Saturday.

But he could not identify his intended prey among the people on the sidewalks of Millville's block-long business district.

Somebody asked, "What're you doing over here on Saturday, Dolf?"

He turned and saw a guy named Walt Huff, who worked in the stockroom at the plant. Huff was wearing a canvas jacket and a corduroy hunting cap. Over his shoulder he carried a twelve-gauge shotgun, broken open at the breech.

Without acknowledgment of his greeting Dolf asked, "Know a guy comes around here to this hardware, a railroad dick named Reverton?"

Huff grinned. "I was just down the dump, potting a few rats with this new gun of mine. I just bought it from Bud."

"Bud's Hardware?"

Huff said, "There ain't much left of any rat who gets it with double-O buckshot. I splattered a few across the landscape."

"Bud's Hardware sells guns?"

"I guess they all do, don't they?"

Dolf had never owned a gun, not even an air rifle. He had never cared for the outdoor sports. His game was duckpins.

"I got this gun for rabbit," said Huff. "I got the double-O just to hit rats, to break in the gun. There was some kids downere with twenny-twos. They couldn't hit a thing. They like to shit when they seen me blast a rat. . . . Reverton, huh? He wouldn't be that cousin of Bud's, would he?"

"Sure he is: guy with little beady eyes and he wears a full suit of clothes, shirt and tie, and a felt fedora."

"I guess I've seen him around. I never knew he was a railroad dick."

"He claims to be," said Dolf. "If you see him, tell him I'm looking for him."

"I think Reverton's his first name," said Huff, "now that I think of it. He was Bud's uncle's son on his mother's side. His last name would be Kirby."

Dolf scowled. "Well, you do know him, don't you?"

"Only a little. Bud's wife and mine are sisters. Bud Bullard's my brother-in-law, but I don't keep up that much with his side."

So here was a guy who came out of nowhere, a fellow Dolf knew only at work and not well even there, and he turned out to have none-too-distant family ties to the enemy. Huff would now go into the store and hear from his brother-in-law, and nephew as well, the story of Dolf Beeler's humiliation.

"What should I tell him you want him for?" Huff asked. "Or is it confidential?"

"That's right," said Dolf.

"Well, I'll tell him."

"You know him pretty well?" Dolf was developing a hatred for Huff.

"I forgot. Me and him seen them play softball down at the Legion field."

"I wouldn't be surprised," said Dolf, "if you two turned out to be real close."

"Naw." Huff started to grin, then checked the impulse. "I don't know him that well."

Dolf wondered whether he was being made a fool of. "Listen," he said. "I want to give him a five-spot."

Huff whistled. "By George, he will sure be glad to hear about that."

Dolf nodded and got into his car, which was parked at the curb a step away. If Huff went into the store and learned of the incident, it would be all over the plant on Monday morning.

When he reached home he left the car in the driveway outside the garage: washing it was among his son Tony's duties on Saturday. Tony, a thickset lad of seventeen who wore glasses, was raking the leaves that had fallen from an elm in the corner of the yard. He was a responsible boy and had never given Dolf any trouble, perhaps because of his poor vision. Boys that had some physical defect were almost invariably hardworking and good-natured: Dolf knew that for a fact.

"Say, Tony," he said, walking to the boy, "you know many kids from Millville? I know you know some, from that summer job at the plant. And maybe playing football?"

Despite his glasses, Tony played left guard on the high-school team, wearing a mask over his specs, which furthermore he taped to his head at the temples. He was a powerful lineman who could cast fear into the opposing players.

"A few I guess," he said now to his dad. "Any one in particular?"

"I was wondering if you knew anybody named Bullard?" As a young fellow Dolf had had a build something like Tony's, and when he was near his son nowadays he stood a little straighter and sucked his belly in somewhat, though he considered himself too old and too fat to be able to make much difference. He felt both pride and envy when he supposed that already Tony could probably take him. Though not yet as tall as his father, Tony was more muscular because of the weight lifting he did daily.

Tony now said, "I'll have to think about that." Behind the glasses he had his mother's face, more sensitive than Dolf's. He banged the tines of the rake on the ground, so as to free the leaves stuck there. It was not the implement made specifically for leaves, but rather the iron-spiked rake used to scratch the ground for gardening.

Tony asked, "Does it have to be a guy?"

Dolf raised his eyebrows. "I guess not."

"Well, there was this girl," said Tony. When seen through the thickest part of the lenses his eyes always seemed to be staring intensely.

"Girl?"

"They have those park dances on Friday nights over in Millville," Tony said. "I went over there once or twice."

Dolf lowered his head. "What was her name?"

"It might of been Bullard."

"Oh yeah?" Dolf decided he wasn't interested in the womenfolk of that family.

"I think her name was Eva Bullard."

"You wouldn't know if her father owned that hardware store over there, would you?"

"Naw, I don't know."

Dolf asked sharply, "You didn't take her out or anything?"

Tony looked down and kicked the ground with the rubber toe of his gym shoe. "I only danced with her once."

Dolf thrust out his chin. "You didn't try . . ." He left the rest unsaid.

Tony colored violently. "No, nothing like that."

Dolf said, "I don't know if you have ever heard of what they call a social disease," said Dolf. "I'll tell you this, you wanna be an athlete or get an appointment to Annapolis, or be respected in life, you have to watch yourself. I'm sorry I got to use this kind of language, but you ought to get to know what a cundrum is and how to use one." Now Dolf could feel himself color, and in reaction he said angrily, "Goddammit, Tony, you got to realize them Bullards are no good!"

"You know them?"

Dolf imposed a calm upon himself. He did not want to lose his dignity before his son. "I had a run-in with a few of them just now. They're not much. But they're sneaky, and they know all the dirty tricks. They'll spit in your eye and hit below the belt." He breathed awhile, looking past his son. "They're all skinny little monkeys, and they're yellow and crafty."

"What did they do to you?"

Dolf was offended by the form of the question, which implied that he had been whipped. "I didn't let 'em get away with anything, but"—he shook his finger—"I'm going to teach them a lesson they won't soon forget."

Tony hesitated for a moment and then he said, "Dad, I'm sorry about that Bullard girl, but I didn't know—"

"Tony, there wasn't nothing wrong with that at the time." Dolf patted his son's broad shoulder. "I never heard of these Bullards until today, though as it turned out, they're related to a guy name of Walt Huff, who works over at the plant in the stockroom."

"Huff?" asked Tony. "Would he have a boy about my age?"

"This guy wouldn't be old enough, I don't think. But maybe he's got older brothers or sisters."

"I had a fight with a kid named Al Huff last winter," Tony said. "After the basketball game with Millville, in that empty lot back of school? He bumped into me when we was all leaving, and he called me a four-eyed slob."

Dolf asked fiercely, "Did you whip the son of a bitch?"

"I think I hurt him. I don't see too good with my specs off. I hit him a coupla good ones, I know that. It was his friends stopped the fight." He looked worried. "I wonder if he's related to the Bullards?"

"I hope so," said Dolf. "The goddam dirty trash! . . . Tony, you're a good boy. I wanna give you something, a little piece of change. Maybe you can get yourself a date with some nice girl tonight. Not a pig like that Bullard, but some real nice girl like Mary Catherine Lutz." He pointed diagonally across the back alley to the Lutz residence, in the back yard of which was an empty dog house: their Airedale, a valuable, supposedly pedigreed animal, had broken his chain last year and run away in pursuit of a mongrel bitch in heat and never returned. Dolf found a dollar bill in his pants pocket and surrendered it to his son.

Tony backed away.

Dolf pressed the bill on him. "Come on, you got it coming. You're a good boy, and I'm proud to call you son." He had a very fine feeling with regard to this interchange: there weren't many lads in this day and age with the kind of principles to refuse offered money.

Tony finally took the dollar and mumbled his thanks.

Dolf socked his son affectionately in the meatiest part of the biceps: it felt like hitting a country ham. Too bad about Tony's bad eyes: he would have made a real prizefighter.

Dolf had climbed the back-door steps and was about to go in the kitchen door when his wife opened it to come out.

She backed up. "I was just going to holler that lunch is ready."

The idea of food was suddenly repulsive to him, he who usually packed it away. He said, "Say, Bobby, when I finally get around to stripping your old dresser, what do you know? I get in a fight."

She put her hands on her broad hips. "You didn't get hurt?"

"Not me! You oughta see the other guy." Having made the weary joke, he went to the oilcloth-covered table that was in the ell of the big kitchen and took the chair at its head. He lowered his face into his hands and then took it out to look at his wife, who was still watching him carefully. He proceeded to tell her the truth about the incident at Bullard's hardware.

"Well," said she in her comfortable and comforting

voice, "you can't call that a fight. There wasn't nothing much you could do with a gun in your belly."

"That might be right," said Dolf. "It might not of been my fault, any of it, but *God damn it*, I feel real bad. I feel like somebody threw filth on me for no reason. I've got to pay them back, Bobby."

"What I was wondering," said she, standing in the middle of the kitchen, "was is it legal for somebody who isn't a real policeman to pull a gun that way on a person who isn't doing anything wrong?"

Dolf shook his head. "You mean, I should hire a lawyer? I don't have that kinda money. Why, he'd charge me five bucks just to answer the question. Anyhow, that's the yellow way out."

Roberta said, "What I mean is you could go to the police in Millville, the real ones, and prefer charges."

"I tell you what that would lead to," said Dolf, with a gesture of hopelessness. "Just their word against mine, and there was twó of them, not even counting the kid. Anyway, the local police always favor a merchant in their own town: that figures." He shook his head. "For that matter, they might have a relative on the force."

Bobby crossed her big arms, which were bare below the elbow. Except for church services on Sunday she wore loose housedresses she made herself. She had a good deal of gray in her hair, but her plump cheeks, flecked with permanent freckles below the hazel eyes, had a youthful color and sheen.

"But you would be telling the truth."

Dolf groaned, "Aw, I don't know, Bobby." But talking with his wife as usual made him feel better, and when she said, "Let me get some soup in you before you do anything," his appetite suddenly returned.

Roberta went to call their other boy from upstairs. Meanwhile Tony came in unsummoned from outside. Seeing him vigorously wash his hands at the sink reminded Dolf that he should make his own ablutions, and he did so, accepting from the patiently waiting Tony the coarse, outsized off-white towel, a former flour bag that had been hemmed up.

Bobby returned to the kitchen and served four large bowls of thick vegetable soup that swarmed with yellow dumplings. She waited patiently for hers to cool, but both Dolf and Tony, with much spoon-blowing, had swallowed half their portions by the time the second son arrived. His formal name was Adolf, Jr., but so as to forestall confusion he had since childhood been called Jack. He was a studious sort and spent most of his time reading books, yet, as luck would have it, enjoyed perfect vision. At fifteen he was of average size, a couple of inches shorter than his brother. His assigned chores were, according to his own preference, indoors if possible, cleaning the basement and the like, though he carried out the garbage. He and Tony, being of different temperaments, had always got on well. They were rarely seen together except on such occasions as this.

Dolf himself hardly did more than glance at the newspaper, and he resented Jack's obsession with reading more than he himself understood, and he was usually, secretly, exasperated with him. For example, in distinction to Tony, Jack was never so eager for a meal that he came to it without being called. When he *was* summoned, however, he arrived with reasonable promptness and therefore could not be criticized.

Vapors from the hot soup put a fog onto Tony's glasses. He removed them and cleaned them on some folded squares of toilet paper he carried in his pocket for that purpose. His face had the funny blurred look that habitual wearers of eyeglasses seemed to have when they took them off: as if the spectacles are normally worn instead by the other person. Dolf couldn't help feeling that the boy would be defenseless at such a time, but if he had whipped the Huff kid he was far from it.

Squinting at his father, Tony said, "I thought of somebody else I know over in Millville: the oculist who makes my glasses."

Dolf swallowed some soup without chewing the soft solids therein. That was a luxury; his teeth were not all they should be. "That's right. But I don't see how he would be involved."

Tony returned the glasses to his face. "I think he's in that family."

"Doctor Adams?" Dolf knew the name well, having to pay the bills.

"He's married to a Huff," said Tony.

"I'll be damn." This man had made plenty off Tony, who though careful was often involved in the sort of strenuous activity in which glasses were broken.

Bobby gently reproved her husband. "I wish you could find a better word."

"I'm sorry," said Dolf, "I wasn't thinking." He looked toward Jack. You didn't have to worry that Tony would pick up foul language, but Jack might be another case.

Jack however was interested in the greater matter. " 'Involved'?" he asked. "What does that mean, Dad?"

Dolf dipped his spoon in the soup. "Gosh, it's a long story, Jack." Telling it to his younger son would be almost like disclosing embarrassing information to a stranger.

But Jack chided him. "Tony seems to have heard it."

His mother now remonstrated with Jack. "I wish you would respect your dad," she said. "He'll tell what he tells to whoever he wants, because he puts the food in our mouths."

Dolf was cast in the unusual but gratifying role of defending his second son. "He don't mean disrespect. I know that. He's right." He smiled at Jack. "It's your right to know. It's a family thing." Dolf suddenly felt a strong sense of affinity with them all, including Jack, and he proceeded to give a less personally degrading version of the unhappy incident in the hardware store.

That night Bud's Hardware burned to the ground, despite the strenuous efforts of not only the local volunteer firemen but also the Hornbeck department, called in for the emergency. There had been simply too much flammable merchandise on the premises, chiefly in the form of liquids like paint and turpentine, etc., but the sporting ammunition contributed as well, its explosions serving to discourage the firemen from getting as close as they might otherwise have come.

CHAPTER

2

When Bud Bullard's son, Bud Jr., told Dolf Beeler about the fire insurance that required the keeping of highly flammable substances in the back room, he was only passing on what his father had told *him*. But the truth was that the hardware store had not been insured.

"I couldn't afford the premiums," said Bud. "I figured if we was just real careful, we could get by until we got in the black." He stood there on Sunday morning, looking into the jagged, blackened, still-smoking ruin of his business.

The second shift of Millville volunteer firemen—those who had not been available the night before—had taken over from the fellows who had been called out just before midnight and had pumped water until morning. The fire companies from the neighboring towns—one of them from Beewix, eight miles away—had left by now. Bud had been on the site since someone remembered him at 4:14 A.M. and phoned his home. He wore a lumber jacket over his striped pajama shirt, the bent collar of which protruded.

He was talking to his brother-in-law, Walter Huff, who was a fireman but had not come with the company the night before, because he had been at a bowling tournament up in Medford, the county seat, and after the match the guys had drunk beer late at a Medford roadhouse to celebrate their moral victory against a team who had greatly outclassed them in every way but guts.

Bud's eyes smarted from the smoke; otherwise he had no identifiable feeling of body or soul. He could not understand why he was seemingly so stoical. The store represented not only all his own savings, but also—he had been turned down by the local bank—considerable loans from his relatives, both blood and in-law. Cousin Reverton, for example, a bachelor, had contributed the sum of money he had been awarded in a lawsuit against an interstate bus company, one of whose vehicles had smashed his car and broken his right leg and left collarbone some years before. Even Aunt Ethel Murdal had contributed a widow's mite. Bud's brother Herman, though father of four, had kicked in, as had his sister Ada and his second cousin on his mother's side, Charley Hoople.

Bud realized that he should probably shoot himself, for he could not possibly make restitution in one lifetime. The store had not been a raving success before the fire, for reasons that were not immediately understandable, but the only one that made sense was that it was a new enterprise, whereas the hardware in Hornbeck had long been established and offered prices that Bud could not match and make any kind of profit.

Walt Huff, however, had put no money in the store, claiming he had none to spare, what with the mortgage on his house and other obligations, yet he was prosperous enough to buy quite a bit of sporting goods, a state of affairs toward which Bud's feelings were complex—after all, Walt did at least purchase the shotgun, rod, reel, ammunition, etc., from him and not from his competitors, who were able to charge less—and trade was more satisfying, more professional, than any loan.

Walt's helmet was a little too large for him, coming down so low on his forehead that his eyes were almost cut off.

Bud told him, "I just feel sorry for the people that had money in this. Jesus." Sooner or later he would have to confess to them about the lack of insurance, of which they had been kept in ignorance. It had seemed useful to experiment by telling Walt, who was not involved.

Walt said, "I sure wouldn't relish the job of telling them."

"That piece of money was the only thing Rev had, you know," said Bud, who was getting a kind of comfort from putting the worst face on it. "He don't have a real home, you know. He's got a furnished room up near the railroad yard in Hamburg. He's been on his own since a kid. His old man drank himself to death, and his mom passed away from T.B. Rev was raised in the orphan asylum."

"Say," said Walt, "you mean your cousin Reverton? Guy I know from the plant was asking about him yesterday. Said he wanted to give him five dollars."

Bud shrugged. Five bucks was hardly the answer at this point.

"Speak of the devil," said Walt, nodding in indication of something beyond Bud's shoulder.

Bud turned and saw Reverton, who was dressed as always in a navy-blue serge suit, white shirt, and hat, tie, and shoes in black.

Reverton's expression was habitually somewhat sour, owing to the bony nose and the lines coming down from it to the sides of the mouth, but he was known to have strong emotions that did not always appear on his countenance.

"I was eating my Sunday flapjacks at the Railway Café," he said, "when an engineer come in who heard about this." Bud felt even worse when he saw Reverton. He said, "I don't know how it started, but it was too far gone before they put any water on it."

Walt greeted Reverton, whom he didn't know well, and then he went to join the other firemen, who were raking the debris for still-glowing embers and, when they found some, soaked them down. Of the store only a jagged wall-and-a-half and a brick chimney remained standing. Luckily there had been little wind the night before, and the building was situated between two vacant lots at the edge of the business district, having originally been constructed, just before the war, for a dairy, which grew out of the space in twenty years.

Reverton scowled at his cousin. "Them insurance are all crooked," said he. "They won't wanna pay a penny, mark my words. They'll want to prove you burned it down yourself."

Bud did not have the heart to straighten him out at this point. He said, "I figure it must of been some old wiring."

Reverton was still occupied with anticipatory bitterness. "Them insurance oughta be put outa business, if you ask me. What good are they if they won't pay off on a honest claim?" He had always believed he should have got more in damages when he had been hit by that bus, and regretted having been persuaded by the insurance company's lawyer to settle out of court. Bud knew, but would never have rubbed his nose in it, that Reverton had been at a great disadvantage in acting as his own lawyer, owing to his distrust of attorneys. Nor had his broken leg been set as well as it might have been. After receiving emergency treatment at a hospital, he had insisted on going to his own doctor for the rest of it, and the latter was not a real physician but rather an osteopath. It seemed to Bud that Reverton had a gift for blaming the wrong people for his difficulties, but of course he would never mention that theory to his cousin, of whom he was genuinely fond. He could remember him as a boy in the orphan asylum, with his hair cut an inch above the ears. Bud's parents could not afford to raise Rev along with their six other children, but on holidays they would go by streetcar to fetch him for the occasion and give him a meal and a treat to put in his pocket, an orange or something, before taking him back. He was exactly Bud's age and had been a dark, wiry kid with skinny legs below his knickers.

Bud lightly kicked the brass junction linking two lengths of dirty canvas firehose that stretched near him. "Those boys did everything they could," said he. "I know that." He turned. "Wellsir, no reason to stay around here anymore. Want to go on up home, Reverton? You're staying for Sunday dinner, I hope."

"I thought I might nose around some," Reverton said, pushing forward the organ he named, with its nostrils arched and twitching. "There might be somepin still in working order. Them little anvils you had and anything else that's all metal, wrenches or something. Axheads'll be all shot, 'cause they'll lose their temper."

Bud was amazed to hear that Reverton had noticed the merchandise at all. He had never seemed to, on his visits; and living in the furnished room as he did, he had rarely needed any kind of hardware.

"O.K., then, Rev. I think I'll go home. I don't have the

heart to poke through this mess right now. I'll see you later. You can talk to Walt if you want, though he wasn't here last night."

"Where was he?" Reverton's question was surly.

"Out of town. He didn't know about the fire."

His cousin scowled in the direction of Huff. "Fire hat's too big for him, ain't it?"

"He's a nice guy, Rev. It's just too bad my wife don't get along too good with her sister, or we'd see more of him. Say, he told me he knows some guy owes you five dollars."

Reverton immediately acquired a hunted look. "Somebody's a liar," said he. "I don't loan money and I don't gamble. Anybody says I do is a dirty dog and better not say it to my face." He called to Huff, who was knee-deep in blackened, broken wood. There had been no cellar under this structure. Given his firemanly duties, Walt would have been within his rights had he postponed acting on the summons, but he came promptly, wading out of the ruins.

"What's this story about me being owed five dollars?" Reverton asked aggressively.

"Sure," said Huff, grinning. "Dolf Beeler. I know him from down at the plant."

"That's the big fat slob was in the store yestidday!" cried Reverton. "There's who started your fire with his stinkweed cigar."

Bud said, "I forget his name. But that cigar of his wasn't lit." You had to be fair.

Walt Huff said, "I've seen him smoking his stogie many a time." He said this neutrally, however. "Anyway, you ought to collect the five-spot."

"We're gonna collect a lot more than that from the sumbitch!" Reverton had violence in his voice. "He burnt down our store! I had to call him on some lip he was giving

Junior. I pinned his ears back, and he done this dirty deed
to get even."

At first Bud was less than enthusiastic about this theory.
He put his head on the side and said, "Wellll, I donnn . . ."
But then it occurred to him that if Reverton were distracted
by the possibility of arson, the lack of fire insurance would
not seem so important to him. " 'Course," he said, "I don't
know how you can prove it."

Reverton patted his suit coat in the area of his holstered
revolver. "You just let me at him. You seen what I did to
the sumbitch yestidday."

Huff wore a quizzical expression. He pushed the fire
helmet up off his forehead, but it soon fell back, and he
took it off altogether. Big as it was, it proved unwieldy to
hold, and he returned it to his head.

"I don't know," he said. "I seen him outside the store
myself yesserday, and I think he was chewing on a dead
butt."

Reverton peered at him with little angry eyes. "Sure,
cuz he flicked off the burning part on the floor."

Bud's doubts returned. "If he did that, we would of seen
him, wouldn't we? And then what happened, it took all
day for the fire to start?"

"That's the way them things go," said Reverton. "Why,
down in the coal country they got mines that been burning
real quiet since the Year One. All of a sudden smoke and
fire shoots out of the cracks in the ground, and boils the
water in the ponds, and the ladies do their wash there."

"Is that right?" said Walt.

Reverton said, "That's how it works sometimes."

"I still say it would be hard to prove," said Bud.

"Why," said Reverton, "me and you and Junior'll say
we saw him do it."

Bud didn't much like that approach. He wasn't a saint, but to tell a downright lie about another man in a serious situation like this was not to his taste. Fortunately he was not forced to reject his cousin's idea: Walt Huff came up with the conclusive reason why it wouldn't work.

"If all of you saw him drop the hot ash off his cigar onto the wood floor," asked Walt, "why didn't none of you put it out?"

Reverton turned away for a moment with a face made dark by exasperation. When he turned back he asked Huff, "You gonna fight every idea that we cook up to look out for our family?"

Walt said, "You can figure my argument's gonna be a lot easier to handle than what the other side comes up with. If Dolf Beeler gets him a lawyer he'll make mincemeat of you unless you got some real proof."

Reverton stared hatefully at him for an instant and then he dropped his head. "Them dirty rotten shitass lawyers!"

Bud was relieved to see that Rev was conquered by reason. He himself knew very well that Beeler's dead cigar had had nothing to do with the fire. Besides, Beeler certainly hadn't looked like a man who would be rich enough to refund the damages if he *had* been guilty. That's all that would have meant anything to Bud. A Beeler imprisoned for arson would not bring back his store.

But Reverton had merely been diverted into another channel. "That makes it easier if we don't have to mess with the law. We'll just get even in our own way."

This had a chilling sound to Bud, who was a merchant, not a fighting man. "Maybe we ought to think about it first, Rev. I don't know what good any revenge would do, even if the fire was caused by some particular person." He was beginning to feel the physical effects of adversity and wondered whether he could make the half-mile walk home.

"You think too long about anything, and you won't do it," said Reverton. "We got our pride at stake here. They get away with that, and the next thing you know they'll be riding us down like dogs and violating our women and all."

Walt raised his eyebrows. "You put it pretty strong, Reverton. I've worked not with but pretty near to Beeler for some years, and I seen his wife come to the plant oncet to bring his lunch that he forgot, and then his boy had a summer job down there, heavy labor. He's a good football player. Hornbeck whipped us last Thanksgiving if you recall—"

"You're running off at the mouth," said Reverton. "And you oughta get yourself some other hat. That one's too big for you."

Walt was a good-natured soul. He just smirked and said, "I'm just saying you're exaggerating, is all. And all these helmets is the same size. They got a webbing inside that your head fits in. This one should be tighter, is all." He asked Bud, "You didn't ever put a penny in the slot when a fuse blew, didja?"

Reverton had walked away in annoyance. Bud nodded at his cousin's back and said to his brother-in-law, "Rev eats with us most every Sunday. I sure wish we could get you and Bess to come up, but she and Frieda are still on the outs, I guess."

Walt shook his head inside the helmet, which did not turn. "*Women!*" said he.

Though usually deserving of his father's characterization of him, "honest as the day is long," Tony Beeler had not been thoroughly truthful about his encounter with the Bullard girl at the Millville public park the summer before. She was somewhat shorter than average and not heavy, but she had large, firm breasts that rubbed against him when they danced, while his right hand, on her back, could feel the tense brassiere strap that crossed the deep groove of her spine. He immediately got an erection that was so powerful as to embarrass him, and he drew his pelvis in while pushing forward with his upper half, and he found his face so intimate with hers that his glasses were put at a crazy angle and their lenses were fogged by the combined breaths.

It was something of a relief, as well as a definite loss, when the next record to be heard was too fast for Tony's modest talent at dancing. He led her off the slab of concrete that served as dance floor, and took off his specs and cleaned them on the tail of his sports shirt, conveniently worn outside the trousers, squinted ritualistically before returning the glasses to his nose and, when they were once again in place, looked not at her but rather over the heads of the nearby jitterbugs.

He said, "I guess you're from Millville."

"Yeah."

"I thought you was." He now looked at the concrete in front of his own shoes, the toes of which he had freshly whitened before leaving the house. "I'm from Hornbeck."

"I thought you were," said the girl, looking earnestly at him. "Or someplace else than here."

This could have been insulting. He met her eyes at last. "You mean I look like I ain't good enough for Millville? I look like a hillbilly or something?"

She had the bluest eyes in the world, and light brown hair that hung in long strands, and a soft, wide mouth that now widened farther in a slow smile. "It's just I know most of the Millville boys. This town isn't all that big."

"Neither is Hornbeck," said Tony, "but I like it. I wish we had these dances over there, though."

"Why?" She stood almost as close to him as if they were

still dancing. He continued to be aroused though no longer in actual contact.

"I always feel better in my own town. I play football against your guys."

"I couldn't recognize you with your helmet off," the girl said, "but I have probably seen you. Two of my cousins are on the team: Gene and Norman Walmsley?"

"Norman's right halfback, I think. Gene's second string, ain't he?"

"Well, you do know them, don't you?"

"It was me who tackled Norman when his collarbone got busted."

"I remember that. You did that?"

Tony assumed a noble look. "I didn't do it to hurt him, I swear. I just play to win. I hit hard but clean."

She lowered her head. "Gee."

Suddenly Tony was completely exhausted of things to say, and he felt foolish, standing there silently next to a girl. He believed that if his friends were to see him now, they would make jeering remarks and elbow one another.

Therefore he said, "Well, I got to get going."

"O.K."

"Listen, if you see your cousin, why, you tell him I hope there's no hard feelings. I been hurt myself more than once, had some ribs busted and hurt my knee real bad: it's never been the same since. I don't blame the other guys."

"I'll be glad to tell him, but I don't know your name."

He told her and got hers in return: Eva Bullard.

"I'll see you around then, Eva." He remembered his manners, from the course in social dancing given on three successive Wednesday nights at the high-school gymnasium the year before. "Thank you very much for the pleasure of your company."

"You're welcome, I'm sure." She had probably taken a similar course at the Millville school.

He regretted that his own had not included instructions on how to jitterbug: you had to learn that on your own, but you needed a kind of nimbleness he did not naturally possess.

"I'll see you then, Eva," he said again, and he was about to leave when she punched him smartly but not painfully in the belly, giggled, and dashed away, leaving the lighted concrete plateau (tennis courts in the daytime) for the shadowy descent of the surrounding lawn. Her bouncing hair ribbon looked like a butterfly. She had fine sturdy legs, and her skirt was shorter than if it had been brand-new, because it was last year's and she was still growing. Tony liked everything he had seen of her, and he was thrilled to recognize that she had invented something to do so that he was not forced to pretend he had business elsewhere.

The night grew darker as they ran, for there was no moon or stars and the park lights, mounted on high standards, were focused on the dance floor. By the time Tony had reached the level ground and its little grove of bushes and young trees, he could no longer see so much as a flicker of Eva's dress of washed-out blue. Obviously she was hiding somewhere. His bone-on returned in the suspense of tracking her down.

But defective sight in daytime does not improve in the dark. His lenses barred some of the little light available, and he was none too reckless about peering into foliage, lest his spectacles be caught in the twigs. So after a while what he did was just to come to a stop and stand between two evergreens and flex his thick shoulders.

"Hey, Eva," he called softly in admiration. "You're nuts. You know that?"

"Oh, yeah?"

This came from behind him, but when he turned she was not there. A few more such exchanges took place, genial chidings answered by gentle taunts, and then he went around a bush and found her waiting in an attitude of mock defiance.

"I guess you think you can beat me up," she said. "Hoho, we'll just see about that. Put up your dukes." Her little balled fists were in the air between them.

"Hoho," Tony excitedly echoed. "Now you're in trouble. You're going to have some trouble sitting down after I get ahold of you."

"Oh-oh," wailed Eva, dropping her hands and putting them in back of her, probably to cup the halves of her round behind: her breasts were thereby made even more prominent. Her gestures invariably fanned Tony's ardor. He had never known a girl with that knack. She proceeded to increase his sweet torment. "I should have padded my pants!"

He managed to stay with the style of mock severity. "Well then, little girl, you mind and you won't get spanked."

"I promise," she piped in falsetto, and then before he was aware of what she was doing, she was pressed against him. She had a sweet, damp smell, like the bathtub after it had been used by his sister, who had left home by now and worked in the city as cashier in a moviehouse, and therefore he hadn't smelled that in a while: it was not perfume as such.

Since it was Eva's idea to embrace him and not vice versa, it seemed O.K. not to retract his crotch as on the dance floor, but rather to allow it to enjoy the rich friendship of her warm belly.

But then she pushed away abruptly and went running

again, out of the park now, across the street, and along the line of darkened shops. Tony did not understand the purpose of these maneuvers and felt at once exhilarated and ridiculous. He was about to be a senior in high school and had earned an all-county reputation at football, and here he was, chasing a girl along streets that did not even belong to his home town. Unknown as he was here, the police might take him for a sex fiend. Nevertheless he continued to pursue Eva until she willfully plunged into the dead end of a deep shop doorway.

Over in the park the lighted dance floor and its throng had dwindled to miniature, and the recorded music, which blared so loudly when one faced the loudspeakers, was comfortingly faint. The nearest streetlamp provided a discreet glow. No one else was on this sidewalk: the world was giving them privacy.

Eva crossed her arms behind her back, and out came her breasts again. They could not be resisted. He put a hand on each, in the most natural way in the world. They were substantial and resilient but amazingly weightless all the same. So palpable in flesh, to his vision she was just a shadow now. His wide body blocked such light as came from the streetlamp.

She was looking at him. "You're fresh." It seemed a simple statement, devoid of moral judgment, and required no answer. Tony's experience with breasts was limited. He had thus far in life managed only a few gropings, all of which had been fiercely resisted by the owners of the target organs, and when it came to whatever females possessed between the waist and, say, midway between knee and groin, he might not be so ignorant as those who were sisterless, but he had never been there even as a tourist.

Eva asked, in her softest voice, "Why did you ask me to dance? Because you thought you could get fresh with me?"

He still held her breasts. He finally said, "Huh-uh."

"Then *why*?"

She certainly liked to talk. "I guess I liked the way you look."

She said, "What I meant was, you're a senior, aren't you?"

Tony found it embarrassing to converse while in such an intimate situation. "Sure." He wished she would stay quiet so he could figure out what to do next. Try to kiss her? Or continue in the same area where he was being so successful: open her dress and invade her brassiere? But they were in a place of which the privacy could at any moment prove illusory.

Then for too long an interval she *was* silent, and not having been able to conceive a plan, he spoke next. "What are you, a junior?"

She chuckled in a deep note. "I'll just be a freshman!"

"This coming *fall*?" he asked. "You just got out of the *eighth grade*? How old are you?"

"Fourteen," said Eva. "In just a couple of weeks."

"You're thirteen right now, though?"

"Not for much longer."

Now, and only now, did he at last remember to take his hands from her breasts. "I'm sorry." He stepped back a pace. "How was I to know? You look as old as me. I guess you're growing up faster than usual." She seemed to be smiling serenely. He said, "Listen, I got to go." It would have helped had his hard-on lessened, but it had not, and it weighed him down, slowed his movements.

She followed him out of the alcove. "Are you coming to the dance next week again?"

"I don't know," Tony said. "Maybe not. Maybe I'll just stay over in Hornbeck and do something with these guys I know: lift weights or something." He had never known a

Hornbeck girl of thirteen to have had such a big milk fund: it was weird and made him feel lousy. Could she be lying about her age? But that was usually done in the other direction, so as to seem older for the purpose of buying cigarettes or beer. He wasn't a sex maniac.

"I really hope I can see you again," Eva said plaintively. "You're very nice." All at once she departed, walking at a rapid, almost military pace and not looking back.

Tony felt both relieved and bereft. He wondered what she meant by calling him "nice": because he had felt her jugs? Or because he had stopped there? The sad thing was that he *really* liked her: face, voice, eyes, hair, and, of course, body, the works. But even if he waited a year and neither of them had anybody else by the end of that time, he would be out of high school while she was just a sophomore, and so it would be as weird as ever and no more decent. Any way you looked at it, this had been a punk experience. From now on he intended to ask a girl's age before he danced with her. *Thirteen?* He could only hope that if anybody noticed them together—even just dancing, let alone running out into the dark—that such a person would not be aware of the discrepancy in their ages. He could be ruined by the kind of derision that might come from public knowledge of such a thing.

The fact was that though Tony's proficiency at football was well known, his position on the team was not one of the glamorous roles. What he did was to make the heroics of the backfield possible, but he was not himself a hero or, except while running out of the locker room with the rest of the players, a celebrity at Hornbeck High. With his thick glasses he was hardly considered a collar ad, nor was he a good dancer, nor given to witty repartee borrowed from radio comedians. He had no confidence when it came to girls, and he had had but few dates. Only two, in fact;

both with Mary Catherine Lutz, who lived across the back alley from his house, was his own age and a tomboy, and with whom, when they were younger, he had shot baskets or tossed ball—on days when he couldn't find another guy. Mary Catherine's breasts were still almost undiscernible and she was as tall as he.

It was by accident that he had come upon the dance in the Millville park. He had been taking one of his long, lone walks, and if you went more than a mile in a westerly direction you were out of Hornbeck. At the edge of the concrete floor he had seen this large-breasted, round-faced girl in the short blue wash-dress. He had found the nerve to ask her to dance because, one, she was alone, and, two, he was a stranger in Millville. He should have stayed home.

However, he returned on the same evening a week later. He had no plan beyond a vague intention to spy on Eva without her knowing he was there. He wondered whether she made a practice of letting boys feel her up, and he wanted to settle this question by personal observation. But search as he did, he could not find her on this Friday evening. After several careful tours around the concrete and the ultimate descent to the shrubs, he even went across to and along the doorways of the shops. Until he had completed his rounds it did not occur to him that he had not been prepared for what might have happened if he had seen her with a guy. He did not own her, and he wasn't a cop. It was foolish to think of making a citizen's arrest of the guy for molestation of a minor, when the boy would probably be, like Tony, himself underaged and not a notorious Hollywood movie star.

He finally walked back to Hornbeck with the conviction that Eva was just a little smart aleck, still wet behind the ears, and deserved to be taught a lesson but he hoped would not really get one unless it was administered by him.

"You know, you really ought to be more ladylike or you might find yourself in a situation too hot to handle. Some hillbilly might get the wrong idea, the way you flirt with guys, and you could find yourself in a lot of trouble. Of course, if I was around nearby someplace, and I heard you scream or cry, I'd come and I would kill him. I would beat him to death. I wouldn't care if he had a knife or a club, or if he pulled a gun on me. I'd make him eat it, I swear. You can rely on me! But you oughtn't to get yourself in this kinda spot in the first place, hanging around with bad company."

This was a new idiom for Tony. He had never before been passionately, madly, hopelessly in love. In fact, anything of that sort had always turned his stomach, and if he possibly could, he avoided movies that had to do with romance, though even comedies might spring that theme on you without warning, somewhere along the line.

But what was so rotten about this state of affairs was that no matter how great his ardor, Eva would, even after her coming birthday, be only fourteen years of age. There was no way to change that. However, when he was twenty-three she would be all of twenty, and at his thirty she would have twenty-seven, and when he was eighty, she'd be seventy-seven, so the solution was to live a long time. In the short run he continued to be a pervert, but it wasn't as bad as if he had met her when *he* was thirteen—and she nine. Of course she would not have had breasts at that age, and therefore he would not have noticed her at all. The truth was that Eva was a woman whatever her years, and they were being kept apart only by some phony theory: so, in the privacy of his room, when the lights were out, did he sometimes believe, only to see it differently on awakening in the realistic morning.

On the following Friday evening Tony was back in

Millville again, and this time he was not the only Horn-
becker at the park dance. Bill Plunkett and Wally Hines,
classmates of his, stood at the edge of the concrete slab,
staring sullenly at the dancers. He thought he might slip
behind them without attracting their attention, but no such
luck: Wally was scraping one heel, to free it of gum or
dogshit, and he lifted it for inspection, looking down over
his shoulder and then raising his eyes just as Tony came into
range.

"Hey, there's Tony Beeler," he said to Plunkett, but
speaking toward Tony, and Plunkett turned and said, "Hi,
Tony. You slumming too?"

Tony had no choice but to join them, as dreary a prospect
as that was: they weren't even particular friends of his,
just guys in the same class, and Hines had blackheads in
his nose and Plunkett looked like he might have bad
breath, his teeth being of a dingy hue. Encountering them
in Hornbeck, Tony would have been only acting naturally
if he gave them a nod and a wide berth. They would have
expected no better, not being his close associates. But the
code of normality—which he was already secretly defying
in his search for Eva Bullard—ordained that loyalty must
be extended to compatriots when on alien ground, and
even your enemy at home would be first a fellow American
if you came across him in China.

Plunkett said, "Lotsa pigs in this town." He wrinkled
his nose and tossed his head. His hair had been combed
with a lot of water and had dried hard, with the comb-
tracks still showing.

"I don't know, though, what *you'd* want with nookie,"
Plunkett told Hines, "because you're a big fruit."

"Oh, yeah?" Wally rejoined, punching the arm that Bill
raised, biceps distended, for just that purpose. "You're a
big fairy."

"Well," Tony said, "I didn't know about this dance here. I got to go and do some things for my dad. I'll see you guys." He started away.

"Hey, wait," Plunkett said. "You going back home? We'll go with you."

Tony had never had much reason to be guileful, and the only thing he could come up with now by way of discouragement was: "Naw, I got to go in the other direction."

Hines said, "Hell, that's Coontown, Tony. What are you gonna do for your old man over there? You got some relatives who are boogies?" He howled and slapped his thigh.

What bad luck to run into these two lousy guys! Tony couldn't let Hines's insult go unchallenged. He squared off in front of him.

"I don't like the way you talk, Hines," he said. "You want me to take off my glasses?"

The color left Wally's face. He said, "I was just kidding. I didn't mean it."

Plunkett looked miserable. "Come on, Tony. He was just kidding. He ain't saying you got jig blood."

"It's just dumb, see," said Tony. "I got to go now." He realized that Hines's stupid joke had turned out to be an advantage: he could use it as an excuse for escape. But he was not quick enough.

Plunkett moved closer, cupped a hand at his mouth, and said, "Here comes fresh meat." His breath lived up to Tony's worst expectations.

Tony then looked where Plunkett's elbow indicated, and he saw Eva Bullard coming toward them. She was still some forty yards away. He was aware that if he let her reach him she would speak in a manner that would reveal to Hines and Plunkett that she knew him personally. Therefore he moved rapidly in interception.

When he reached her he spoke in a low, intense voice.

"Listen, I want you to leave me alone. If those guys knew I was hanging around with some young kid they would never let me forget it." He didn't want to look at her too closely, being under such surveillance, so he turned his head toward the dance floor, where the couples were gliding to the slow music that would have suited him.

Eva was not quick to reply. When she did finally speak, it was terribly stark. "All right." She walked away. He felt horrible but did not even have the courage to watch where she went.

Instead he came back to the two lousy guys. "My cousin," he said. "That was what I was supposed to do over here: give her father a message for my dad."

Plunkett and Hines, who ordinarily would have hooted derisively as he returned to them, had been cautious now, owing to the earlier foot-in-the-mouth (*feet*, if you counted Plunkett's coarse announcement of Eva's approach), and they received his explanation impassively.

Then Hines said, "O.K., if you got your business all settled let's go home. This town stinks."

So it had ended in the worst way that could be imagined, and once over the Hornbeck line, though they respected Tony's person, Hines and Plunkett themselves traded punches and gooses and catcalls, and it was an eternity of misery before Tony could turn off at his house.

The disaster had occurred in the middle of August, which by the calendar was only two months in the past, but in emotional time the summer had become almost remote. Tony had decided to wait until Eva grew up or at least was firmly established in high school. He had now just about determined that the moment would soon be ripe to submit a bid for forgiveness. Young girls must surely have short memories, and despite her extreme youth Eva seemed a generous and understanding person: that kind of character was almost ordained by her large breasts and round face and soft brown hair. Had she been a blonde, for example, or of an angular build, or with a long upper lip, he would have had no hope. But if she had been one of those, he would not have been likely to feel as he did, or to have betrayed her, or to have been in a position to do so.

But everything had been changed by the disastrous episode involving his father in what he had to assume was *her* father's hardware store.

A heroic gesture was needed at this point. The situation had so deteriorated that only a desperate courage would do. Therefore, after rising from the dinner table early Sunday afternoon and letting it be known that he was heading for the matinee at the Hornbeck movie house, Tony instead kept going when he reached that theater and crossed over into Millville, en route to Eva's home, if he could find it.

Most people in Millville lived north of the business district, so after having walked past the establishments there, most of which were closed on the day of rest, with the exception of the only real restaurant in town, Tom's, which had both a counter and a double line of booths (and in off hours was a hangout for high-school kids with their ten-cent orders of Coke-and-potato-chips, and therefore he looked through the windows to see if Eva might perchance be within), Tony wended northward and went a block or two past one- and two-story family houses, some of which had not yet taken in the porch swings for the winter, until he saw a kid of about twelve round the next corner and come in his direction. The boy wore a knitted cap and a green plaid lumber jacket.

When the kid was about to pass him they exchanged hi's, after which Tony said, "Hey, you know where the Bullards live?"

"Sure," the boy answered. "On Macklin Street. That's

it right up there. It's about the middle of the block. You should find it easy, because there's a lot of people coming and going on account of the fire."

"Fire?"

"Their hardware store burnt down."

Tony was emotionally confused by this news. He felt even more of the kind of guilt which had been evoked by his father's account of the quarrel—for the fact was that he suspected it had been his father's fault. He was all too familiar with his old man's tendency to act in a way that was disagreeable to certain people. But on the other hand the fire could be seen as a useful distraction. By contrast the incident involving his father and Eva's relatives might already have faded from the Bullards' consciousness, occupied as it must be with the major disaster. Things might actually be better for him now that things had gone bad for the Bullards.

"I'll seeya," Tony told the kid, and went on. He turned the corner and walked about halfway down the block, and not seeing any house at which crowds were coming and going as predicted, he continued on to the next corner and was standing there in a quandary when a man came along.

"Say," Tony said, "you don't know where—"

"A lad your age addresses me as 'sir,' " said the man. "And, by God, you say 'please' when you ask something of me."

"Well, can you please tell me—"

"Sir!"

"Sir, I'm looking for the Bullard residence."

The man squinted at him. He was smaller than Tony and of a skinny build. "It might interest you to know," he said in a menacing manner, "that I am connected with that family, and I look out for them. You got that straight? Now what's your name?"

"Anton."

The man squinted again. "What's your first name? You some kinda foreigner?"

"That *is* the first," said Tony. "I think it's from some book my mother read one time. We're Americans."

The man gestured with twitching fingers, as if in reference to money. "Let's have the last name."

Tony had been postponing this information as long as possible, should this Bullard have heard about the quarrel. But now that the moment had come, he saw no reason why he should not be proud, maybe even defiant. His dad might have caused that run-in, and he himself might be somewhat warped in being interested in so young a girl as Eva, but his family was not shameful.

"It's Beeler."

The man nodded and at first spoke calmly enough. "Uh-huh. You wouldn't be from over in Hornbeck, wouldja? . . . Uh-huh. . . . I'm taking this nice and careful, see." He said this as if to himself. "You wouldn't be related to a heavyset gent what comes over and trades in the hardware, which is now burned to the ground?"

Tony lowered his eyes and nodded. This wasn't going well, but he didn't see how bad the situation had become until he looked up. The man had pulled a pistol on him.

"Looky here who I caught sneaking around outside," said the man, having pushed Tony into the Bullard living room ahead of himself. He had holstered his gun as he crossed the porch. He had no need of it in a room filled with his own crowd.

The people there stared dumbly at Tony. They were all strangers to him. Though residents of the neighboring town, they could have been Frenchmen for all he had in common with them at that moment.

"Here's your firebug," said the man. "If it wasn't his dad."

The nearest person to Tony was a heavyset middle-aged woman, seated at the end of the sofa. She was eating a piece of cake from a plate on her lap. A card table had been erected farther along the couch, but it was too far for her to reach without rising, and her coffee cup sat on the floor near the left heel of her stout shoes. She looked blankly at Tony and then forked up a morsel of cake and deposited it in her mouth.

The man peered around the room with his angry eyes. "Where's Bud?"

Someone said, "I don't know. He was here a while ago." And a man said, "Maybe down cellar."

"All right, you," his captor growled at Tony, whose wrist he clasped with bony fingers that felt like handcuffs. "Just you get marching, and remember: your life ain't worth a plugged nickel if you get smart."

"Yessir," Tony said readily. He wondered what Eva would think, if she were there, when she saw him being led as a prisoner through her house, but he was not embarrassed by this prospect, because it certainly was not his own idea or fault.

But she was not in the dining room, nor was anyone else who could be called young. The table held a number of cakes, but the people who stood around it were talking and not eating. One tall, skinny woman with a faint mustache said, "Oh; hi there, Cousin Reverton," and to Tony, whom she assumed was a legitimate member of the party, "Hi there, sonny. Now which one are you?" But Reverton pulled him onward.

In the kitchen a friendly, motherly-looking woman was tending to the enamel percolator on the stove. She gave Tony a warm smile.

But Reverton forestalled her. "He's a bad-un, Frieda. He's a Beeler!"

She acquired the same blank expression as had been displayed by those in the front room. Tony assumed she was Eva's mother. There was a certain resemblance in the shape of the face and also the plump bosom.

Reverton opened a door next to the kitchen cabinet, and with a push directed Tony to go down the rough wooden stairs. Stacks of newspapers and magazines, neatly tied, sat on the concrete floor near the bottom of the steps, no doubt awaiting collection by the Boy Scouts. There was a toilet in the Bullard basement, with a crude door of wood slats, wide open at the moment: the seat was in the raised position and looked split. Beyond this were the stationary washtubs of soapy-textured galvanized metal, and then one entire corner was filled with a workbench and its attendant tools, the smaller ones hung neatly on wall hooks and the largest, a wood-turning lathe, mounted at one end of the long bench top. Toward the other extremity was a vise of the under-table type. Everything was very clean, but it looked as if it had seen use enough: the blades of the edged tools had that subdued sheen of veteran steel, and the wooden handles were darkened and polished with the natural oils of the hand.

Reverton said, "Yessir, Bud, this pretty well settles it for my money, when it comes to who set the fire."

Tony looked around to see whom he was talking to. In the shadows beyond the furnace was a man's figure, standing in the doorway to the coal bin. He mumbled something.

Reverton said impatiently, "I tell you I found this here monkey hanging around out front. He's a Beeler! He never come here for our own good, I'll tell you that." He elbowed Tony. "You tell 'im, boy: what's your name?"

"Anton Beeler."

"How do you like that moniker?" Reverton asked. "That's some Hunky for you! . . . What are you doing over here onna peaceful Sunday, boy? How come you ain't with your own kind, eating a nice dinner if you can steal one?"

Bud came out of the coal bin. He looked as if he had been crying and then had wiped his face with hands that were dirty from coal dust.

"Just what is this, Rev?"

Reverton said to Tony, "You tell the truth, or by God I won't be responsible for your health."

Tony shrugged and addressed the man who must be Eva's father, and because of that he could not tell all the truth, for trafficking with a girl who was too young was a good deal more shameful than setting a fire. "I was just taking a walk," said he.

"That's rich!" jeered Reverton. "There's a whole town of his own to walk in, and even if he would want to come over here, it's full of plenty other streets."

Bud addressed him sternly but not unkindly. "Is that right? Did you come over here to start some trouble?"

"No sir."

"Did you start that fire?"

"No sir."

Bud asked, "Who did?"

"I didn't even know anything about it till just now when I was coming over—"

"I guess you think it's pretty funny, though?" Bud said this in melancholy irony, but Reverton made a strangling sound of rage.

"I just wish I'd been there when you struck the match," he said. "I'd of blown your goddam hand off at the wrist, you dirty little pup."

"I didn't do it," Tony said, "and I don't think it's funny, and I came over here today just on a walk, I swear. I didn't know where you lived." He could see nothing of Eva in her father's face, but when Bud turned and walked to the workbench he was reminded of her stride, which was somewhat irregular. He had previously believed it mere girlish jauntiness.

"*I'll* sweat it outa him!" said Reverton.

Bud turned around and told Tony, "You get out of here. You get out of this town. And don't you come back, or you'll be in real trouble, and that goes for your father and all the rest of you Beelers. I'm real good friends with the police over here, and I'm going to tell them to look out for any or all of you. This is our town, and we don't want you in it."

"Yes, sir," said Tony. "But—"

Bud pointed a finger in his face. "Don't you give me any back talk. You just keep your mouth shut and get out of this town."

Without warning Reverton gave Tony a tremendous shove in the back. "Get going!"

Tony climbed the stairs, Reverton behind him. Eva's mother was gone from the kitchen when they arrived there. The conversation continued in the front part of the house. It sounded lively and good-humored and was accompanied by the clinking of the silverware against china. This family convocation reminded Tony of the one held after his grandfather's funeral.

Reverton did not march him through the entire house again. They went out the kitchen door, across the back porch, and down into the yard. There he saw it, a girl's bicycle with pale blue fenders and a very worn seat: pretty soon the springs would come through and hurt her bottom. He knew it was Eva's, without knowing whether there were any other girls in the family. She had come home while he was down cellar with the men.

Reverton said, "Now we're gonna go to the town line, buster, and don't forget I'm right behind you all the way, and I can draw faster than you can move."

Suppose *she* would look out the window!

"I swear I'll go right back to Hornbeck," Tony said. "You don't have to follow me. I give you my word."

"What's a Beeler word worth?" Reverton asked the middle distance. "I'd like to know." He nodded at Tony and patted his coat at the place where he carried his gun. "Get going. I won't tell you again."

Tony obeyed. His feeling toward Eva made it impossible for him to think badly even of Reverton, who was her relative and, in protecting the Bullard family from what he honestly believed were its enemies, was guarding *her*. But Tony couldn't think of any way to commend the man without incurring his wrath, so he just applied himself quietly to the walk toward the town line and was relieved when his captor chose the closer portion of it, reached through the back streets, rather than that which ran through the contiguous business districts of the two towns.

When he saw the Hornbeck sign ahead—a modest one on this block of industrial garage, empty lots, and back yards of houses so old that one or two still had privies—and looked over his shoulder to check on his captor, he saw nobody close behind him. Furthermore, only two middle-sized kids were in view for an entire two blocks beyond, and farther up the street was only a man burning leaves in the gutter: they had passed him earlier.

So Tony once again had his freedom, a state of which one is ignorant until it is taken away, but the strange thing was that he felt more loneliness than elation. As a captive of the Bullards he had been a sort of member of the family and in a way closer to Eva than he had ever been before, despite his not seeing her at all.

A few blocks from home he turned a corner and saw his brother just ahead. Tony was not really all that close to Jack, though they had shared a room before their sister left home, and were only two years apart, and he did not feel like talking with him now on any subject, let alone his own experiences in Millville. There was not one person in the world who would not think, erroneously, that he had had a disastrous afternoon: not one but perhaps Eva Bullard, if it could be explained, and at the moment he was at a loss for a means of communicating with her.

However, only a lunatic would walk fifteen yards behind his brother without saying anything, and Tony called "Hi" to Jack.

Jack suspected that Tony had shouted to him more than once before getting his attention, and he was briefly unnerved, for he believed it an immutable law that he himself had an awareness superior to the rest of the world's. He resolved never again to fall into such a deep distraction when he was outside, but to reserve such states for the splendid isolation of his own room.

He returned his brother's hi. "Did you go to the picture?" It would have been quite possible for them both to have been in the big, crowded theater at the same time without seeing each other.

"Huh?" said Tony. "Oh, yeah."

"Did you like it?"

The question seemed to take his brother aback. He finally answered, "Oh, sure . . . You?"

"Not much," said Jack. "I don't ever like all that singing and dancing. That's a girl's kind of movie."

"I guess you're right about that," said Tony.

Jack complained, "That's all they ever have there now. It's never realistic. Some guy starts singing to a girl, and an orchestra begins to play somewhere you can't even see."

"Yeah," said Tony. "That's right."

Jack saw a little woolly dog running up the sidewalk toward them, and in the distance he heard a woman's shrill voice calling it.

"Here comes Mopsy." In a moment the dog arrived, wagging its entire body violently. "Hi, Mops. Oh you nice dog you." He bent and petted the animal. The unseen woman continued to cry its name. "You go on home now you bad dog." He straightened up and pointed, but the dog ignored the order. Seeing that he would pat it no more, it ran on.

When they started to walk again, Tony said, "What I was thinking was maybe you could do me a favor. I would be willing to pay you."

Jack could assume that his brother meant something other than common domestic chores: those they sometimes traded, usually because of Tony's football schedule. He practiced every weekday after school, and the games were played on Friday nights. Jack did not go in much for what were called "activities" at school, yet in practice he was not as much of a loner as his brother. He always had one intimate. He had just parted from this pal, currently a fellow named Dickie Herkimer.

Tony looked from side to side, as if to make sure they would not be overheard. "This is confidential. You know that Bullard family that Dad had trouble with in their hardware store over in Millville? Well, that store burned down last night, and they are blaming us."

"Us? You mean the whole family?"

"That's what I hear," said Tony, whose eye Jack could see, at an angle, between lens and cheek, in its naked and vulnerable state.

"Where'd they get that idea?"

"How do I know?" Tony asked. "I guess because they had that argument with Dad yesterday and then the fire broke out at night. And the argument had been about him smoking and maybe causing a fire. Maybe it seems too much of a coincidence."

They were both silent for a while, and then Jack asked, "Did it burn to the ground?"

"I guess."

"What favor do you want me to do you?" From the

corner of his eye Jack could see that the dog Mopsy was returning from wherever it had been.

Tony said, "This is changing the subject, but I met a girl over at one of those park dances in Millville last summer."

Mopsy had not gone past them but was trotting smartly at Jack's heels. Jack stopped and pointed down the sidewalk. "Go home, Mops!" The dog ignored him. The woman's calls could no longer be heard.

Tony said, "I want you to write a letter to this girl I am talking about. I'll pay you for it. You can write a lot better than me. I never know what to say. You always get good grades on compositions. I remember that thing you wrote about How I Spent My Summer Vacation got an A plus, and it was hung up for Exhibit."

Jack chuckled. "Boy, I really made up a lot of crap for that! . . . What did you want me to write about to this girl?" To Mopsy he said, "Go on, Mops, take off."

"She's a nice girl," said Tony. "You know, she's not snooty or anything, and she ain't silly."

"She good-looking?"

"She's all right," Tony said. "She's nice and neat, you know? She's not phony." He shook his head. "I just would like to make a good impression on her."

Jack didn't understand exactly what was wanted, but his brother was a nice guy. Some people didn't get along with their brothers at all, but Jack liked Tony, even though he probably wouldn't have known him had they not been related. But of course the same was true of Jack so far as his father went.

"Sure," he told Tony. "I guess I could write it. And you won't have to pay me anything. We belong to the same family."

They were passing a brick house with a gray concrete

porch, the roof of which was supported by more thick, squat pillars than would seem necessary. It was one of the houses Jack most hated to look at. He stopped there and pointed at it for the dog's benefit.

"Go. There's your home."

"Hi there, Tony. Hi Jack. You come on up here, Mopsy!" These words were spoken by an enormously fat woman who emerged from the door of the ugly house and stood between the porch pillars, being more than a match for them. The dog now obeyed her and scampered toward the house. The Beeler boys returned the greeting to Mrs. Munsenmeyer, and she went indoors with Mopsy.

"Boy," Jack said, "is that an ugly house."

"I wouldn't talk so loud," said Tony, always the cautious one. "Somebody might hear you."

He was right, but this town was beginning to be too small for Jack. He would have liked to open the door one day and gaze upon a sweep of greensward which gently descended to blue water, or again, undulating prairie as far as the eye could see, or the clustered masts of the Old Port: to mention only a few of the infinite possibilities.

The Beeler residence was just around the corner. The brothers went around to the back door, as was the custom, and entered the kitchen, and there, at the table, was their sister. It was the first time they had seen her with bright red hair.

Jack didn't know if he liked it or not: it had been sprung on him too quickly. "Hi, Bernice," said he.

"Hi Jack, hi Tony," Bernice said. Her mother sat across from her, and before each was a cup with a teabag tab dangling from it. Bernice touched the back of her coiffure, which in addition to being red was frizzed in a funny way. "You like it?"

"Hi, Bernice," Tony said sadly.

Jack said, "I don't know yet. It's different."

She said, "It's the latest thing."

"Oh, yeah?" Jack asked, though not defiantly. "I thought I saw in the newsreel that it was something else."

"What was?"

"The latest."

"No," said Bernice. "This is it."

"You boys want something to eat?" their mother asked.

"No thanks," said Tony.

Jack said, "Huh-uh. Say, Bernice, how's the—"

His mother interrupted. "Is that the way to answer?"

"I'm sorry. No, ma'am, thank you." He resumed with Bernice: "How's the movie business?"

She smiled. "I'm outa that line now, Jack. I got me a swell new job as a manicurist. You know where?"

Boy, did that ever sound dreary! At least when she worked as a movie-theater cashier she got to see all the new pictures for nothing. "Naw," he said.

"In a swell men's *barbershop*," said Bernice. "In the Hotel Continentale. How about that? You oughta come down sometime and see me there, you and Tony too, and I'll treat you to free manicures. You're on your own for the haircut, though. They cost too much for me."

"How much?" asked Jack's mother.

"Six bits. And then in a place like that you gotta tip, and if you left a dime you might be thought a piker. So it'd cost you a buck or the better part of it."

Jack screamed, "A *buck*? For a *haircut*?"

"That wouldn't seem anything if you had a lot of dough." Bernice giggled smugly and plucked the sodden teabag from the cup and deposited it in the saucer. She was wearing the brightest nail polish ever seen on earth, and her lipstick matched it, and she was all powdered and rouged, or whatever.

That Tony remained silent was not unusual, but at the moment he was subtly communicating his impatience to Jack, so the latter said, "Well, see you later, Bernice. Staying for supper?"

"If they'll have me."

Her mother said, "Go awn."

Jack had Bernice's old room. It was nicer than the one he had always shared with Tony, but Tony wanted to stay in that one, being fixed in his ways, so Jack had been happy to move into the larger, deeper-closeted room, with the better view, among the features of which was a perspective on the private quarters of Mary Catherine Lutz, on the second floor across the alleyway. With his one-dollar drugstore binoculars Jack had more than once seen Mary Catherine in her slip. He had certainly never bragged about this to Tony, who had gone out with her on occasion.

When he and Tony reached the second floor now, Jack said, "I guess you want me to write that letter, huh?"

"If you don't mind," said Tony. He followed Jack into the latter's room.

Jack's desk had formerly been Bernice's vanity table. You could take the mirror off it, unscrewing the whole thing frame and all, and he had done that. Though the ivory-colored legs might not seem professionally desklike, the glass top made a nice smooth writing surface.

Jack sat down at the desk, and Tony took the edge of the bed nearby. Jack found a ring notebook in the lefthand drawer and turned to the first clean page and tore it out. He picked up the stub of a pencil.

Tony grimaced.

"What's the matter?"

Tony asked, "Don't you think it'd be nice if you opened the rings and took it out, so the holes wouldn't be all torn?"

"I wasn't going to send this piece of paper," Jack explained. "This is just a worksheet. When we get the letter just the way we want it, then we should copy it on a nice piece of writing paper. You wouldn't want these lines and holes in the one you send."

Tony was somewhat embarrassed by his erroneous assumption. He said brusquely, "Oh. Well, how do you think we should begin? 'Dear Eva' might be kinda fresh—? Can you say 'dear' to someone you don't know very well?"

"That's a good question," said Jack. "But it's my impression that people in business begin a letter that way to a total stranger. We could ask Bernice. She'd know. . . . O.K., so we'll have whatever goes at the beginning. Then what do you want to say?" Jack was hoping to be elegant. To write to a girl was a kind of aristocratic thing to do, as opposed to the plebeian conversation-by-voice: it gave one the opportunity to employ all the otherwise unusable words that one acquired through reading. "What's she like?"

"Huh?"

"You know, her personal traits of character, like hobbies or extracurricular interests."

Tony shrugged. "Gosh, I don't know. She's just a high-school kid."

"She would have liked that movie this afternoon, probably," said Jack. "That was real girl stuff." He had yet to put down a word. He looked up at the ceiling. "How about, 'Dear Eva, Do you enjoy the cinema? Speaking for myself, I do.' " He looked at Tony and saw him shaking his head. Jack squinted. "It would be better if I knew just what you want this letter to do: just pass the time of day or what?"

"I don't know," said Tony.

Jack changed the subject. "Is that right about those Bullards blaming all of us?"

"Yeah."

"What are they going to do?"

"I don't know," Tony said. "But we're not supposed to go over to Millville, I know that."

"That's crazy. I mean, I can't go over to the bike shop to get an inner tube?"

"Not according to this theory of theirs."

"How could they get away with that?" asked Jack. "Set up guard posts at every entrance to the town?"

"I don't know," said Tony.

Jack asked, with reference to his family, "Do the rest of them know about this ban on us going to Millville? Because how's Dad going to get to work?"

Tony said, "God, I never thought of that."

"I'd better tell him." He left the room and went downstairs, skipping every second step, which was not really much faster but simply his current style of descent.

Wanting to avoid the womenfolk when on such a mission, he went out the rarely used front door and around to the garage, where his father could usually be found when not inside. The garage was empty now, but its doors were closed. If they were left open, birds flew in and might be hard to get out when the car came back, and would crap on it.

Just as Jack was ready to go back to the house, along came the little dog Mopsy, who was once again taking a breather from its mistress. He had just bent over to pat its wagging behind when the familiar blue sedan, its windshield badly yellowed, came rolling up the alley. Mopsy being the kind of sappy pooch that might well run barking into the roadway and get flattened, Jack swatted the animal's hairy butt, and it skittered into the yard.

Jack's father pulled up on the little apron between garage and alley: this was surfaced with coal ashes. Whenever Jack heard the crunching sound, he was unpleasantly reminded of how cruel a terrain this was to bare feet. He took the stick out of the hasp and opened the garage doors, and was just barely able to clear the right side past the nearer fender.

But his father climbed ponderously from the car: apparently he wasn't ready to garage it.

"Say, Dad," Jack said, "there's this thing—"

"Don't bother me now, Jack," his father said brusquely, passing him without a glance.

Jack pursued him. "This is real important, Dad."

His father stopped and turned. "God damn you, not now!" He plodded toward the house.

Jack obeyed to the degree that he did not at once try again to get his news across, but he did follow his father into the kitchen.

"Hiya, Papa," said Bernice, from her place at the table.

Jack's mother got up. "I'll give you some coffee, Dolf, and a piece uh pie."

"Naw, I ain't hungry," said he. "Hi, Bernice. I'm glad you came." He went to the table, but not to the head, instead taking what was usually Tony's seat, across from Jack's, where Bernice was sitting now.

When he had got himself seated he noticed that Jack was still in attendance. "Hey, you," he said threateningly. "I thought I told you to leave me alone."

Bernice said, "Aw, Papa, take it easy on the kid." She winked at Jack. "He ain't all bad." She always stuck up for him.

His father stared at Jack for a while, and then he said, "Is your brother to home?"

"He's upstairs."

"Go get him."

Jack went to the front of the house and shouted up the stairs, and in a few moments Tony joined the rest of the family at the kitchen table.

Jack's father said to Tony, "While you was at the movies we got a phone call here from somebody who wouldn't give their name."

Bernice asked, "Who was that?"

"I don't know. It sounded like a fake voice of some kind, talking through a rag or something. But what he said was he knew I burnt down Bullard's hardware last night."

Jack was tempted to look for Tony's reaction, but he restrained himself.

His father went on. "So I says to this person on the phone that I never knew anything about that, and he says, 'You're a liar. You set that fire, and I seen you do it, and the Bullards are gonna get even.'"

"I just wish I had been on that telephone," said Bernice. "I'd of given that customer a piece of my mind."

"Well," said her father, "he hung up right away then. But I got to thinking it was maybe that one calls himself Reverton, though it never sounded like him, except if he was disguising his voice some way, which he could of been doing. So I went over to see the chief. You know I went all through school with Harve. I told him about this business, and I says, 'You know me, Harve, I wouldn't hurt a fly, but this guy carries a pistol. I need me some protection. I want to get me a permit. If he's got this crazy idea I set that fire, he might try and plug me one of these days.'" He breathed heavily for a moment.

Jack's mother rose from the table. "I'm gonna get some coffee for you, Dolf. You need to calm down some."

"I don't know if that will do it," Bernice said brightly. "Ain't you ever heard of Coffee Nerves?"

"So Harve says, 'If he carries a concealed weapon he's breaking the law, Dolf. He can't get away with that.' But I says, 'He's a railroad detective,' and Harve says, 'Oh well then, he's got a permit, but he ain't got no right to draw on just anybody he argues with. Besides, that permit's only good for the towns where the railroad passes through and would have to be okayed by all of them. If I catch him over in Hornbeck wearing a gun, I'll pinch him. We ain't got no railroad here.' But I says to Harve, 'I don't know if he ever would come over here for any reason at all. The trouble is, I work over in Millville. If he jumps me over there I could get killed.' But Harve says a permit he could give me for Hornbeck wouldn't be no good in Millville, and he says, 'You'd have to get another one over there if you carried a weapon across the line. And I don't think their chief would give you one. He's a mean man,' Harve says. 'I couldn't do you no good with him. We don't get along a-tall.' "

Jack's mother put in front of his father a cup of coffee that was colored blue from all the milk in it.

Bernice screwed her face up so that it seemed to converge on her scarlet lips. "Gee, Papa, it's all pretty punk."

Tony was looking miserable. "Maybe it'll all get straightened out in a couple days," he said hopelessly.

Jack waited in vain for his brother to go on. "Hey, Tony," he said at last. "Don't you have something to tell Dad?"

Tony stared at him in alarm. "Huh?"

"About how the Bull—"

The explosion came at this point, making such a loud noise that for a moment its source could not be identified: it seemed to embrace everything in the universe.

Despite his apparent moral confusion just prior to the blast, Tony was quickest to respond. He was at the door in an instant, and before Jack got off his own chair, Tony was well into the yard. When Jack reached the corner of the garage he saw that one side of the car's hood had been blown off and lay in the alley.

Tony emerged from the garage, carrying an old blanket of oil-stained felt: this he quickly hurled over the smoking engine. He was amazingly cool in such an operation.

Their father arrived, and the neighbors were beginning to come out of the nearby houses. Mr. Petty, who lived to their immediate west, got there first. He wore no tie, and the neck of his shirt was open, showing that he had already, this early in the season, put on his long johns.

"What happened here, Dolf?"

Jack's father glared impersonally, crazily, at Petty or really past him, and said in disbelief, "I think that one was supposed to have my name on it."

When her mother went out to the scene of the blast, Bernice dashed upstairs, presumably to go to the toilet but actually to check on her makeup and hairdo before joining the crowd in the alley. She was aware that all of the women would be observing her enviously. She was the only sophisticated person yet to emerge from that neighborhood, or for that matter from anywhere in Hornbeck, which was a pretty corny place and thought by the other usherettes with whom she had recently worked as being out in the sticks though it was only fifteen miles from downtown. Bernice had not really been a cashier but had named herself as such for the sheer prestige of it, and she had been safe enough from discovery, for no one from Hornbeck was likely to go to a city moviehouse, which charged half a buck for a climb to a balcony in which there was never a seat this side of the last two rows of Peanut Gallery.

As Bernice had told her family, she was no longer employed by that theater. But the truth was that she had been fired because she was invariably distracted from her duties by the picture on the screen, which was enormous when you worked on the main floor. Nor had she taken a job as a manicurist in a hotel barbershop. She was altogether out of work at the moment, with no prospects, and in arrears on the rent for her furnished room in the city. And since her period had been overdue for a week, she had begun to suspect she was pregnant and had no means by which to determine which man might be responsible. But being naturally an optimist, she was not downcast.

Now she touched up her lipstick and blinked her eyes rapidly many times so as to brighten their luster, and did little things to her hair with a rattail comb. She pulled her stockings taut under the rolled garters just above the knee and checked the seams in the long mirror on the front of the wardrobe in her parents' room.

Before going outside, she donned her coat with the fake fox collar, and then, wearing her famous cocky but not snotty grin, she appeared in the back yard.

Mrs. Petty, from next door, said, "Why, Bernice, I never knew you was out home today! And looking like a million." Mrs. Petty was a very thin woman with ugly features, but as nice as she could be. The Pettys had no children, and when the Beeler kids were smaller they had called them Aunt Harriet and Uncle Clem. Bernice was too old for that now but lacked the assurance to use the first name without the title, and of course could not at this late date say "Mrs.," so she did not preface her remarks with any address at all.

She grinned even more brightly and said, "A bad penny will always turn up, they say!"

"Shaw," said Mrs. Petty, beaming on her. "I keep tabs on you, Bernice, and I know you're doing just swell. I say more power to you."

"How about that?" said Bernice, and moved on toward the crowd back of the garage, and while she was on her

way the police cruiser came rolling slowly up the alley.
Everybody said "Hi" to her, and she went among them and
found Jack, put her arm through his, and said, "Hi, hand-
some. What's going on?"

"I guess it was some kind of bomb." He looked at the
police car. "Who called him?"

Harvey Yelton, Hornbeck's chief of police, was sliding
out of the car, holding his holstered pistol so that it
didn't catch on the steering wheel. He was the first man
who had ever had Bernice, who was seventeen at the time.
It was doubtful that he knew she was a virgin, because she
had lost her thing riding a bike as a kid.

"Hi there," Harvey greeted her now. He certainly had the
right build for a cop, being well over six feet tall and
weighing probably two-fifty, more or less. He lumbered
over to join her father and Tony at the wounded automobile. Tony had taken the felt blanket off the engine,
and the chief leaned down, sniffing with his big nose.

Bernice's father said piteously, "See what I mean?"

Harvey straightened up and looked suspiciously though
impersonally around a half-circle of the nearest people.
Bernice no longer regarded him as being as important as
she had at the time he did it to her.

What happened was that he had caught her smoking a
cigarette with Charlie Conley, one summer night, sitting
on a bench at the ballpark. Harvey ran Charlie off with a
warning, but he brought Bernice to the cruiser and drove
her out to the cemetery, where he stopped with the motor
running and gave her a good talking to, the point of which
was that he had known her father all his life and her since
she was born and he wouldn't stand by and see her go to
the dogs by way of cigarettes, which led to drinking and
worse. Then Bernice begged him not to tell her father, and
the chief said, Well, he would think about it, and Bernice

began to cry, and Harvey patted her knee with his big hand with its heavy lodge ring twinkling in the lights of the dashboard, and said, Now, now, I'll think it over, and then later somehow he was in the passenger's seat with her straddling his lap, and she could feel, with various parts of her body, the various pieces of hardware he wore at his belt, and he was breathing fast and hot into her face and smelling of fried food, and then he pulled back of a sudden and caught at himself. And when he was done he said, Now you needn't to worry because you ain't going to have any kid because of this, and she did not. Pity that at least one of the people who had enjoyed her favors in more recent times had not been as careful as Harvey.

She was still holding on to Jack. She tugged on his arm now and said, "You breaking the girlies' hearts yet?"

Jack said, "Let's go over and see what Yelton has to say."

Bernice asked, "Do you really like my new hair?"

"Sure." He got loose from her and went to join the men.

Bernice sighed in boredom. As long as she could remember, her father was always worked up about something. He took life too seriously and often thought somebody was cheating him or insulting him when probably they never had the least intent to do so. They were probably just forgetful or something. Bernice never had any enemies, because she lived and let. You'd drive yourself crazy otherwise in this old world.

She looked around. Her mother was talking to old Mrs. Smiley, who lived three doors up the street. Bernice had used to do it with her son Ben in the loft over the Smiley garage, where there was no ventilation and the air in summer was stifling. When, after a time, she discovered that Ben had a weak heart, she discontinued the practice, not relishing the idea of suddenly having a corpse on top of her.

Tony was handing some things to Harvey. Now that she

remembered it, the police chief had had her only that one time. He simply never got hold of her again, but that she was no longer innocent must somehow have shown on her face, for not too long after the incident with Harvey, a number of guys began to approach her with one thing in mind, and she did not disappoint them if they weren't too crude about it. As the saying went, it was good for the complexion.

The chief lowered the hand in which he held whatever Tony had given him, and he addressed the crowd in a loud voice.

"Any uh you people seen anybody in the alley here just before this went off?" He put his free hand at his pistol belt, thumb hooked over it, and waited, looking slowly around. No response came. "Well, you just let me know if you remember later on. You know where to get hold uh me."

Bernice was curious as to whether Harvey would still like her looks. She went over to the group around the car.

Tony was fooling with something down in the engine. He said, without looking up, "It might still run if we got a new distributor cap. Be worth trying. Then we could pound out the hood and repaint 'er, and be back in business."

Bernice sidled up near Harvey. It wouldn't be long before he smelled her Evening in Paris.

Her father said desperately, "They mean business, all right. I hope this proves it. I need that gun permit."

Harvey threw back his big head. His police-chief's cap had ventilating wickerwork below the cloth crown. He said, "I'll tell you, Dolf. You want a good self-defense weapon, you do better to get yourself a twelve-gauge double. You don't need a permit for that. You're legal 'slong as you carry it broke open and unloaded and you don't cut it down or conceal it. Heck, you could be going trap shooting, perfectly legal. But I tell you this, anybody sees what you're carrying, they ain't gonna give you any trouble."

"Unless they drill you from ambush!" said Jack. "Bushwhack you."

Tony said, "You know who might have a distributor cap? Shorty Rundle. He's got everything down in that junkyard. And he's always around on Sundays, 'cause he lives there. I'm gonna go see. O.K. to use your bike, Jack?"

"It's yours, isn't it?"

"I gave it to you," said Tony. "You know that." He went into the garage.

Harvey said, "I got to get on over to the ball field now, Dolf. The kids been coming there lately of a Sunday to play touch football, and they get in trouble sometime if you don't watch 'em."

Tony shot out of the garage on the bicycle he had ridden for years and only recently given to Jack, and pedaled rapidly up the alley. Bernice was fond of both of her brothers, who were some distance from her in age and of course experience of life. Jack was good-looking enough to be a real lady-killer when the time came. When she was eighteen and he ten, Bernice used to wrestle with him: sometimes she could feel that his little thing, pressed against her in some hold, was hard as a nut.

Harvey went toward the cruiser. Jack followed, asking, "You want me to interrogate these people, Chief? Maybe they will remember something when the dust settles."

"You leave them alone," said Harvey. He opened the door of the car, and then looked over at Bernice for the first time. "You want a lift to the bus stop?"

She gave him a dazzling smile. "Why sure, if you don't mind. That'd be real nice."

"I thought you were staying for supper," said Jack, surprised by this new move.

Bernice wrinkled her nose. "Gee, I'd of liked to, but somepin came up." She went to her father, who was still staring dolefully at the car. "It turns out I got to go back to town now, Papa, and Harvey's gonna gimme a lift to the bus, so you don't have to, and anyway your car's on the fritz now, ain't it?"

He nodded sluggishly. "Sure, Bernice. Now you just take care." This thing was hitting him hard.

"It'll all come out all right," Bernice said, patting him on his fat back. She had seen her mother talking to Mrs. Kunkle, from across the alley three houses down, and she did not want to approach them, for Mrs. Kunkle suspected her of having done it with Mr. Kunkle, who taught civics at the high school, whereas Bernice was innocent for once, having only let him kiss and feel her sometimes after hours, so as to get a passing grade. She now asked her dad, "Tell Mama for me. I got to go now."

She went to the cruiser and got in. Harvey did not look as old as her father did, maybe because he had no kids. His wife was known as a sickly person and was hardly ever seen out of the house.

Harvey remained silent until he pulled out of the alley onto the street. Then he said, "I hear you been doing all right for yourself, Bernice, and I'm glad to hear that."

"Oh, I ain't in the poorhouse yet, Harvey. I'm still working on my first million, but I got nice friends."

A striped rubber ball came from nowhere and rolled across the street, half a block ahead. Harvey drove to it, stopped the cruiser, and got out. By this time a kid about ten years of age had come running from between the houses. He skidded to a halt when he saw the police car.

Harvey said, "You know better than that, Willis. You oughtn't play ball so it comes into the street. You know why? It could hit somebody's automobile and scare them so they would lose control of the wheel and drive up over the curb and turn over and burst into flames, and everybody in the car would be burned to a crisp, see? Or the driver might just lose his head and turn and run over your pooch. Or you and your friends might tear after the ball onto the road and you'd all be killed if a big Mack truck was coming along real fast, or you'd scare the truckdriver and he'd smash into them high-tension wires, which would fall down and electrocute the whole neighborhood and kill everybody and burn up all your houses, maybe get outa control and burn everything in the whole town, see. Now, you wouldn't want that to happen, wouldja?"

"Huh-uh." Willis had blond hair in a butch cut. His face was expressionless.

Harvey picked up the ball. He weighed it in his hand and said, "I oughta take this ball away from yuh." He stared at Willis. "Now you wouldn't like that, wouldja?"

"Huh-uh."

Harvey thought for a long moment. To Bernice it sure seemed like a storm in a teacup, but then she wasn't a policeman, and you did have to keep kids in line or they'd grow up to be bums.

Finally he tossed the ball to the boy, returned to the cruiser, and put it in gear. He said, "Little snotnose."

Bernice crossed her legs. The hem of her skirt was caught just above the roll of her stockings, but if Harvey looked at this, she did not see him.

He asked, staring straight ahead through the windshield, "What time you got to get back?"

"Well," said she, "I ain't in any real big hurry."

He kept driving as slowly as ever through the neighborhood streets. Now and again he nodded to people through the window or even rolled it down and said "Hi." In Hornbeck's business district he slowed to a crawl when passing a driverless rattletrap flivver at the curb in front of the butcher shop, and stopped altogether when parallel to a shiny, new-looking maroon coupe that was parked outside the drugstore. The man and the woman in the front seats were colored people.

Harvey leaned across Bernice, his elbow on her knees, and rolled down the window. He asked, "Can I help you folks find something?"

"Yes sir," said the colored man. "We was looking for a drugstore that was open on Sunday."

"You won't find one in this town," said the chief. "That's against the law here."

"Yes sir. You don't know of any that is open anyplace else?"

"If you want to find one, you better move along."

"Yes sir," said the colored man, "we was fixing to do that."

Bernice said with a smile, "You go down to the city, you might find one."

"Yes ma'am."

The chief kept the cruiser where it was until those people drove away, and then he followed them, at a distance, to where Hornbeck gave way to unincorporated territory to the south, mainly weed fields.

"I'd of asked for their papers," said Harvey, driving the cruiser into the entrance of a coal yard. He shifted into reverse and turned back before he completed the statement. "But every time I done that recently with one of them, he's owned it, sure enough. You wonder how it is they can afford that when white folks got to drive old heaps." He glanced at Bernice. "I ain't holding you up for your bus?"

"Naw, I got time."

"Sundays is real quiet," Harvey said. "My radio's broke, besides. But I make my rounds."

They reached the high school, and he drove the police car into the service alleyway behind the building, stopping at the base of an iron fire escape.

"We got kids around here who have figured out a way to pick the lock up there and they sneak in on weekends and fool around." He gave Bernice a look and then climbed from the car and began to mount the metallic stairs of the fire escape.

Bernice followed him. When Harvey reached the door at the top, which was on the second floor of the three-story structure, he took a key from a ring of many attached to his belt along with the other gadgets, and he opened the door and entered.

Bernice closed the iron door when she was inside. It made a loud noise that echoed along the dark, empty corridor with its shining floor and the peculiar smell of a school in the off hours.

About halfway along the hall Harvey turned in at the entrance to the women teachers' lounge. When Bernice came in, she stepped out of her shoes, pulled up her skirt and took her pants off, and lay down on the old leather couch there. The chief removed only his equipment belt, the tunic of his uniform, and his cap, and he unbuttoned his fly.

He was not awfully good at it, but she enjoyed it more than she had seven years earlier. When they were finished the chief went into the toilet part of the lounge and presumably washed himself, but Bernice just put back on what she had taken off. She figured she had now got herself a father for the baby, in case she ended up being stuck with one.

Harvey dropped her off at the bus stop near the First National Bank, but before she had waited very long a nice

big black car pulled up and the driver, a white-haired gentleman in suit and tie, leaned over to ask from the passenger's
window whether she would be going to the city, for if so
he could offer her a ride. Bernice accepted. This Good
Samaritan turned out to be the Presbyterian preacher in
Hornbeck, Reverend Finch. Bernice did not know him, because her family was of a different persuasion, being
nominally Methodists though none of them ever went to
church except sometimes her mother, and her father had
been born Catholic but had stopped being one when he got
married.

The minister was driving to the city for some church
conference, and in Millville he stopped at the Presbyterian
manse of that town to pick up a fellow preacher.

"Say, Jim," said Finch, "I want you to make the
acquaintance of Bernice Beeler. She's from my town but
not my congregation. This is Reverend Amburgy, Bernice."

Amburgy waved off Bernice's offer of the corner of the
front seat, she sliding toward the middle, and he entered
the rear door. He was a pudgy individual, who wore eyeglasses above fat cheeks.

When they started to roll Amburgy leaned forward and
said, "Bernice, is it your family that has gotten into some
disagreement with the Bullards who come to my church?—
though not as often as they should, I must say!" He
simpered, but corrected himself with a cough. "I do hope
that can be straightened out, and if I can be of any help . . ."

Bernice had forgotten about that subject, but now that
she was reminded she permitted herself some indignation.
"I should *say* it's a disagreement and then some! Those
Bullards ought to be arrested. They just blew up my dad's
automobile."

"Good grief," said Amburgy, withdrawing to the rear of

the seat. "It certainly is a troublesome matter. I was hoping it would simmer down. But it doesn't sound like it has, does it?" He had begun to assume a cute intonation. "Oh, dear me. These things can get out of hand. Burning down a store, blowing up an automobile. What ever could happen next?"

Reverend Finch said, from behind the wheel, which he steered with rigid arms in his blue-serge suit, "I'd sure be willing to offer my 'umble services if they wouldn't be taken the wrong way, but I bet you'd want to go to your own minister, Bernice, who is? . . ."

"I'll tellya," she said, "I probly ought to be seeing him right now, now that you mention it. I oughtn't go back downtown till I got that settled. You want to let me off right at this corner?"

Finch was startled by the request, but he glided to a slow stop at the place indicated. He turned gravely and said, "Bernice, I think you're a pret-ty fine young lady."

"I join in those sentiments," said Amburgy, in that voice of his, from the back seat. "I'm sure all this will be cleared up soon enough, and you'll all be even greater friends than before."

Bernice hopped out onto the main street of Millville, which was a direct continuation of Hornbeck's main drag and on the same city-bus route. She looked for the sign that marked a stop and saw it ahead in the next block and was about to walk there when she thought about those Bullards and what trouble they were causing her father, and feeling full of confidence now that she had worked out a possible solution to her own predicament, she decided to call them up and tell them to let her father alone, or else. She had always been known for her spunk.

She walked a couple of blocks to the business district and went into Tom's Restaurant, the only place open and with a telephone, and she consulted the directory, which was mounted on an outside wall of the varnished wooden booth, on a sloping shelf beneath a brass lamp.

Three Bullards were listed, none under the name of Bud, but one was an Ada and could therefore be eliminated, which left Cornelius and Herman, and of these two, the former would be more likely to be called Bud, so she committed that number to memory and went inside and dialed it.

The phone at the other end was answered by the voice of a young girl.

As those things went, Bernice had expected to be speaking immediately to someone in Bullard authority, if not Bud, then another male, and for a moment she was almost embarrassed.

But then she recovered and asked, "Who's this?"

"Eva."

"Is this the Bullard residence?"

"Yes."

Bernice had regained her strength. "Well, you just go tell Mr. Bud Bullard that I want to speak to him and pronto," said she.

"He can't come right now."

Eva had a soft, sweet voice. In the current situation Bernice found it annoying. She growled, "Well, he better if he knows what's good for him."

Eva said, "He's sick in bed. The doctor said he's having a nervous breakdown."

Again Bernice was taken aback. She was silent for a moment, and then she said, but with no real assurance, "I've heard that one before. Is he hiding out? Is that it?"

"He just tried to kill himself," said Eva. "Maybe you could call back when he feels better."

* * *

There was a gas burner in the Bullard cellar that Bud's wife, Frieda, had used, before he bought her the washing machine, to heat a copper tub of water, and what Bud did after Reverton had marched Tony Beeler away was to lock the cellar door from the inside and then put a big paper shopping bag over his head, which he lowered near the burner, and turned on the gas. The gas stank like rotten eggs, and it was all Bud could do to keep breathing till he passed out.

When he woke up, the bag had fallen from his head and he was on hands and knees, vomiting onto the concrete floor. He was still there when some of his male relatives broke the door open and came down to the cellar and turned off the gas and opened all the little windows that were set in the walls just under the joists of the floor above.

After a while they helped him up the steps and out through the living room, the women staring at him, and up the stairs to the bedroom, where Frieda took over, shooing them out, and got his outer clothes off him and put him to bed in his BVD's. Before leaving the room, she pulled the blind down, and Bud went into further darkness by drawing the covers over his head.

But he was still awake when the doctor came, twenty minutes later, and rolled the shade up again and even lighted the lamp on the bedside table.

"We need to get a little light on these matters," said Dr. Swan, who had brought Bud into the world more than four decades earlier and prided himself on still going strong. He had a brushy mustache, all salt-and-pepper, though given his age it was a wonder it was not snow-white. He whipped a stethoscope from his bag and, having opened the first two buttons of the BVD top, pressed the cold hard-rubber cup against Bud's chest and asked him to cough. Then he took his pulse, after which he put the shiny mirror on his forehead and examined eyes, nose, mouth, and ears with that flashlight the little front of which came to a point.

"You'll live," the doctor said when he had put away the instruments. "But what is it that ails you?"

Bud started to answer, but his head hurt too much: it was as if a barrel of pain. He managed to communicate this to the doctor, who flipped open that part of his bag in which were mounted, within little leather straps, rows of vials, and from one of them he removed two fat pink capsules. Bud barely got them down, with water from the pitcher his wife brought.

When the doctor left, Bud fingered at Frieda to come close, and he croaked into her ear, "Don't . . . tell . . . Rev." For luckily his cousin had left the house before the unsuccessful attempt at suicide.

Bud slept throughout the remainder of Sunday and did not wake up till Monday noon. He felt physically exhausted, but his soul was, oddly enough, refreshed. Though his predicament was exactly the same as it had been when he put his head into the shopping bag and turned on the gas, his morale was high. He still had not the least idea of how to inform his relatives of the lack of fire insurance, let alone how he would get through the remainder of his life: yet simply living, at the moment, was rewarding.

When Frieda quietly opened the door and peeped in, he said brightly, "Hi. How're you doing?"

"Why," said she, having raised the window blind, "you look fit as a fiddle."

Bud said, "Mom, I been thinking. Maybe this is a blessing in disguise. Maybe we're being told to start off on a new foot."

Frieda was puzzled. "Huh?"

Bud pointed at the ceiling, but then he shrugged. "Aw, I don't know, maybe we should get outa this place."

"Then where'd we go, Bud? It's our home. And how'd we go anywhere, now?"

"I'm thinking," he said. "I know hardware inside and out. I could probly get a nice position with a chain, but if so we'd have to move."

Frieda was wearing a very gloomy expression. Clearly, this wasn't the time to pursue the matter.

"Say," he said, "I wouldn't mind tying on the feedbag. I think I missed supper. I could stand some breakfast."

She brightened. "You missed breakfast too, but I can still make some for you."

When he discovered what time it was—twenty to twelve —he said he would as usual eat lunch with the family, and got up and went to the bathroom to shave.

Eva had come home by bike promptly at a few minutes past noon, washed her hands, and was sitting at the kitchen table when her mother was dishing up the chicken-and-noodle soup.

"Why do you think it's taking your brother so long to get home?" Bud asked. He hadn't seen Junior since the store burned down. That boy actually went to the early Sunday matinee at the moviehouse in Hornbeck, having made and gobbled a pot-roast sandwich and passed up Sunday dinner. Bud himself would never have permitted this, but he had been distracted at the time, and Frieda was a notorious pushover for her only son. Now he was lagging in his return from school, though so far as he knew, his father was lying in a sickbed. This was the son to whom Bud's Hardware would eventually have been turned over.

"I don't know," said Eva. "I don't see him at school very much. The seniors are all on the first floor, and the freshmen never go down there except on the way to gym."

Bud approved of his daughter, who had always been an

obedient child and a diligent student, whereas it was just
the other way around with Junior, who as quite a young
boy began to play the smart aleck and had been sent home
many times throughout the years with a teacher's complain-
ing note and never once got a higher rating than Fair in
the space for Conduct on his report cards and never a
better grade than C in anything, including Phys. Ed. Junior
was the only boy in the history of the school to tangle with
the gym instructor, who was also the track coach, a fine big
man's man habitually worshiped by the male students. But
leave it to Junior, when only a sophomore, to be caught in
the locker room drinking stolen elderberry wine from a jam
jar, the little snot. He was just doing it to show off because
he wasn't good at sports. Bud himself, being of the same
light build, and by nature lacking in coordination, had been
no great shakes as an athlete, but he never tried to dis-
tinguish himself by acting like a little turd; he used the
old noggin, and in a positive way. He got through school,
and then he started out as an errand boy for Old Man
Kuntz, the stingiest man in the world, and drudged and
trudged, and finally acquired his own little business, which
had never gotten in the black before it burned to the
ground. He didn't know if the Beelers had done that, but
he was sure that, whatever, they were gloating now—and
not only them, but most of his neighbors right in Millville,
for people don't like their friends to succeed, as everybody
knows. Bud was well aware of that truth. When Kuntz was
the proprietor of the only hardware in town, people lined
up at the counter, and he was a real bastard. Nobody
realized that they seldom got more than twelve–fourteen
ounces in a pound of tenpenny nails and the old man would
put tools to extended personal use and then polish them
up and sell them as new.

Junior finally arrived at 12:23. The others had finished their soup and were well into sandwiches of ham salad and American cheese.

Bud said, " 'Bout time."

Junior seemed startled to see his father. "You up?" he asked.

"What's it look like?" Bud replied.

Frieda served Junior his soup, which she had kept hot in the pan, and passed him a box of soda crackers. He sank his hand into the latter and seized several at once and began to crush them before he got anywhere near the bowl, crumbs snowing down onto the oilcloth.

Bud watched Junior hide with broken crackers the entire surface of the liquid. He hated his son's ways at the table. He said, "That's gonna be thick enough to eat with a fork."

Junior said, "Yeah, well."

Bud looked at Frieda and then Eva and then came back to Junior. What he said was addressed to them all. "I was under the weather there for a few hours, but that's nobody's business. That's just between you, me, and the gatepost. There isn't anybody else in even the family who ought to know about it, because they would get the wrong idea. We got to keep a stiff upper lip at this time." Junior had acquired an expression that infuriated Bud, who said, in a quiet but savage tone, "Are you making fun of me?"

Junior swallowed. "Huh-uh."

"Because, by God, if you are . . ."

"Bud," said Frieda, "are you ready for dessert?" She could be counted on to protect her cub.

Bud said, "If we was in the spring now I might be able to slap up a temporary structure of some kind and do enough business to get into better quarters by next fall, but it's rough now, heading towards the winter."

Eva was nibbling her sandwich in a ladylike way, being a clean and neat girl, and she was listening respectfully to what her father said. It was just a pity she hadn't been a boy. Bud took a sip from the inch of now cold coffee in his cup, but waved off Frieda's attempt to get him a hot refill.

"But maybe," said he, "somebody's got some space in town that I can use. It was Rev of all people who pointed out there's probably some merchandise that can be saved, like anything made of metal, wrench sets and the like. And the fact is there's always some stuff survives a fire, or anyway ain't ruined totally, maybe just smoked up a little or slightly charred. So maybe I can bring in something with a fire sale. That kinda thing appeals to people. They'll buy damaged stuff at a bargain they wouldn't have wanted when new at the best price."

He took a speculative bite of his sandwich as Junior paused between spoonfuls of soup to say, "You won't find nothing left by now."

"What does that mean?"

Junior said, as if shamefacedly, "There ain't anything left."

"Goddammit, I asked you what that meant!"

"I wish you wouldn't—" Frieda began, but Bud's fierce gesture shut her up.

"What it *means*," Junior said, "is they are cleaning you out."

"Looters?"

Junior nodded curtly. "When I got there, not till noon, some kids was fishing around in the ashes. I run them off, at least the littler ones than me, but—"

"You mean the bigger ones defied you?" asked Bud. He sensed in himself a new capacity for violence of emotion: yesterday he had been ready to die. "By God, they better not try that on me, those dirty scum!" His hand gripped the sandwich as if it were a weapon, and his teeth bit down upon it like the shutting of a steel trap.

Junior shrugged and dug into his soup. "It don't matter now. It's all gone."

Bud suddenly spat the mouthful of sandwich into his hand, dumped it on the plate before him, shoved his chair back, and left the kitchen. In the bedroom he dressed in his usual workday outfit, a sleeveless coat sweater under the gray suit coat and over the white shirt and bow tie. From the back corner of the closet he took a twelve-gauge pump gun which he had never yet fired, having brought it home from the store just to keep for home protection. He rapidly ejected all the shells onto the bedspread until the magazine was empty, and then he reloaded them into the shotgun, pumped one into the chamber, and put on the safety. He wrapped the weapon in a colorful Indian blanket he and Frieda had bought on their honeymoon, in the gift shop at Badger Lake, where the proprietor had worn a warbonnet but, with glasses and a mustache, was thought to be not a full-blooded redskin, but more likely a gentleman of the Hebrew persuasion. Frieda had also purchased a pink sateen pillow, suitably inscribed with the name of the resort.

She came in now while he was engaged in his task. She said, "Bud, you know I never stick my nose in—"

"Well then, don't do it now," said he. "I been pushed too far, Frieda. They're doing me dirty. All I ever done was keep my nose to the grindstone year in year out. I never said boo to a soul. And look where it got me."

"Well," Frieda said, "you're still alive."

"Am I supposed to settle for that?" He hefted the wrapped weapon in one hand, but then decided to carry it in two, as if it were some harmless implement or piece of pipe. He went downstairs and through the kitchen to the back door. Eva was still there, placidly drinking her milk. Junior was already gone.

She said, "Bye, Dad."

"So long," said Bud, making it impersonal, and adding, "Don't worry 'bout me!"

Dolf's morning entry into Millville, en route to the plant, had been uneventful, and he realized that the Bullards' threat to keep him out of their town had been so much hot air if it was meant to be taken literally. Tony had found a distributor cap and ignition wire at Shorty Rundle's, and working until late at night, in the light of an extension lamp, he had managed to get the engine to run, but something was basically wrong with it: it made a bad noise and, worse, Dolf smelled gas while driving to work. The carburetor was probably cracked or something. It was only amazing that the explosion had not ignited the fuel the day before.

Tony had reshaped the hood-half with a ballpeen hammer until it could be rested in place and wired down, but the result really looked like hell, and some punk kids on their way to school had jeered and hooted at the car as Dolf chugged past them that morning, and in the parking lot at the plant he was humiliated to be seen getting out of a maimed automobile that looked like something driven by a hillbilly or a shine of the sort who when he had a bunion cut a hole right out of his shoe.

At lunchtime Dolf tended to avoid the men who worked under him, on the machines, and to take his lunchbox not to the large, noisy, crowded room set aside for the purpose, but to a relatively peaceful corner near the stockroom, where sitting on one crate he could put his sandwiches and thermos on another and while eating gaze with a certain satisfaction on the momentarily quiet factory-scape, crane and catwalks overhead, machinery below. Dolf had come here after dropping out of high school, and he had never worked anywhere else.

This noon he had just put his first sandwich in order—taking out the piece of lettuce that Bobby insisted on including, which was always wilted by lunchtime and reminded him of garbage; and folding the bread, if it was white, upon itself so that there were four layers instead of two, because white bread tended to compress to nothing when chompéd—he had just arranged all that was necessary for the first taste when who should emerge from the adjacent door but Walt Huff, formerly a neutral personage but now of course to be identified with the enemy.

"I be darn," said Huff, in a not unfriendly voice. "So you did show up, after all."

Dolf lowered his sandwich. He got the reference but would not admit it. "What's that mean?"

Huff moved his lower jaw from side to side and said almost shyly, "I don't know, I thought them guys was making threats."

Dolf put it right to him. "You mean your relatives?"

Huff jerked his shoulder. "By marriage. I ain't all that close."

"Any uh you wanna make something of it," said Dolf,

"you know where to find me." He had previously made a decision to say nothing directly about the damage to his car to any member of the Bullard crowd. Anybody who would do such a thing would only derive enjoyment from hearing the outrage evoked by it; therefore the only effective response was not words but an act of revenge.

"I never had anything against you, Dolf," said Huff. "You know that."

Dolf realized for the first time that Huff had a yellow streak up his back. He pressed his advantage. "By God," he said with quiet savagery, "I'll take all of you on, one by one, or all at once. I don't give a good goddam."

"Well, that's got nothing to do with yours truly," said Walt. "You 'n' me ain't got no quarrel. Guy who causes all the trouble is that Reverton. He's half-cracked. He spends too much time with hoboes, if you ask me."

"Yeah," Dolf said, still holding his doubled sandwich. "Well, you just tell him I'm getting me a twelve-gauge, and if he makes one move towards that popgun of his, he won't have no belly."

Huff didn't look as impressed as he should have. He said, "Well, if there's too many guns on the scene you can't tell who's gonna get hurt. You and Bud could probably make it up, whatever the argument's about, if Rev would keep out of the way. Trouble is, he's got a lot of pride. If he thinks you're trying to show him up—"

"Aw, the hell with that son of a bitch," said Dolf. "Shit on him. Is he the only one in the world who's got pride? Is he God Almighty because he carries a pistol?"

Huff ducked his head in a yellow way. "I'm just saying it would be too bad if anybody'd get really hurt, you know?"

Dolf sneered at him. "You mean you're worried about yourself. Well, you just crawl aside with your tail between your legs, and you won't get hurt."

Huff grinned at him for a while. Walt was as chicken-hearted as they came. Then he said, "Go to hell, you bastard."

Dolf put down his sandwich, stood up, and swung a roundhouse at Huff, who stepped out of its way, and just as Dolf had completed the follow-through forced on him by the momentum, Walt gave him a big one in the gut. Luckily it was too low for the solar plexus, and though it hurt him, he was not put out of action: behind the fat he still had solid stomach muscles, dating from his early days of strenuous labor.

His own next blow hit Huff's nose: blood gushed from it like water from an open tap. Huff tried to continue, but he was bleeding too much. He put both hands to his face and walked rapidly away in the direction of the toilet.

While Dolf was watching Huff's retreat he was struck in the chest by the sledgehammer of a heart attack, and he fell writhing to the concrete floor.

It took a while for Walt to stanch the flow of blood from his nose: he was a notorious bleeder. He snuffed a lot of water from the cup of his hand, and from time to time he threw his head back as far as it would go.

He had been wrong to start at Beeler's belly, which had not proved that weak; he too should have gone for the face. Luckily no one else had seen the fight. Being ten years younger, he would have been humiliated the way it turned out. However, that brief encounter was only Round One so far as he was concerned. The blow he took could be considered as pretty much a sucker punch. It had been gentlemanly of him to strike at the body, whereas Beeler had obviously been out to disfigure his own opponent: he was a dirty fighter, a yellowbelly, and a bum.

Walt gingerly fingered his face while looking into the

discolored mirror over the washbowl in the toilet. His swollen nose definitely changed the upper part of his face; even his eyes were affected. The guys had a softball team that sometimes practiced at the nearby Legion field after work, and for safekeeping stashed their equipment in the stockroom, which was either always manned or stoutly locked. Walt was thinking he would go get one of the baseball bats and settle the score with Beeler, who had really, if you thought about it, jumped him from behind without warning, the shit-heel. He himself had been in the right and had suffered for it. If Beeler dared to come into the toilet at the moment, Walt would have shoved his face in a pisspot.

When finally someone did appear, it was a guy with whom he had had no dealings and whose face was only vaguely familiar. This man went to the urinals and assumed the standard spread-legged stance. After a moment he looked over at Walt.

"Know a foreman named Beeler? They just took him away in an ambulance."

"Huh?"

"There's blood all over. They don't know what happened."

Walt ran out to the scene of the recent fight. The old colored janitor, wearing a suit coat on top of overalls, was mopping the floor, but nobody else was there.

"What happened here?"

"Don't know if he was daid or not," said the janitor.

"Who was it?" It could have been somebody else. Dolf was perfectly O.K. when last seen. The guy in the toilet could have been wrong about the identification.

"That heavy guy," said the colored man, "you know? What they call Ralph?"

It was tempting to take him at face value, but having had experience with our dusky friends, Walt was aware they were none too reliable with the names of white men. "You don't mean Dolf?"

"Yes indeed, that is it," said the janitor, grinning affirmatively. "They was hauling him out when I come, and I says, 'Who's that?' and they says, 'Ralph.' "

As Walt hastened out toward the parking lot he met a group of men who were returning.

He asked, "Was that Dolf Beeler?"

Somebody said, "That's right. He just keeled over."

Someone else said, "He had a hemorrhage. There was blood all over the floor."

Walt tried to oppose panic with reason. *He* had been the one who bled. His only blow had sunk into five or six inches of fat: a man didn't die from that or even lose a drop of blood. Yet who could say what might happen to a man of Beeler's age if he took a punch? It wasn't as if he had just collapsed in the normal course of his day. He might well have a legal case against a younger guy like Walt. Walt knew a man on whose property a door-to-door magazine salesman had tripped coming down the front-porch steps, twisted his ankle, and claimed he couldn't ever walk right thereafter, and a shyster lawyer had won him a bundle, to pay off which the poor devil lost his home.

The Millville volunteer ambulance corps had the same personnel as the fire department, except that fewer guys were needed for most calls. If Walt had not been oblivious to the situation while in the toilet, he would certainly have considered himself as being on duty with respect to the fallen Dolf, and would have been the first to put in the emergency call and then to grab an end of the stretcher—all this when maybe it was he who had killed the victim.

His nose started to bleed again, and he returned to the toilet.

Merryvale Hospital, where the Millville ambulance boys had taken Tony's father, was up on the county line and could not be reached from Hornbeck by public transportation except by taking two buses whose routes did not quite intersect. Though Tony was handy around engines and could drive very well, he could legally operate a motor vehicle only when accompanied by a licensed adult. His mother had never been behind the wheel of a car, and wishing to maintain Dolf's code of independence and self-sufficiency (he hated being beholden to relatives or friends), especially now that he was on the flat of his back, Bobby realized that if she expected to get to the hospital, someone in the immediate and available family would have to drive her. Bernice had a license but could not be reached at the moment—on hearing that she had left the employment of the Majestic Theatre, Bobby strongly suspected that her daughter had been fired and was fibbing about being a manicurist, and phone calls now confirmed these suspicions—and therefore Tony was elected willy-nilly.

He came home from school within ten minutes of her call to the principal's office and brought Jack with him. Jack was wearing a sweater that had been handed down, like so much of his clothing, from Tony. It was darned in one small place, under the arm, where the moths had got to it because he had not given it to his mother to put away for the summer, owing to an aversion to the smell of mothballs, which he said made him queasy.

"I guess you'll want to change that," said Bobby, pulling the wool at the elbow.

"O.K." He went upstairs.

"I'm sure glad Dad didn't die," said Tony.

"People don't always die from a heart attack," Bobby said. She had put on her foundation and her Sunday best, including a hat, and powdered her face: all of this really did help to support a person's spirit. "Heck, a lot of people have had one and lived to see a better day."

"Where's the car?" Tony asked. "Still over at the plant? I better hike over there, be quicker than the bus. And then I'll run back and pickya up." He too was wearing a sweater over a shirt and tie. It was nice and neat, but as the man in the group he should be dressed like one.

"Fella from work's bringing it over, some pal of your dad's. While we're waiting, why don't you go upstairs and put on a suit, Tony? You know what I mean."

"Sure." He almost bumped into Jack, who was just returning in a brown coat sweater, all neatly buttoned. They really were good boys.

Tony had just gone upstairs when from her post at the back kitchen window Bobby saw the automobile come up the alley.

She gathered her coat together at the waist: it was a little too snug to button in comfort. She picked up her purse and said to Jack, "Car's here. Tell Tony I went on out."

Going down the back stairs she was cautious. She wore high heels only on such official occasions, weddings, funerals, and the like, which happily were not that frequent. When she reached the alley she was amazed to see that the man who had returned the car was some distance away and striding rapidly.

She called, "Hey there."

He stopped and turned. "Miz Beeler? Key's right there in the ignition."

"Say," she said, "don't you wanna cuppa coffee and some pie?"

"No ma'am. No thanks."

It was the least she could do to walk up to him and say, "It was real nice of you to run it over. I know Dolf will appreciate it." She smiled at him. He looked some years younger than her husband. "Would you be Ozzie Walsh?"

"No ma'am." He looked shyly away. His nose looked red, as though he had a cold.

"I was wondering who to tell Dolf it was," said Bobby. "We're going over now, so we'll be there's soon's they let us see him."

"Izzat the hospital?"

"Merryvale," said Bobby.

"He's holding on, then?" This question was anxious.

"Yes he is. But you never know what the future holds," she said superstitiously. "With the heart you just have to wait. They'll keep him for a while. I just thank the Lord this first one wasn't fatal. . . . Well, he will sure appreciate you bringing the car over. If you don't mind, I'd like to tell . . ."

He got the idea, and said, "Tell him Walt Huff hopes he gets better real soon. Tell him Walt is real sincere. Tell him I . . . tell him I will sure miss him at work and hope he gets back there before long. I mean it!"

"I certainly will. It's real nice of you. My name's Bobby. We been married twenty-three years."

"Is that right?" He still looked uneasy. Bobby decided he was one of those people who were always shy around somebody else's wife when alone with her, as opposed to the kind like Harvey Yelton, who when everybody was younger would naturally take such an occasion as an opportunity to get fresh, and how far can you go in fending off a policeman? It made a real difference when a man carried a gun and a nightstick, even though Harvey never made a threat of any kind and would have laughed off her fear.

It was a relief that they had both gotten too old long since for him to think any more about such things, though if the truth be known she had never really blamed him altogether, considering that awful wife of his.

"You married and have a family, Walt?"

He nodded sadly. "Yes, I do. I live over in Millville, you know. I just walk to work. It's real convenient. I go home for lunch. I live so close there's plenty of time in the half hour. The missus has a ham 'n' cheese samwich ready or a bowl of chili . . ." He seemed to get more nervous as he talked.

"I guess we better get going," Bobby said, "though they said we can't see him right away. It might help just to be there." Suddenly she felt weak, and it was in appeal to male sympathy that she said, "I hope to God he'll pull through. He's a real good man, Walt. He's had some trouble lately with some mean people over in Millville. Maybe you know 'em? The Bullards?"

He got an awful look. Given her worry, she had spoken without thinking. He might be friendly with some of them: far as she was concerned that wouldn't necessarily be a crime. Some of them might be all right: it wasn't your fault into which family you were born.

Walt finally said, "Well, it was nice meeting you."

Bobby could hear the boys coming. "Listen here," she said, "we'll just give you a lift back to Millville. That's the same way we're headed."

He looked scared. "Oh, now that won't be—"

"Nosir," said Bobby. "We're not going to let you walk! You just come on." With that shy sort of person you just had to bully them for their own good.

"This here's Mister Huff works with your father," Bobby told the boys when everybody converged on the car.

They said "Hi" to Walt, and Tony checked the hood

to see if it was still holding. Bobby insisted that Walt climb into the front passenger's seat. It was at such times she was pleased that Dolf had had the foresight to buy a four-door: a person of her bulk would have had a tough time climbing over a folded seat.

Jack entered through the far side. He had tried to comb his hair, but in back he had a persistent cowlick that wouldn't stay down without grease, which he hated. He said he would make his hair slick only if he had a cookie-duster mustache to go with it.

He leaned forward and said to the back of his brother's neck, "Let me know if you wanna move the seat forward: I'll push."

"I must of grown some more," said Tony. "Seat's just right."

Walt was staring out his window. Jack addressed him. "Just let us know where you want off."

Bobby said to Jack, "Mister Huff."

"I'm sorry. Say, Mister Huff, please let us know where you want to go."

"Sure," Walt said nervously. "Anyplace, anyplace at all will be just fine." He was silent until they crossed the Millville line. At the first corner inside his town he said urgently, "Right here!"

Tony pulled to the curb, and Huff got out. He stared wildly in through the back window at Bobby, and she cranked the glass down.

He cried, "I never meant no harm. As God is my witness, I never did!"

"Nobody said you did, I'm sure," Bobby gently replied.

But Huff looked ready to burst into tears. "They will!" He continued to stand there, though he said nothing more.

Tony pulled away. Jack said, "Who was that guy? He's sure got a big nose. He acts like some kind of screwball.

What does he do at the plant, sort the nuts?" He looked grinning at his mother.

"I don't know as how it ought to be a joke, Jack," said she. "I think Mister Huff just feels real bad about your father."

Tony's shoulders heaved slightly. He said, "I wonder if he knows I had a fight with a kid of his last year after the basketball game with Millville."

Jack made a cackling sound. "I bet you whipped him, Tone."

"Tony!" Bobby chided. "You know I don't like you to fight."

"You got to sometimes, Mom," said Tony. "You just got to." He was calm behind the wheel and didn't get angry at other drivers as Dolf often did.

"I just hope you didn't hurt that poor boy," said Bobby. She naturally assumed that Tony himself was invulnerable. "It would be a shame, considering how nice a man his father is. You know, you're awful strong, lifting those bells of yours."

Jack snickered. "Barbells, Mom, or dumbbells. Not just bells."

"I guess you're calling me a dumbbell?" asked Bobby, but behind all of this she was worried sick about Dolf. If he was laid up for any length of time, they'd lose their house, having only something like seventy-six dollars in savings.

Tony thought he'd go crazy if he didn't get to Eva sometime soon. Everything was getting worse and worse, and he was still stuck with the last memory of how he got rid of her so that those two assholes wouldn't think less of him. Now this had happened to his father, and he still hadn't even got Jack to write that letter for him.

He put the car into a space in the parking lot, and they all went into the hospital. After his mother had inquired at the main reception desk, she came back and said, "It hasn't changed. He still can't have visitors, but I called Doc Kinney from home and asked him to take over. He said he'd get there soon's he can. Maybe we could get Dad switched to Jewish. That's Doc Kinney's hospital."

Jack asked, "I didn't know he was Jewish."

"You don't have to be, either as doctor or patient," said Bobby. "It's just the name of the place."

Tony said, "Hey, Jack, you want to look for the coffee shop?" He added, hypocritically, because he yearned for some privacy, "You wanna Coke or something, Mom?"

"No, Tony. I'll just sit over there in that waiting room. If anything happens before you two get back, I'll come looking for you."

That was a relief. He and Jack explored the corridors until they found what they wanted, which had the usual counter and booths. There were not many customers during the middle of the day. Of a wide offering of stools Tony took the farthest from the door.

Jack said worriedly, "I hope you have dough. *I* don't."

Tony sank his hand into the pants pocket where he carried his cash if any. He saw he had a dime. When the waitress came he ordered two small Cokes.

"Wait a minute," said Jack. "Have you got root beer?"

The waitress shook her head.

"O.K., Coke then." Jack turned to his brother. "You know anything about heart attacks? What does that mean? The heart just stops? Christ sakes."

"Doc Kinney'll handle it," said Tony, and added piously, "The rest is in the hands of the Guy Upstairs. We just got to wait." After a decent interval of silence he said, "As long as we're waiting, I was wondering if you might get going on that letter again."

"Huh?"

Tony was annoyed. "You know, the bomb and all came before you really got started."

The waitress brought the Cokes. When she had gone Jack said, "What's eating her, I wonder?"

"Huh?"

"She's sorta snippy."

"I'm serious, Jack. If you ain't got nothing better to do at the moment, maybe you could start writing that letter."

Jack gulped half the Coke in one gulp and briefly chewed some of the shaved ice. "I would if I had some paper and something to write with."

Tony said, "Here." He produced some folded sheets of paper from the pocket of his suit coat, and a fountain pen.

"This is nice stuff," said Jack, taking the paper and feeling the top sheet with his thumb. "Real smooth and thick. . . . Hey, aren't these pages from *books*?"

"Those pages at the beginning and end that don't have any printing on them, you know? Nobody will miss 'em."

"The owner might," said Jack. "What're they from, one of Mom's books in the living-room cabinet?"

"Naw, I wouldn't touch *them*. Schoolbooks, you know: English, history . . ."

"You're a wild man," Jack said. "You'll have to pay a fine at the end of the year, I bet."

Tony said impatiently, "So what? Let's get that letter going."

"Right here?" Jack thoughtfully took a paper napkin from the chromium holder and cleaned the counter top. He unfolded the sheets of paper, then unscrewed the cap of the pen, and put it onto the end of the shaft. He tested the point on the napkin, making a blue-black blob. He began to write: *Dear* . . . "Uh, what'd you say her name was again?"

Tony found it hard to believe that the name that was so precious to him could be forgotten by his brother in one day. "Eva." He leaned against Jack's narrow shoulder so that he could watch the writing.

"Now, what was it we were going to say?" Jack asked.

" 'Dear Eva,' " said Tony, "I want to apologize to you, Eva, for the dumb stunt I pulled last summer, the second time we ran into each other at those dances, when I was with those guys from Hornbeck, though I didn't come there *with* them, I just ran into them by acci—' "

Jack said, "If I'm supposed to write that down, go slower, willya? So far I haven't got the whole first sentence, and I've forgotten the rest of it."

"O.K." Tony took a swig from the glass before him. As he put it down, the sixth sense by which one sees through the sides and even the back of the head sent him a signal to look to his left. When he obeyed this command he saw Eva Bullard. She was just entering the coffee shop, wearing a green sweater and a pleated plaid skirt. For an instant he assumed she was alone, but then behind her came the woman he recognized, from that trip Reverton had taken him on through their kitchen, as her mother, and then came a kid his own age, and then some adult fat guy wearing rimless glasses. They all definitely proved to be together when they took the same booth.

Eva and her mother sat on the same side, their backs at an angle to Tony. Had they occupied the other side of the booth, they could have seen him. As it was, he was safe enough unless she turned to scan the room, which of course people will sometimes do for no reason at all, and she was seated on the outside. The other difficulty was that to leave the coffee shop he would have to go right past her, and her group had just come in, meaning that they would be there for a while, whereas Jack had long since finished his Coke, and neither of them had any money for a refill.

But some time could be gained by giving Jack his own glass, which he had scarcely touched.

Jack was suspiciously incredulous. "Something wrong with it?"

"Naw. I just ain't thirsty."

Jack made a moue, accepted the glass, and drained it. He said, in a perversely louder voice than he had been using, "I got it! How about, 'Dear E—' "

The athlete's reflexes came in handy here. Tony was able to get his hand across his brother's mouth before more than the initial sound of her name emerged.

Jack was dumfounded. "What was that supposed to be?"

"Look," Tony said in a low voice, "I don't want my business broadcast to the world."

Jack was good enough to reply in a whisper, "But there's nobody to hear, except those people who just came in." The waitress, who appeared to be the only functionary on duty at the moment, had gone over to the booth.

"Yeah, well," said Tony.

Jack would have done better to stop at this point, but he had to add, still in the near-whisper, "When we get this letter done, I think I'll write one to that girl with them over there. She's really neat."

Tony felt like punching someone—not his brother, who was totally innocent, but something inanimate that could represent the face of the god of Chance. Why, on the same day of his father's sickness, should *she* be chosen to come to the coffee shop of the Merryvale Hospital?

He inhaled and said to Jack, "Listen, let the letter go for a while, and go out and see if Mom's all right. O.K.?" Again

Jack looked astonished. Tony added, "I'm worried about her, see? Maybe she should have a cup of coffee to calm her down."

Jack lowered the pen, but then he picked it up again and screwed the top on it. "So it won't dry up? You know? Did you ever try to write with one that—"

"Would you mind getting going?" Tony asked.

Jack shook his head. "Gee, Tony, you're getting pretty nervous these days, aren't you?"

Frieda Bullard was telling the Reverend Amburgy of some of the events that had preceded her husband's admission to the mental ward of Merryvale Hospital. She suppressed certain details, not only because of the presence of the children: she would not have wanted to tell the whole story to the preacher.

"Junior went down the store at noontime, before he came home for his dinner, and he says looters had already cleaned out a good deal of the merchandise as was left after the fire. Well, you know that store was everything to Bud. He worked and saved and scraped—" Suddenly she was on the verge of tears, and to come back to normal she told her daughter, "You can have pop or plain milk."

Eva made a face. "I was going to have a sundae."

Frieda said, "I figured you had that in mind, but we got to watch our pennies now."

The Reverend Amburgy looked uncomfortable. He cleared his throat and said, "Please permit me to pay for my own order." Some people called him stingy, but Frieda was aware that his salary was not large; though it was true that his rent was free and the church bought his car, and he was a single man.

Junior said, in the almost angry voice he had been using for the past few days, "I'll just have ice water."

"Now, that's not necessary," Frieda said. "You have whatever you want, Junior."

Eva wailed, "But I only get pop?"

"I'd think you could figure it out, Eva," Frieda told her. "There isn't any danger that Junie would order something expensive." Eva went into a sulk. She didn't need ice cream: it looked as though she was already getting a hickey on her chin. Her mother resumed the story.

"So Junior says there was still some kids around poking through the ashes, and he run 'em off. But some of the bigger ones sassed him even though he says he was the owner's boy, and—"

Junior interrupted angrily. "There was three or four, and I didn't know any of 'em. I don't think they're in school. Probly some of them hillbilly kids that quit when they're sixteen. I ain't yella, but they were three or four and real tall."

The Reverend Amburgy smiled on Junior, who sat next to him, and he said, "Why, now, you mustn't blame yourself. We all know you are a brave young man. That was a job for the police." He patted Junior's hand on the tabletop.

Frieda went on, "So uh course when Bud heard that he— well, he couldn't even eat any of his dinner. He just went upstairs and got his gun."

"Oh dear me," said Amburgy, pursing the little lips in his chubby face.

"He always sold guns but he never even hunted, himself," Frieda said. "So when he takes this shotgun—"

Amburgy said, "Was it loaded?" And when Frieda said yes, he murmured, "Oh, my."

The waitress came and took their orders, and Frieda resumed. "So I was sure worried when he goes out with that gun. I knew he was headed for the store, or what was left of it, but there's no arguing with Bud when he's got his mind set on something, so I never said beans. Of course a man's got a perfect right to protect his own property . . ."

"Certainly," the preacher agreed, turning to smile at Junior.

Junior said in anger, "He should of shot them down like dogs."

Amburgy's expression turned to something like fright, and he turned back to Frieda.

She said, "I don't think he actually shot *at* anybody personally. From what I hear, he was firing mostly up into the air. But I guess he kept it up for quite some time, even when there wasn't nobody there any more, and then if some car just came by he got the idea that they might be some looters coming back, and so he'd shoot off his gun again. Ray Dooley was on duty at the station, and nobody reported it or anything: he could hear the shots from town hall, so he runs over in the cruiser, and there's Bud shooting away.

" 'Say, Bud,' Ray says, 'I can't letcha keep doing that. It's against the law.' 'You just mind your own business, Ray,' says Bud, 'I'm only protecting what's mine. A man's gotta do that. He can't leave it to others.' 'Near as I can see, Bud,' Ray says, 'ain't got nothing left to protect. Come on now, gimme that shotgun.' But Bud he wouldn't put it down, so Ray finally says, pointing, 'Oh-oh, they're creeping up behind your back, Bud,' and Bud he whirls around and shoots into the ashes, and Ray conks him with his nightstick, lays him out cold.

"Then he hauls him back home, and he says, 'Let's get this poor devil in bed, Frieda. You take this here gun and keep it away from him until he settles down. Somebody might get hurt otherwise, and it would sure be a shame, with all the bad luck Bud's been having lately.' "

She stopped talking so that the waitress could serve their refreshments: two coffees, one Coke, and an Orange Crush for the preacher.

"You put lots uh cream in that," Frieda urged Junior. "Don't want to stunt your growth." She told Amburgy, "Some won't let a young person drink coffee at all, but I think it's O.K. if diluted."

The stout minister said, "Speaking for myself, it gives me acid stomach." His drink had come in the bottle, with a straw: he now sucked at the latter while raising his eyebrows toward Frieda.

She resumed, "Bud came to with quite a headache, as you might expect, but what could Ray have done otherwise to stop him from shooting up the town? He seemed to understand that himself, and was real sorry about the whole thing." What she did not say was that when an attempt was made to put Bud properly to bed, he began to fight with the policeman, who was a head taller than he and had forty pounds on him, and Ray had to restrain him in a pair of handcuffs. Dr. Swan came and put him under with a shot, and the ambulance boys, who said they were just back from another emergency down at the mill, hauled him here to Merryvale, where at present he was technically under observation, though practically he was still out.

"So anyway Doc Swan thought they might figure out what was ailing him if he stayed here overnight, but naturally we're worried, and I sure thank you for giving us the ride. It's times like this I regret I never learned to drive."

The Reverend Amburgy looked solemn. "Only too glad to help out, Frieda. That's what I'm for. I call on all folks from the congregation who get sick. The kind of thing that is troubling Bud, well, maybe I can talk to him some: that might be the sort of medicine which would do him more benefit than morphine."

Frieda shook her head. "Is that what the doctor gave him?"

"I would imagine," said Amburgy, his gaze drifting away.

"That's awful strong stuff, isn't it? I didn't think he was in that bad uh trouble."

The preacher looked at something off to the left for another instant or two, and then he came back to her. He said, "Excuse me. I couldn't help but notice a young boy at the counter over there. Earlier he was sitting with another boy, the one who just a minute ago walked right past here on his way out, if you noticed. But the second one sat there for a minute longer, and then he left the stool and went around the other side of the counter, but then all at once disappeared. He must have scrooched down below it. He still hasn't come up. I wonder where he went?"

They all looked in the appropriate direction, Frieda and her daughter turning in the booth.

Seeing the group movement, the waitress came to them. "Check?"

The Reverend Amburgy said, "We were just curious about where that boy went, that other boy at the counter."

The waitress, a stringy-haired woman wearing earrings, said, "I'll find out." And off she went.

Amburgy simpered in a certain embarrassment. "I don't know," said he, "if it's *that* important."

Frieda turned back, but Eva kept looking toward the counter. Junior was still blowing on his coffee. "See," said his mother, "you probably should have got a cool drink of some kind."

When the waitress came back she was snickering. "He went out through the kitchen. Cook saw him come walking in, all bent over, and thought he got sick." She laughed raucously. "Ptomaine, you know? Anyway, out he goes by the service door. I guess it was some kinda joke he was playing. He wasn't sneaking out, anyway. He paid the check."

Junior, with a sneer, tried his coffee. The Reverend chuckled briefly, and then he siphoned up the remainder of his orange drink. "I do have to make my other rounds," said he. "Should I look in later on you in the waiting room? Do you have any idea how long you'll stay?"

"Gosh, I don't," said Frieda. "I just figure we ought to be here, so that when Bud comes to, he won't feel like we deserted him. But I don't know what the rules are. Maybe they'll want to kick us out by a certain time."

Amburgy extricated himself from the booth, the edge of the tabletop temporarily scoring his belly. When he was out and standing erect, he said, "I'm afraid I can't be here tonight because of the regular weekly meeting of the Bible Club. I can't bring you home if you stay that late."

"Now, don't you worry yourself none about that, Reverend," said Frieda. "We'll make out O.K. There's the bus, and then who knows if we won't run into somebody going our way."

As Jack came back to the coffee shop he stared with interest at the girl with the group in the booth. She did not return his glance or give any indication that she was aware of his passing. He went to the empty counter and shrugged. The waitress came over to him.

"Looking for your friend?" She giggled stupidly. "He just left."

"Oh."

"You didn't see him in that hall," she explained, "because he snuck out the kitchen." She laughed some more.

"So?" That might seem like a funny thing to do, but why admit it to this person?

"He's a real nut!" said she.

Jack left the coffee shop. Going in this direction, he could see only the back of the head and shoulders of the girl in the booth. She had not appeared to be as sophisticated as Mary Catherine Lutz, because she was younger, but he liked her a lot. However, he and she were like ships that pass at sea and never the twain shall meet again.

If Tony had left via the kitchen, he had gone outside, probably en route to the car for some reason. Therefore instead of returning directly to the waiting room, Jack left the building by the front door and walked to the parking lot. Nope, the car was there, but no Tony. Nearby a fat man with glasses was rolling down the window and smiling at him from the driver's seat of another automobile. He smiled back.

"Hi, there," said the fat guy. "Weren't you in the coffee shop just now?"

"That's right." Jack was somewhat flattered.

"I couldn't help but notice you and your friend. He left in an unusual way while you were gone."

Tony seemed to have acquired an instant fame for this episode. "Yeah. He's my brother."

"Ah . . ." The man smiled a while longer. He wasn't the sort of older person Jack found very interesting: he seemed sissified. "Say, you wouldn't like a ride back to Millville?"

"No thanks," said Jack. "We got a car. Anyhow, we're from Hornbeck."

This information seemed to please the fat man. "Oh, how nice," he said. "But that's not far away. Maybe we'll meet again sometime. You're welcome to come over at any time to our Young People's Nights in the church basement. I'm the minister there." He told Jack where the church could be found.

That explained a lot. Jack had begun to get the uncomfortable suspicion that this guy might have it in mind to corner him somewhere and slide a fat hand between his legs, which had happened once the previous summer with a man who was parked near the public swimming pool; he said he was lost and couldn't figure out where he was on the state road map, and Jack's showing him with a fingernail did not do the job, because the map was upside down; so he got into the passenger's seat, and the man slipped a hand under the map as he held it and rubbed his crotch with strong fingers; at first this didn't feel bad, but then he thought about it and saw that it was creepy; so having indicated where Hornbeck could be located, he politely left the car.

He said good-bye to the preacher now and went into the waiting room, where not only Tony but also Dr. Kinney had joined his mother.

Whatever the doctor had reported, he was finished by the time Jack arrived and, holding his black bag, was obviously anxious to get going elsewhere.

The doctor was saying, "—easy, Bobby. Worrying yourself to a frazzle won't help, now will it?" He clapped her on the shoulder, and then he looked at Jack and said, "Don't tell me this is who I think it is? Looks like you put on a few ounces, Jackson."

Jack had always had difficulty in gaining weight. He had never eaten much because he was rarely hungry. Dr. Kinney had prescribed a tonic for him that was supposed to increase the appetite, but he couldn't feel any difference. However, he didn't want to insult the doctor, who was only doing a job, and therefore he said yes, he was eating better.

After the doctor had departed, his mother said, "We'll just go home and keep our fingers crossed."

As usual, Jack had to ask what had happened. He seemed always to be somewhere else when information was handed out.

"Nothing," said his mother. "They're keeping Dad real quiet. There's nothing to do but wait, so I guess we can do that at home. I gave Doctor Kinney Dad's pajamas and shaving stuff to take in."

"Where'd you have that all this while?"

"Didn't you notice that shopping bag I was carrying?"

Darned if he did. He was aware that some details eluded him, and that was annoying, because he thought of himself as a keen observer as well as a shrewd judge of character: though so far as the latter went, he had been wrong about the preacher, who might not even be really a sissy. He might be just a gentleman, who spoke in that very clear way in the fashion of those actors who wore Ascots and velvet smoking jackets with fringed belts, who were sometimes Englishmen or just imitating them.

On their way out to the car Jack said to Tony, "Did you take an exit through the kitchen of the coffee shop?"

His brother glared suspiciously at him. "What do you know about that?"

Jack said, "It was noticed."

Tony seemed hard hit by this news. "They *saw* me?"

"The waitress did. She just thought it was strange, I guess."

"Well, it was *my* business."

"That's what I told 'em," said Jack. "When we get home, I'll work on that letter."

"Don't say anything to Mom on that subject," Tony said in an undertone, leaning close. Their mother was coming along in the rear: she didn't walk fast in her good shoes.

"I met this preacher. He's not such a bad guy. He invited me to come over to these young people's affairs at his church: it's in Millville."

"I guess you ain't about to take him up on *that*," said Tony. He opened the car door for his mother.

Whereas in reality Jack was secretly thinking of doing that very thing. He had somehow hoped, foolishly, that Tony might give him some encouragement. For a moment he had forgotten about the trouble with the Bullards and was occupied utterly by the idea that if the preacher had been sitting with those people in the coffee shop, they probably went to his church and that girl attended the functions for young people. Jack had not yet learned to dance, despite some rudimentary lessons from Bernice, but he could play games, drink punch, and eat ham-salad sandwiches as well as the next. He had done those things on occasion in the basement of the Hornbeck church to which his family nominally belonged, and given the other young people in attendance, he had been unspeakably bored, but having a girl you liked nearby could transform such an event. This one had the kind of face to which he was sure he could bring laughter with some of the jokes he had memorized from the witty repartee he heard on the radio.

Instead of returning via the direct route, going south on the county pike until they hit the main west-east thoroughfare, Tony unaccountably turned off into a maze of back streets when they reached the former.

Jack asked, "This a shortcut?"

"Yeah," said his brother. "I sorta wanna keep outa downtown, without a regular license and all. You can't ever tell."

"I forgot about that," said Jack. "It's crazy. I bet you're the best driver on the road." Jack did not yearn to drive; he looked forward to being rich enough to have a chauffeur. Tony was great at any kind of practical pursuit, yet he seemed none too certain of where he was going at the moment. In the middle of this block he had slowed down almost to a stop, and he was staring across Jack and out the passenger's window. There was nothing there but an ordinary house.

Jack said, "Are we lost?"

"I guess not." Tony shifted gears and picked up speed, turning right at the corner.

Their mother had been silent since leaving the hospital. Jack turned and spoke to her.

"I hope Dad gets some rest," he said. "He's had a lot of aggravation lately. I think that made him nervous and put a strain on his constitution."

His mother smiled in a sad way, and then she seemed to cheer up. "What sounds good to you fellas for supper? Pork chops? Tony, stop at the butcher's on the way home, willya?"

Over his mother's shoulder, through the rear window, Jack saw a police cruiser approaching a couple of blocks behind them. It was rolling considerably faster than they were. The red light behind its windshield was flashing, and in the next moment its siren was heard.

"Looks like there's a bank robbery in progress," Jack said in some excitement.

But Tony groaned. "You mean, it looks like my goose is cooked. I think I went through a stop sign back there." He pulled into the curb.

Jack still assumed that the cop was en route toward big criminal game, until the Millville police car passed them and swung into the gutter just ahead. The officer took his own good time in emerging. When he finally appeared, he was a stocky man in navy-blue uniform pants striped in yellow, and a white shirt and a black tie, but the jacket he wore seemed to be a civilian windbreaker. He put on a police cap as he approached them.

Tony moaned, and his mother said, "Now, don't you worry." She leaned forward and patted his shoulder. "I'll explain."

The cop stuck his large face into the opening of the window which Tony had just lowered.

"You look like a stranger here," said the officer.

"Yessir, we are," said Jack's mother. "Our dad has just been rushed to the hospital."

"Then," the cop went on to Tony, "I guess you don't know we require respect for our traffic laws." He smiled, but not kindly.

"Wellsir," said Jack's mother, "you just tell us what we did wrong, and we'll apologize."

"You got a driver's license?" the cop asked Tony.

Tony shrugged hopelessly, leaned forward, and dug his wallet out of his left rump pocket. He probed within one of its compartments.

"See," his mother said urgently, "our poor dad just had a heart attack and—"

The policeman poked a thick, blunt finger toward her. "Lady, you keep your goddam trap shut."

Tony violently hurled the door open, knocking the cop backwards and almost off his feet.

He shouted, "Don't you talk to my mother that way!"

The officer recovered and began to claw at his holstered revolver. He was detained by the strap that ran around its hammer and snap-buttoned below. He began to yell in the filthiest language Jack had ever heard in public.

This caused Tony to go wild. He hurled himself at the cop and gave him a series of punches too fast to count, but one or more of them knocked his enemy down, and out. The policeman lay prone on the asphalt.

Their mother called from the car. "Oh, my, Tony! You haven't killed him, have ya?"

Tony's glasses were disarranged, though he had not been touched. He adjusted them and peered carefully down at the officer.

"Naw," he said. "He's breathing. . . . Come on, we better clear out fast."

Jack was thoroughly shaken by observing this episode. His brother might be an old hand at violence of various kinds, but he himself was entirely innocent of it. He had never had a single fight, and managed for the most part to avoid rough sports.

No doubt with the realization that as long as the cop was unconscious no one could nab him for speeding, Tony now took the direct route and zoomed through Millville.

Until they crossed the Hornbeck line nobody said a word. Then Tony looked at his mother in the rearview mirror. "I'm sorry about that," said he. "I should of shut him up before he opened his foul mouth, that filthy skunk."

His mother leaned forward and patted his shoulder. "You did fine, Tony. You're a real good boy. I guess us Beelers don't have much luck in Millville. We ought to stay out from now on."

It took Jack a while to form the words. He had never seen anyone attack a policeman, for God's sake, let alone his own brother. "Boy," he finally managed to say, "if he was trying to get out his gun when you hadn't even socked him, what's he going to do when he comes to?"

Tony slowed to make the turn into the alley behind their house. He said, "What choice did I have? What kinda man sits there and lets his mother be insulted? He's lucky I never took that gun of his and shot him with it. He's a disgrace to his uniform."

This interpretation had not occurred to Jack. He realized that his brother had a more complex conscience than he had previously supposed.

He said, "You got all the nerve in the world, Tony."

"Listen, you would of done the same." Tony here revealed how little he knew his brother. Jack would no more have done anything of the sort, regardless of the provocation, than he would have set himself on fire. He knew that very well, and he felt guilty about this inability and tried to tell himself that using the brain could often be courageous, but he did not really believe that theory. Columbus had been brave not because of his insistence that the world was round, but rather because he had sailed three flimsy boats into uncharted seas to prove it. And though Galileo knew very well that the earth moved around the sun instead of vice versa, he lied about it so that the Catholics wouldn't burn him at the stake: which was not brave, but it was certainly intelligent.

When they got home, Jack's mother said, "In all the commotion I forgot to stop for the pork chops. There isn't much to eat here. I better go down Dorfman's and buy some wienies' and a couple cans baked beans."

Jack made the unprecedented offer to fetch the order from the grocery that was two blocks away. He was not usually the one to volunteer for a job, but Tony's feat continued to stir him in odd ways.

"Why, that would be real nice," said his mother. "That'll gimme the chance to tell Harvey Yelton about what happened over there. Gosh knows what report that Millville cop will put out."

She began to make a list of needed foodstuffs with a stub pencil on a fragment of brown wrapping paper from a drawer in the kitchen cabinet. But when her elder son had gone upstairs, she suddenly seized Jack and pressed him to her.

She said, "I don't know what we'll do if they take Tony away."

When he was released Jack said, "Maybe he'll have to go on the lam for a while till this blows over." But those were just words. He was as worried as he could be, and in times of crisis he felt as if he were no older than eleven or twelve and thus was disqualified from anything but the observer's role.

"He *what*?" said the Hornbeck police chief. "Oh, boy, is that right? He knocked Clive Shell on his big fat keister?" He howled.

Bobby did not join Harvey in his merriment. She waited till his laughter diminished in volume, and then she said, "Thing is, I believe Tony did go through a stop sign." She cleared her throat: after all, Harvey was himself a cop.

He stopped chuckling for a moment. "Well, what was it he said, or ain't it fit to repeat?"

"It isn't," said Bobby, demurely. "But it wouldna mattered that much to me: I wasn't born yesterday. It's just that Tony would not stand for anybody talking like that to his mom."

Harvey suddenly became grave. "By God, I'd shoot the man through the heart who would utter foul language before any lady, let alone my sainted mother: I cooden answer for my behavior in that case."

"But what're we gonna do," asked Bobby, "when he comes to?"

Harvey began to roar with laughter again. "He knocked

him out *cold*?" Finally he was able to say, "He won't ever be able to hold his head up again. That bum!"

It took Bobby an unhappy moment or two to realize that he meant the Hornbeck police chief and not her son.

She said, "Tony lifts a lot of weights. I guess he's stronger than he knows. He didn't mean to hit him that hard."

"I'll say this," said Harvey, "I envy him. I allus wanted to do it to that fat slob myself." He laughed awhile.

Bobby said, "But when all's said and done, I guess we're in pretty bad trouble, wouldn't you say, Harvey? Knocking out a policeman who was performing his duty . . ."

The chief grew solemn for a moment. "Ordinarily," he said, "there wouldn't be much that was worse, for you got to maintain respect for the law and them hired to enforce it. That's right!" He snorted. "But when you're talking about Millville, at least since old Clive took over the force, you got a different kettle of fish. They give him an appropriation over there a whole lot bigger than I get here, and he's supposed to use it to hire a part-time patrolman in addition to himself, but what old Clive does is just hire one, his cousin Ray Dooley, and I bet my bottom dollar Clive don't pay Ray even a decent salary, but pockets the difference. Ray ain't a bad guy. He's generally on duty around noon, when Clive is eating his lunch for about three hours. Too bad you dint go through Millville at that time. Ray ain't got a foul mouth: you can say that for him."

"But this Clive Shell can cause us trouble, can't he?" asked Bobby, with the purpose of bringing Harvey back to the subject, away from his personal gripe against the rival police chief.

Harvey said in a harsh voice, "He might if I wasn't here. As it is, he knows he'd never hear the end of it: knocked on his—excuse me—butt by a high-school kid? Tell me this: was there any witnesses?"

"I didn't see anybody."

"Well, there you are," said Harvey. "Mark my words, that guy ain't gonna wanna advertise what happened. He'd be a laffinstalk from here on. You know, us chiefs get together and have us a picnic from all over the county every spring: old Clive wouldn't never show up there again. He loves that picnic—on account of all the eats and beer."

"You wouldn't kid me, wouldja, Harvey?" Bobby asked, in an almost seductive voice. He had taken pleasure in her in the old days.

The chief did not react to the personal note. "But I hope alla you got enough sense to stay out of Millville from now on. I can't help yuz if he catches yuz over there. Clive'll throw the book atcha."

Bobby was greatly relieved. She exchanged her Sunday clothes for her everyday attire of wash-dress and apron, and was down in the kitchen when Jack returned from the store. She boiled the wieners and heated the baked beans.

At the table she said to Jack as she passed him a bowl, "I wish I'd remembered to tell you *not* German potato salad."

"Oh, yeah? What kind should I have got?"

"My own preference is with mayonnaise," she said, grimacing, "not so much sour vinegar. And I'll tell you this: I'm not so crazy about pieces of greasy bacon, either."

Jack said, wrinkling his nose, "I don't much like *any* kind."

"Well, you eat some, anyway. It's good for your health." He took two spoonfuls. "I thought you liked wienies, though, and baked beans—? Then I hope you're gonna eat some. You're too skinny, Jack." She was avoiding Tony, for what she took to be good maternal reasons. It had always been better to let him alone when he stared stonily into space. He was doing it now, even though she had told him what the chief had said. But at least he was eating. He was like her, in that trouble seemed to whet his appetite: of a dozen wieners Jack ate only one and a half, and maybe four tablespoonfuls of baked beans, of which she had opened two large cans. She and Tony polished off all else, even the potato salad, and when clearing the table for dessert (chunks of pound cake covered with canned shredded pineapple, topped with whipped cream), she ate the half-sausage Jack had left on his plate.

Just as they began dessert Bernice walked in the back door.

Bernice had been evicted from her rooming house. She had been in arrears for some time, and had gone as far as she could go in kidding the landlord along without actually putting out. He was a big fat greasy foreigner of some kind, with lots of hair in his nose and baggy eyes. Luckily he had never put a hand on her, or else she would have lambasted him with a hot curling iron, but if looks meant anything, he had done it to her plenty. She could have lived there rent-free for the rest of her life if she had given him a little of what he was dying for, but she was no tramp.

That's what hurt, when he called her one, though she should have considered the source and seen it was just sour grapes.

She had only smiled and said, "Maybe we can work something out till my ship comes in."

"No danks," said he. "You see your sailors someplace else! Dis ain't no cat-houze. Now you pull dat bathrobe shut, and den you pack up and get out inna morning."

"Hi, everybody!" she said now. "Didja dream you'd be seeing me so soon again?" But they didn't look that excited. Her mother got up and went to the cupboard. "The pineapple's all gone, but I got cling peaches, Bernice—?"

"Cuppa java will be fine," Bernice said. "That's all I need."

" 'Java,' " said Jack. "Is that what they say in the city, Bernice?"

"Ain't you ever heard that inna movies, Jack? 'Hey, you bozo, gimme a cuppa java. The flatfeet are out to get me, see.' Ain't you ever heard 'em say that in the movies?" Bernice was an authority on certain moving pictures: as an usherette she had seen and heard the same film over and over again and could therefore quote a lot of dialogue by heart.

Her mother brought the coffee. "Don't you wannany cake, Bernice? I sure hope you ate. We just polished off everything else in the house."

"Not me," Bernice said jauntily. "I couldn't swallow a morsel. Hey," she turned to Jack, "how do you like that one: morsel? Pretty classy, huh?" She went into an English accent that soon put him in stitches: words like "veddy" this and that, and "by Jove."

Her mother sat down at the table. "We got some bad news, Bernice. If you're wonnering where your dad is, he's in the hospital."

"Awwww—"

"Now, it's not fatal, thank the Lord. He had a heart attack over at the mill, and they came with the ambulance and took him right to the Merryvale Hospital."

"Awwww—" Bernice was really hit hard by this information. She had always thought her old man was the Rock of Gibraltar.

"He's all right, so far. We just have to wait, I guess."

Bernice hung her head. She had always been closer to her mother than to her father. She realized guiltily that she didn't know much about him at all. She remembered seeing a snapshot of him, once, wearing a uniform in which he looked funny because of the cap and also the leggings that were like bandages and gave him toothpick legs. But he was a lot skinnier all over in those days.

She said now, "I guess he had a tough time inna war."

Her mother shook her head. "He wasn't in the war."

Bernice mentioned the photo.

"Oh," said her mother, chuckling. "I recall that. He had that taken in a penny arcade. You didn't put the costumes on: you just stood in back of 'em and stuck your head through a hole: the different clothes were painted on big sheets of cardboard or whatnot. You know what I mean."

Bernice shrugged. Her mother told her of their visit to the hospital, but stopped there.

It was Jack who said, "And then, coming home, we had more trouble." While his mother tried to shush him he told about Tony's punching the cop.

"Oh for God's sake," Bernice said. "Tony."

He looked inscrutably at her through his glasses.

Jack said, "If he has to hide out for a while, can he stay at your place downtown?"

"Harvey Yelton don't think anything'll come of it," said her mother. "He says the Millville cop won't want it known a young boy beat him up."

"Now," said Bernice, grateful for this diversion, "that's somepin Harvey would be the authority on. You can rely on him." She addressed Tony in a lighter tone. "Now don't you go getting into a fight with Harvey too. He's on our side." Or so she hoped, in more ways than one.

Tony doggedly spooned up the rest of his dessert. Then

he said, "I ain't gonna worry about it. I did the right thing. I got no regrets, except I wish I'd of seen that stop sign."

"And see," said her mother, "Tony don't have his final license yet, so he didn't dare get picked up."

"Heck," said Bernice, "I shoulda been here. . . . Well, I'll tell you this, Mama, I intend to stay right here at home as long as Daddy's laid up. I can make myself useful for a change. I'll be the chauffeur!" This also neatly solved her own problem of where to live at the moment and disposed of the otherwise painful job of inventing a story as to why she was leaving the city altogether.

Her mother didn't make as much of a protest as she expected, probably because she was so worried about Dad. "That would sure be swell of you, Bernice, if you could spare the time."

"Why," Bernice said brightly, "I'll just take my vacation a little ahead of the season. You want me to run you back to the hospital when you finish your cake?"

"They wouldn't let us see him yet," said her mother, reflectively working her teaspoon into the dessert. Tony's appetitie did not seem to be affected by his troubles. Jack was like Bernice in not eating much. There were some who said that men preferred plump girls, but Bernice was only too aware that many others liked their meat close to the bone.

Jack said, "The Millville cop would have to get extradition papers. I don't know if that means the G-men would be called in or not."

His mother shook her head. "Now, come on, Jack, let's drop the subject for a while."

Tony had been chewing stolidly and staring at his plate. He now lifted his head. "I'm going to quit school tomorrow and get a job at the mill."

"No, you are not," his mother said firmly. "My Lord, you only got the rest of this year to finish, and you're gonna do it." She lifted the milk bottle and filled his glass to the brim, though it had been only a few seconds since he had given himself a refill and he had not drunk much of it.

"Yeah, Tony," said Bernice. "*Somebody* in this family ought to have a high-school diploma." She herself had left school as soon as she could, when she turned sixteen in the middle of the sophomore year. Her parents had to sign for her, and they did it willingly. She went to work at the local independent five-and-ten, but it had not been long before she and the proprietor, a newcomer to Hornbeck named Chick Willig, had a falling out over some missing cosmetics which the daily sales figures could not justify. Willig was a real cheapskate. Nor would anybody have ever called him a he-man, else he wouldn't have objected to her learning how to use makeup professionally, at a very small expense to himself. But when he fired her, the excuse he gave was that his female customers had complained: she was too stuck-up to wait on anybody. Well, they weren't altogether wrong about that; she had better things to do than wait on that bunch of old biddies.

Tony said stubbornly, "What difference does it make if I graduate? I'm gonna end up at the mill sooner or later anyway, ain't I? If Dad's laid up we're gonna need some money now. It's stupid for me to just sit there and take history and English and that other crap."

Jack said, "I guess you're right, but that junk's useful if you want to be a foreign correspondent."

Bernice smiled at her younger brother. "Izzat what you want to be, Jack?"

He looked shy. "I don't know."

"What is that, sort of like being some kinda spy or something?" Jack was going to be a swell-looking fellow in a couple of years.

"I guess you go to places like Constantinople and Singapore and Paris, France, and write things for the newspaper," said Jack. "You have to carry a portable typewriter, you know, one that folds up into a little suitcase?"

"Well, then we know what to getcha for Christmas, don't we?" said Bernice.

"I'm saving up," Jack said, and then laughed wryly. "I've got a dollar sixty-five so far: that's from selling old papers and stuff to the junkman."

"Does that Hunky still come down the alley with his horse 'n' wagon?" Bernice asked idly. "Does he stink as much as ever? You could smell him all the way upstairs from the cellar."

"Well, it takes all kinds," her mother said. "Say, if you're gonna stay the night, Bernice, I'll give you a pair of Tony's pajamas."

Bernice snapped her fingers, as if she had genuinely forgotten. "My gosh." She got up. "I left it on the porch. I brought out a suitcase full uh dirty wash. Where I stay the boiler busted last night, and there wasn't any hot water all day." She had worked up this story on the bus, coming out; in truth the valise contained such possessions as she owned at this time, apart from things she had left here at home in Hornbeck.

Her mother hastily left the table, went out to the back porch, and brought in the suitcase. "I'll get going onnis right after I do these dishes."

Actually, everything was dirty and could use a good washing, so Bernice didn't protest. Her mother loved working, whereas she herself hated it. Among the many lousy things about leaving home was all the stuff you had to take care of, like laundry, etc., etc., which when your mother took care of it, you hardly knew existed. The only good thing was you had your privacy, but the advantages of that could be exaggerated. There were a lot of rotten people in the world who would rather die than give you a break.

"I was thinking," she said to her mother, "I might just take a little spin inna car to get used to it again. It's been a while since I was back of the wheel."

"Say, that might be an idea," said her mother. "Whyn't you and Tony do that?"

Bernice's idea had been to go by herself, for her own reasons, but when Tony promptly left the table, tossing the car keys in his hand, it seemed simpler to play along.

Jack said, "I'll clear out of your old room, Bernice."

"Gee," she said, "I sure feel bad about that. It'll just be for a little while. I'll make it up tuh yuh, Jack."

"Gosh, that's O.K." It was a pity you couldn't meet any grown men who were anything like Jack, or even Tony, who was a pretty swell guy too, with lots of principles. Never in her life had she met a grown man with any principles worthy of the name, unless her father had some: she wouldn't know about that. They were all liars and cheats and had a yellow streak up their back, and if they ever had a feeling that wasn't purely selfish, she had never detected it. The only trouble was: in spite of this, she had a soft spot in her heart for guys, and though they were all dirty rats, deceitful as they come, she would rather trust any of them than some other woman.

The sun was setting when Bernice and Tony reached the yard. She remembered that she had seldom driven at night and in fact had forgotten exactly how to turn the headlights on. It was therefore just as well that her brother had come along, at least this far.

"Say, Bernice," Tony said when they climbed into their respective seats. "Can I talk to you about something?"

"Sure, Tone. Just let me get this crate started up. . . . Here, right? Have I got the right thing?" She was treading the starter, but nothing happened. Tony told her she'd have to kick it hard. She did that, and the engine whirred for a while and at last caught on. "Gee," she said, "does that sound right?"

"It's a little loud," Tony admitted. "That's because the hood is just wired down, and the vibration, see. . . . What I wanted to talk about was, uh—"

"Just lemme get this backed up," said Bernice, trying all the gears before she found reverse. Some guy had taught her to drive on a different make of car not long after she quit school. He sat her on his lap back of the wheel, like they do with a little kid to pretend he's driving. This man would feel her up while they were rolling along the road. Once he opened his pants and demonstrated the shift pattern using himself. He had quite a sense of humor, but eventually proved himself to be the usual son of a bitch. One time they got into an argument about something, and he threw her out of the car three or four miles out in the country, and she would have had to hike all the way back home had not some kindly hick come along with a load of hay.

Tony waited until she had turned from the alley into the side street, and then he said, "I guess you'd know about this, Bernice. Does a girl hold a grudge for very long?"

"Just let me . . ." said Bernice, probing for the brake without success. "Hey, how do I stop this?" There was a stop sign at the approaching corner.

"*Right* foot," said Tony.

She found it. "I thought that was the clutch."

"Clutch is left foot, Bernice. Gas and brake is right. You better not forget that." When they started up again he resumed, "I wouldn't want this to get beyond you and me, if you don't mind, but would you marry somebody who did something stupid though he didn't mean to?"

She was less nervous now they were rolling freely along. "Well," she said, "if I was to hold something stupid against any men friends of mine, I wouldn't have any, to tell you the truth. Guys are always acting stupid. That's normal for them. They don't ever know how to act for very long. If you didn't know how to take care of yourself, boy, you'd go nuts." Then she realized she was talking to a male, even though it was her brother. "I mean older guys, not a young fellow like yourself. What'sa trouble? You still taking out Mary Catherine Lutz?" Bernice didn't like Mary Catherine; she thought short hair was ugly, and Mary Catherine's legs were as muscled as a boy's. Bernice couldn't understand what Tony saw in her, and she was relieved when he sneered now.

"*Her?* Naw." He hung his head. "The thing is . . . this is really hard to tell anybody. It's so crazy."

They were approaching the intersection with Elm Street. A car was stopped there at the red light. Bernice skillfully pushed the brake pedal and slowed to a halt just behind the car ahead. She was warmed up now, had returned to being a master driver.

"Heck," she said, "you can tell me. You know I wouldn't hold it against yuh." Tony related his thus far mostly dismal connection with Eva Bullard.

When he was finished, Bernice said, "Is *that* all?"

"Ain't it enough?"

She shrugged. The blaring horn of an oncoming auto annoyed her: she wasn't that far over.

"Be me, I wouldn't pay any attention to it," she told Tony, with reference to the trouble between the families.

He said, "It ain't as easy as it sounds. I went over to just her neighborhood the other day, and that one they call

Reverton, who is some kinda detective for the railroad, he put me under arrest. He pulled his gun on me, for God's sake."

Bernice did not really understand what this meant. She believed that Tony had picked up a tendency to exaggerate in the name of puppy love. She certainly had suffered from that malady in her day. In school she had been crazy about Mr. Keeler, who taught Speech and had a headful of tightly curled brown hair and big sensitive glowing eyes. She realized now, looking back, that there had probably been something wrong with him. He had since got into some kind of trouble and left town, though the details of this matter had been hushed up. He had always been nice to her, that was certain, and had given her a passing grade after an entire year of exasperated sighs. "*Honestly,* Bernice! I don't think you're *trying.*"

"You know what they say about a faint heart not getting a fair lady, Tone," she said to her brother. "I bet Eva has a higher opinion of you since you overcame them obstacles. The way to a man's heart might be through his stomach, but a girl likes a guy who would put his hand inna fire for her."

Distracted by the desire to say what she really meant, which she had not as yet come near to doing, she suddenly recognized that she was too rapidly overtaking the car ahead, and braked vigorously. Luckily Tony's reflexes were quick, and he caught himself on the dashboard.

"Sorry," said she. "Gee, these brakes could sure use some adjusting. They stick. . . . Uh, all I can say is, you gotta take a chance to get anything worthwhile in this here life of ours. Think I woulda gone anywhere if I had stuck around town and never went to the city? Oh, it might seem darn nice to stay where your friends are and family and all, like the rest of them I went to school with, and sure, some got married and had kids who already are old enough to get chickenpox and whooping cough, and the husband will get the mortgage paid off in thirty years and by then they'll be ready for the old folks' home, but I can't see myself in that picture. But, sure, you got to take some hard knocks and there are days when you feel real blue, but you can't let 'em see it or they'll just give you some more kicks where you sit down. . . ."

Up ahead she could see the alleyway where Harvey Yelton often parked his cruiser. The townsfolk were aware of this, but people from elsewhere, passing through, were ofttimes caught by him when they tried to run an orange light or exceed the downtown speed limit, which happened to be 5 MPH, as the tiny sign said, which they always protested they hadn't seen. "That's why we use such little letters," Harvey was known to boast. This might be called a dirty trick, but the people caught were usually those who might turn into troublemakers if not stopped in their tracks: this was particularly true of coloreds and hillbillies.

Bernice asked Tony, "Where is it you wanna be left off?"

He seemed amazed. "I wanted to get this thing talked over," he said slowly. "That's what I wanted to talk to you about."

She rolled slowly past the mouth of the alley. Yessir, there was Harvey. "Well, I dunno what else I can tellya, Tony, except not to be so shy. You're a swell guy, you got a winning personality, all you need's some confidence." She pulled to the curb. "I'm gonna stop here and go see the chief back there about some police business. But listen, you come to me any time you wanna talk. You can always count on me. I mean it, Tone."

"Gee," he said. "Thanks a lot, Bernice. I guess you really helped, but I gotta think about it for a while."

"But not too much, Tone! That's what I'm saying. You got to *do* something. You won't win her by just thinking."

Tony left the car frowning and walked slowly up the street. Bernice went into the alleyway and up to the passenger's window of the police car. She tapped on the glass, and when Harvey rolled it down with a scowl, she said, "Spose I could have a few words with you?"

He peered suspiciously through the windshield, and then came back to her. He spoke in a low, coarse voice. "I'll meetcha up at the station, see?" He started the cruiser and pulled out of the alley, turning onto Elm.

Bernice went back to her father's car. Harvey was out of sight by the time she got started. But Tony could still be seen, as slowly as he was walking. Not wanting to be detected by him as she sailed by, she reversed direction, using the mouth of the alley.

The police station was situated in the rear of the town hall. Next door was the firehouse, which was mostly unmanned except when the alarm sounded and the volunteers came from all points. However, at the moment the big garage doors were opened and the red engine had been run out onto the concrete apron, where it was being washed by several of the firemen.

"Hi there, Bernice," said one of them as she climbed out of the car.

"Hi there, Harry."

Then somebody else said, "Hey, Bernice, after we get done we're gonna wet our whistles. You wanna drink? It's on us."

"Well, that's sure the best offer I had in the last five minutes, Ernie," said she. But if those guys had any idea of loosening her up, they had another think coming. She was getting too old for that kind of crap.

She went past the parked cruiser and entered the police

station. Harvey had a little office up front, with a desk and a couple of chairs, and then down a short corridor there was one jail cell. This was the same kind as could be seen in the movies: the furnishings were a toilet without a lid, a small washbasin, and a bunk that hung from the wall on chains.

Bernice did not see the chief when she entered, so she poked down the little corridor, and there was Harvey, taking a pee in the toilet of the cell. She backed up and waited in the office part till he came out, buttoning his fly.

He pointed at the chair in front of the desk as he went behind it. As he sat down, the light of the gooseneck lamp made shadows around the bags under his eyes.

"Now what's your business?" he asked sternly.

She hemmed and hawed for a while, and then she said, "Well, I guess we can talk on the level with one another, Harvey—"

He interrupted. "I don't believe it's right for a girl your age to call me by my first name here in this office. It just don't seem right. There's some respect ought to be due."

"Why, sure," said Bernice. "But it's real funny to call you 'Chief.' "

He scowled. "Now, you're the daughter of my old friend Dolf, and you know I allus been on good terms with your whole family, but darn if I believe you should be disrespectful, girlie."

Bernice couldn't help snickering. "Oh, come on now, *Chief*. I seen you with your hair down."

His face contorted violently, and he stood up. "You think you can march in here and say what you want, you little floozy? Just 'cause you drop your pants once inna while?"

Bernice felt as though she had been set down in a bathtub full of ice water. She had never been so insulted in all of her life, and she might well have struck back, had she not come here in a greater interest than petty pride.

"I'll just pretend you never said that," said she, quoting a remembered speech from a movie. "I admit I might of been out uh line, seeing we're inna police station. But I'm real worried nowadays, see, Harve—uh, Chief . . . For God's sake, am I going to have to call yuh that when your child is born?"

He had continued to glower at her. Now his lower jaw fell. "Huh?"

She moved quickly to seize the advantage. "That's right. I'm overdue for my monthly. I don't have to remind you of what you 'n' me did the other day." He continued to stare stupidly. "Now as a married man I know you're in a tough spot. I wouldn't ask you to get divorced, but I guess I could use a few bucks to go away someplace where I ain't known, and when the time comes, maybe you could show up for a day or two so they would think the baby had a fath—"

The chief broke in, grinning in a mean kind of way. "That was just *yesterday*. I don't know what you're trying to pull, Bernice, unless maybe you really are too goddam dumb to know better. You might take after your dad, who I never thought would light many bulbs in the mental department. But your mother's got some sense. Now, what would she say if she knew you was in this kinda trouble and then tried to blame it on the chief uh police, of all the people inna world?" He shook his big head for a while, and then he took the pistol from his holster and laid it on the desk top. "You see that weapon, Bernice? That's called a Police Special, thirty-eight caliber. Now, let me giveya a piece of free advice—'cause I can remember you since you was a little baby with a load in your diapers, and I ain't got nothing against you—let me tellya this, you don't want never to make any kinda threats against somebody who is legally empowered to carry one of these pistols. I'm telling you that for your own good. I don't mean you got to be worried about *me*. Everybody in the world but you, I guess, would know you can't get pregnant one day after inter-what-do-they-call-it. Now, anybody but me might get real mad about that." He picked up the weapon and pointed it at her for a moment before returning it to the desk. "And if he was carrying a gun, he might shoot you with it."

Bernice was shaking. She said, "I didn't mean no harm. I guess I'm just a dumb kid. I'm not dry yet behind the ears." She began to sob.

The chief rose and came around to her. He leaned over and put his hand down into her blouse, into her brassiere, and lightly pinched her right breast at the nipple. Then he went to the door and locked it. He led her into the cell, put her on the bunk, and he took her.

Probably because he was worried that someone might knock on the door, the chief was a bit too hasty, and Bernice, who had been slower to arouse than usual, owing to her earlier fear of being shot down in cold blood, had not been satisfied. Therefore when Harvey unlocked the door and sent her on her way with a pat on the behind, she walked more slowly past the firehouse than she might otherwise have done. It was twilight. The boys had finished the washing, and the engine had been pulled back inside the garage, but the big doors were still open.

The fellow named Ernie spotted her. "Ready for that little drink, Bernice?" He sounded as if he'd already had a few. He came outside. The other guys were grinning, and somebody whistled.

Bernice spoke in a voice too low for anyone but him to hear. "I ain't crazy about your friends, Ernie. They could use some lessons in good manners."

"Heck, Bernice, we don't need them," said Ernie. He was a short guy with sandy hair. She had known him for years but had never been out with him. "We could just go off someplace by ourself."

"I'd like that," said Bernice. "You wouldn't mind using my car?"

"Not me," said Ernie. "Mine is laid up at the moment anyway. Want me to drive?"

"Yeah," said she. "Might look better."

So Ernie climbed back of the wheel, started the engine, and backed out like he was going to a fire.

"Hey," Bernice said, "this is my old man's ottamobile."

"I ain't doing nothing to it that hasn't already been done," Ernie said. "How'd it get so beat up?"

"You'd be too if you was blown up."

"Oh, yeah?" He slammed the shift into first and shot ahead. Bernice saw the other fireman grinning at them, and she felt like shaking her fist, but she didn't do it.

She asked, "Where we gonna have that drink?"

"You'll see," said Ernie, patting his pocket and winking at her.

"You carrying a pint? I hope it's not some junk like sherry wine you got at the drugstore."

Ernie pretended to be insulted. "You certainly have a small opinion of me, Bernice. I'll have you know it's Rock 'n' Rye."

She raised her eyebrows. "Oh, O.K. . . . Well, what've you been doing with yourself lately, Ernie? Just catting around?"

"I ain't ready to settle down yet, Bernice. I still like to have fun."

"Pretty much the way I always felt till now. I been down the city, you know."

"So I heard. What you doing back here with us hicks?"

"There's a lot to be said for the old hometown, Ernie. I'm thinking about staying for a while. There's just so much wild oats you can sow. There comes a time when you just have got to stop and take a look at where you're heading, if anyplace. Yuh know what I mean?"

"I dunno, Bernice, sometimes I feel there oughta be more to life than pumping gas, but I don't know what. Still, I have me some fun when I'm on my own time."

"Still live with your mom, Ernie?"

"I couldn't afford to live noplace else and have anything left over. 'Course, I pay room and board, but it ain't like what it'd cost me otherwise, and then she'd be all alone, and my dad didn't leave much. She couldn't afford to keep living there without my help. So it works out O.K."

Bernice glanced through the windshield. "Where are we going, the cemetery?" The lovers' lane was not actually inside the graveyard, but on an unpaved lane just behind the wall. It was where Harvey Yelton had had her for the first time.

Ernie shook his head. "Naw. That place's too hot to handle right now. Yelton is there all the time, and he's been getting real nasty, and . . ." He looked at her and lowered his voice, as if he might be overheard. "What he's done more than once lately, if he catches a couple inna back seat, is give the guy a real scare, like threatening to turn him over to the G-men—he claims that's guvment property up there right back of the graveyard—and then he runs him off. But he makes the girl stay behind, and he threatens to tell her folks unless she puts out for *him!* Ain't that somepin?" Ernie hit the steering wheel with his fist. "And there ain't a damn thing anybody can do about it! The dirty old bastard!"

"Well, you don't have to get foulmouthed about it," complained Bernice.

"Oh, I'm sorry," said Ernie. "But that really burns me up. Man, I'd like to get that bird outside his jurisdiction. You know, he can't do nothing to yuh if you're over the town line. The only way he could do that would be if him and the Millville police had what you call a reciprosky agreement, whereby each force could chase somebody into the other's territory in a actual pursuit, you know? But Harvey and the chief over there—name of Shell, I think— hate each other's guts so much that a guy could go over the line from either side, doing a hundred, and they wouldn't let the other cop chase him, and just for spite they wouldn't chase him theirself."

Bernice rubbed her nose. So Harvey'd been getting it regularly all over the place. No wonder she drew a blank when trying to talk to him about her problem. She could forget about the police chief as a possible answer.

"I'd just like to trick him into Millville, you know?" said Ernie. "Just over the line, one of them back streets, so he wouldn't know just exactly where he was. And then I'd take that gun and club away from him, and beat him till he couldn't walk."

"Gee," Bernice said, "you sure got it in for him. You wouldn't happen to be one of the guys he sent home from the cemetery, wouldja?"

Ernie nodded bitterly, and he said, "Maybe."

Bernice decided to lean on him. "Say, I'm getting pretty thirsty. Maybe we just oughta go into the next tavern and have a beer."

"Naw," he said. "I found a better place than the cemetery ever was."

"You have, huh?" She looked out to see where they were by now. It had become pretty dark, and the streetlights, where there were any, had come on. "Where are we?"

"Millville," Ernie said smugly. "There's a real private

place up here. It's an otto body shop. It's where my own car is right now. I banged it up some, and they're gonna pound out the fender. But they all go home at five, and you can drive in around back of them garages." He was pointing: they had already arrived. "Nobody can see you in here from the street back there."

He drove into an enclosed yard that was paved with ashes, the car making a loud crunching noise. He stopped the engine and extinguished the lights. It was so dark inside the automobile that for a moment Bernice could see nothing whatever. But she could hear him opening the bottle of Rock & Rye, and she could smell its peculiar sweet odor.

Ernie said, "Here you go."

She groped out and found the bottle he had extended. She wiped the neck on the heel of her hand and took a belt. Whew. The first one went down the hardest. She returned the bottle to Ernie.

She said, "I guess this is the first me 'n' you been out like this, huh?"

He made the sound of taking a swig and then replied, "I guess that's right, Bernice. I never had the nerve to astya before."

She took the bottle from him. "I guess you was just shy, huh, Ernie?"

He reclaimed the bottle. "Heck, you was always so sophisticated, Bernice. I knew you'd end up in the city."

She chuckled. "Then where'd you get the nerve now, Ern?"

He laughed in return. "From what we're drinking!"

She gargled another slug. "Well, you just listen here, Ernie, you're a real nice fellow. I always did think that. You show respect for a person, and you got real nice manners. That's what a girl likes. You don't have to drive a Packard or wear white spats and carry a cane, you know. Heck, that kind are usually phonies, anyway."

"Is that right?"

"My gosh, yes. I could tell you something about that. But after all's said and done, I still come back here, you notice."

"Yeah," said Ernie. "I sure do." His profile could be dimly seen now as it was joined by the mouth of the bottle. He swallowed, and then handed her the Rock & Rye.

"I'll tell you," Bernice said, "I think I'll pass this one up. I don't like to drink so much so quick. Gives you sour stomach." Ernie said nothing. She realized that for all he had drunk he was still too shy to make the first move. She said, "Fact is, I wouldn't mind resting a little onna back seat, if you don't mind."

"Not me. Nosir, I sure wouldn't mind, Bernice. You just go ahead."

She got out, opened the rear door, and climbed into the back of the car. Ernie took another pull at the bottle and stayed where he was.

Bernice breathed audibly and said, "There, I feel a lot better."

He said, "That's nice."

She waited awhile, and then she lost patience. If he thought her fast, well, there was no help for it. "If you wanna visit back here with me, Ernie," she said, "well, it's perfectly O.K. so far as I'm concerned."

Now he moved quickly, not bothering to get out and go back there but just flipping himself over the top of the seat. In the rear of a car nobody ever did much stripping ordinarily, because of the sheer difficulty of the task, but Ernie was an awfully eager guy once the ice was broken, and in a few moments Bernice was mostly naked, as was he, and both were flopping like captive fish in a net of inter-wound clothing.

It was at their most helpless moment that the lens of an outsized flashlight, large and radiant as a floodlamp, glared in on them through the rear left window, that faced by Bernice, and a furious voice was heard.

"You filthy stinking trash, I'll blow you to kingdom come!"

CHAPTER

7

Tony knew that Bernice was right in her insistence that action was what the situation called for, but what should he do? Meanwhile, he continued in the state of distraction that had caused him to miss the stop sign, thereby bringing about the episode with the Millville cop.

"Hey, Tony," someone shouted behind him. "What's wrong with you?"

He stopped and turned. Joey Wurzel was trotting up the sidewalk.

"Jesus," Joey said, "I was yelling my block off. You getting hard uh hearing?"

"Hi, Joey."

Joey said, "Why didn't you come to practice? Coach was really sore. You know every day counts now." Joey, undersized and peppy, was manager of the football team. "He made me run over to your home on my bike. You wasn't there. *Nobody* was there." He peered at Tony in accusation.

"Oh, uh, my dad got sick."

"Oh. Well, you shoulda told us, Tony. We only got the rest of this week to get the new plays down pat. Those Catholics'll be tough enough as it is, let alone if we ain't working together like a well-oiled machine." He referred to the upcoming Friday-night game against Saint Bonaventure High School, whose team was coming from Beewix to play Hornbeck. Like all Catholic teams that included Italians or Polacks, Saint Bonaventure's was reputed to be made up largely of dirty players, who habitually gouged eyes, kicked groins, and willfully ground faces into the earth, and the coach had devised some new tactics to give them back as good as they dealt out.

"I'll make it up tomorrow," said Tony.

"If we can take 'em," said Joey, who was wearing his usual porkpie hat with the brim pinned up in front, "and then beat the jigs two weeks later, we got a good chance for the champeenship thisheer."

Tony nodded. "I'll be there." He wanted to get away.

But Joey hung on, talking football. The big disappointment of his life was that he was too small to be a player. He talked more about the games than anybody on the team. Ordinarily Tony enjoyed this, but now he was miserably bored. Sports had been his whole existence, and he saw now that his life had been misspent.

He finally got rid of Joey, but not until he was just around the corner from home.

His mother was sewing under a bridge lamp in the corner of the living room. Upstairs, in his own room, he found Jack. He had forgotten that his brother would be on hand while Bernice stayed in the house. Jack was lying flat on the bed that had been his in the past, the one nearer the window. He was reading some book, which he held with stiff arms overhead.

He lowered it now and said, "I didn't know where you wanted the stuff I took off the bed, so I just piled it right here. I'll help you put it away if you want."

It was Tony's practice to drop anything he was carrying onto the unused bed. He also was in the habit of hurling his clothes there as he took them off. Jack had carefully put the schoolbooks, ring binder, and the like on the desk in the corner, and the clothes on the accompanying straight-backed chair.

"That's O.K.," said Tony. "Don't worry about it." There was also a lot of junk on his own bed, but he flopped down on top of it anyway.

Jack said, "I'm reading about this guy who was wrongfully accused of being yellow. Some kid fell into the lake, and he didn't jump in to save him because he couldn't swim, but nobody knew that. So everybody hated his guts, and he had to leave town though he had just got engaged to the best-looking girl. Where I'm at right now, he has gone up to Canada and joined the Northwest Mounted Police and been sent into the trackless wilderness of the Yukon to bring in a half-breed murderer. There's a blizzard, and the snow is already six foot deep. An avalanche came down on top of his sled and buried his dog team, so he's going along now by himself, on snowshoes." Jack grimaced. "It's a terrific story, but I wish he had joined the French Foreign Legion instead. I hate all those winter descriptions. I'd prefer the sand and camels, and just as everybody's dying of thirst they spot an oasis, and they run and jump in the pool of water with their clothes on—but it's a mirage! Nothing there but sand. So they are all dying like dogs— or you think they are, and so do they, but along comes some friendly Arabs with coconuts full of milk."

Jack was as talkative as Joey had been, but with Jack you had to allow for his young age.

Tony said, "Well, don't let me bother you."

"Ken—that's the hero's name—he'll do anything to show this girl he's not a coward," said Jack. "It was her brother who actually saved the little kid from drowning, and later he came up and just gave Ken a look of contempt, and then he took his sister by the arm and led her away."

Tony listened now.

Jack went on. "The one thing that gets me, though, is why in the world Ken just didn't say he couldn't swim? They do that a lot in books. People just won't say the obvious thing. I guess the idea is that there wouldn't be a story otherwise—then why would he go off and join the Mounties? But why couldn't he just go and join the Mounties anyway? That's the best part of the story."

"The French Foreign Legion," Tony asked, "ain't that the thing guys join when they don't know what else to do or where to go?"

"Yeah," said Jack, "sort of. When they're falsely accused of a crime or when they're in disgrace, like this story. I never before heard of anyone joining the Mounties for that reason. In the Foreign Legion you give a false name, and it is an unspoken rule that nobody will ever ask you what your real one is or where you're from or what you did before coming there. If you're killed, you'll be buried in the trackless sands of the Sahara, lost to the outside world, but you might get awarded the Croy de Gwair post-hewmusly."

"What's that?"

"A medal given by the French Army. They kiss you on both cheeks if you receive it while alive."

Tony winced in revulsion. "Sounds like the Fruit Army." He would prefer the Mounties. They were probably closer too. "How far is it from here to Canada?"

Jack said, "Gee, I don't know. But I do know that at

one place it's real close to the American border: Niagara Falls. In fact, I think I read once that the Niagara Falls are really in Canada."

"That can't be right," said Tony. "Niagara Falls have always been American. Somebody's trying to pull a fast one." It occurred to Tony that sometimes brainy people like Jack were easy to fool: just give them something out of the ordinary to think about, and they'd believe anything, just for the novelty of it.

Jack swung himself around and sat on the edge of the bed. "I just remembered, Tone: we never did get that letter written."

"Huh?" For an instant Tony had forgotten about that entirely. "Oh, yeah. Well, I changed my mind. What would it be once we got it written? Just a lot of words."

Jack chuckled. "You're sure right about that. That's all a letter can be. Of course, if you want to get something over to somebody, tell them something, it's pretty hard to do it unless you use words, either talking or writing."

But the process seemed unclean to Tony: explanations, reasons, excuses, they were just the kind of things you did as a substitute for what should be done.

"Thanks anyway," he told his brother. "But you can still help me if you want to." He lowered his voice, though his mother was downstairs. "I might have to go away for a while, see. You wouldn't happen to have any money you could let me have on loan?"

"Sure. I've got that dollar sixty-five I mentioned."

"I know that's what you are saving up to be a foreign correspondent on," said Tony, "and I'll sure get it back to you before that time comes, I swear. But if I could use it now, it would sure come in handy."

"That's O.K.," said Jack. "I was thinking of buying a portable typewriter, but that would cost twenty bucks or more, and it'll be years before I could save up that kind of money, so you're welcome to it." He left the room for a few moments and then was back with the cash.

Tony said, "I won't forget you for this," and shook his brother's hand.

Jack said regretfully, "You sound like you're going on a long trip."

"I'd rather not say where," Tony told him, "so then if anybody tries to get it out of you, you really won't know."

"But what'll I do then if they work me over with a rubber hose?"

Tony was able to smile at Jack's exaggeration. "I don't think that will happen. I meant Mom—and Dad, if he gets better."

"You're becoming a fugitive from justice?"

"I just think if I stay I'm just gonna get in more trouble, and the family don't need any more of that. Now Bernice is back, she can drive Mom around, and since she's made something of herself down the city, she'll know how to handle these problems we got. I betcha Bernice could talk to the Bullards and make everything clear, and everybody'd be friends in no time. Ask her about that when she gets back. There must be worse things than that to deal with in the city every single day, I bet."

Jack asked, "You leaving right now, under cover of darkness?"

"Naw," said Tony. "That might sound good, but it's more practical in daylight."

"You going to walk?"

Tony smiled mysteriously. "I don't wantcha to know too much, Jack. I told you that. I'll be all right. You'll see."

"You'll be coming back someday soon, I hope."

"Why, sure," Tony said. "You betcha."

*　*　*

Junior Bullard had hated his father's guts for several years, but now that he was in the nut ward of the hospital and Junior could do anything he wanted without fear of being discovered by his old man—smoking, drinking, playing with himself while looking at underwear ads in mail-order catalogues—he felt worse. He was also still scared that someone might find evidence in the ruin of the hardware store that he had been there earlier on the evening of the fire, drinking stolen homemade grape wine and masturbating while studying the picture of a woman wearing something called a teddy, which had a buttoned crotch that drove him wild to think about: all this by the light of a candle, in the storeroom, so that the flicker could not be discerned from the street. It was possible that he had left the burning candle behind on his departure an hour later, for he had been somewhat woozy at the time. But what could he do? He had no privacy at home. The only other bedroom was Eva's, just because she was female, even though he was several years her senior, and his own quarters were in the front part of the attic, reached through a closet-staircase from his parents' room. This was too cold in winter and impossible to survive in the intense heat of summer, so in such seasons he had to sleep on a couch in an alcove off the dining room. His parents, his father especially, had always favored Eva over him, and the situation had got even worse since she acquired breasts and began to use Kotex. He had never liked girls, but only in the past year had he realized how unsavory their personal habits could be if you were related to them.

When the three of them had finally been allowed to see his father, they didn't go to where the beds were, but to a waiting room off the mental ward, and some nurse brought out his old man, who seemed all weak and confused and scared in his robe and slippers. And even then he looked mostly at the two women and disregarded Junior. Junior swore to himself that he would never get so helpless in life as to be led around by a nurse. He had previously acquired a determination never to operate a business where you had to kiss the asses of the public.

Getting home that evening was difficult because that fat pansy of a preacher had left and his mother was forced to go about begging for a ride back to Millville. Finally some old guy gave them a lift in an ancient coupe, and since there was room only for three in the front, Junior was relegated to the rumble seat, a place he dreaded riding in, owing to his dislike of being blown around by the wind.

When they got home there wasn't any meat for supper, but his mother went ahead anyway and fixed a meal consisting of eggs scrambled with fried potatoes, and there wasn't any dessert but applesauce. He felt like emptying the bowls in one big heap in the middle of the kitchen floor and then letting all the neighborhood dogs in. He could feel new pimples forming on his forehead, and he resented his sister for her as yet smooth skin.

After supper he said he was going, and when his mother asked where, he answered, "Out."

Eva observed, "You're real fresh when Dad's not here."

He sneered at her. "Shut up, you sap."

"I don't think you should talk to your sister that way, Junior," chided his mother.

"So what?" said he, and he left, letting the screen door slam behind him. One of his chores was taking off the screen door when the summer was done; he had let this go for weeks.

It had long been Junior's habit when heading downtown not to bother to go around to the front walk but simply to cut through the back lawn of the next-door neighbors' and so reach the public sidewalk in the southward direction.

These neighbors, the Durkeys, in summertime put up a low barrier of those white-wire hoops to discourage the crossing of certain flowerbeds, but Junior was none too careful about these and sometimes tripped on them and as a result trampled the flowers more than he would otherwise have done. He felt that this served the Durkeys right. They lacked the stomach to protest outright, but if they caught him at it, they might say, hypocritically, "Look out there, Junior. Wouldn't want you to break a leg."

He couldn't see too well in the darkness now, but he went through the Durkeys' yard anyhow. The Durkey house was dark. They had probably gone to bed already. They were the ugliest people in the world. Mr. Durkey had buck teeth and Mrs., popeyes and a goiter.

When Junior reached the sidewalk, he thought he saw a shadow behind the big elm at the next corner, so he walked out into the street. On reaching the point at which he could see the person behind the tree in the light from the nearby streetlamp, he recognized his father's cousin, Reverton, who was turned toward the sidewalk, apparently waiting in ambush for someone to come along.

"Psst! Hey, Rev," said he.

Reverton was badly startled. He jumped and whirled, and then he said, "By God, it's you, ain't it, Junior?"

"Who'd you think it might be?"

"Listen, I caught that Beeler snot up at the corner just yestidday. Now they know your dad is laid up, God knows what they'll do."

Whoever was responsible for the fire, if that potbellied dummy hadn't mouthed off in the store, they wouldn't have been blamed. It wasn't Junior's fault, but he still didn't like to think about the Beelers.

He said, "Oh yeah?"

Reverton said, "If you got a minute, maybe you could

take over for me here while I run downtown and get me a samwich. I ain't et a bite since noontime."

"Why, sure," said Junior. "But whyn't you just go to the house? Mom's got lotsa eggs 'n' stuff, Rev. She'd wanna feedja if she knew you was out here on guard."

"Mighty white of you, Junior," said Reverton. "I won't be but a minute."

"If I'm taking over," Junior said, "hadn't you better loan me that gun of yours?"

Reverton took a long breath. Then he removed his black fedora and offered a rare view of his naked scalp, which was bald to the back of his crown. He looked completely different, sort of birdlike, when hatless. He returned the fedora to its usual place. "If you saw somepin that looks funny you can jist run and git *me*," he said.

"I'd be outa luck, though, if they shot first and asked questions afterwards," said Junior.

This argument had its effect on Reverton, with his extreme way of looking at things.

Junior added, "And if that happened, you might say my blood would be on your hands."

Reverton took the pistol from his holster, reversed it, and presented it to Junior butt-first. "I guess it'll be O.K. so long as you don't shoot it."

Junior accepted the weapon. He could hardly contain his impatience.

Reverton was frowning. "You better not hold it like that," said he. "Put it away. Anybody seesya with it, they coont miss it. A gun can cause a lotta trouble in the wrong hands."

"This O.K.?" Junior lifted the hem of his sweater and put the barrel behind the waistband of his pants, pulling the sweater down again afterward. The butt made quite a bulge. Junior patted it. The weight felt as though it might pull his pants down.

"You just stay in the shadows," said Reverton. "Nobody'll notice it, then. I'll be right back. Maybe your mom will just fry me a quick egg samwich. I'll squirt a little catchup on it and be right back out." He started off, but then he turned and came back. "You be careful, won't you, Junior?"

"Heck, don't worry about me none, Rev."

Reverton nodded and walked rapidly in the direction of the Bullard house. Junior could hardly wait till he was out of sight. He felt like a new man. All his peevishness was gone. As soon as Reverton turned the corner Junior took the pistol out from under the sweater, and he hefted it in one hand and then in both. He caressed the cylinder and rubbed the scored surface of the grips with the tip of his forefinger. Then he put it back in the waistband of his corduroys and headed downtown to Curly's Luncheonette. He had eaten hardly any of that lousy supper and was ravenous for a bowl of chili con carne with soda crackers broken up in it, and a wiener covered with sauerkraut, followed by a wedge of Dutch apple pie à la mode, and a malted milk drunk through double straws.

The lunch counter was at the easterly edge of Millville's business district, almost on the Hornbeck line. Thus to get there Junior had to walk through most of his town, which was not as taxing as it would have been ordinarily, because the gun against his belly caused him to grasp life in a new way. Usually he avoided walking down the side street where the pool parlor, with attached barroom, could be found, because the tough guys regarded that terrain as their own, and unless you were one of them, they could be relied on to give you a bad time till you were out of earshot. But, armed as he was, he now went eagerly along the sidewalk in front of the place, hoping to encounter some trouble-makers, and he was not disappointed. Three bad-looking guys were under the lamppost there, and another was in a rusty, dented car at the curb. The last had moved over from behind the wheel to the passenger's seat, and his bare arm, adorned with an American Rose tattoo on the broad bicep, was hooked over the window ledge.

The guy in the auto was first to take notice of Junior. "Well, looky what we got coming along here," he said in his whiny voice, "a real piss-ant."

And the three who were lounging around the streetlamp took up various positions on the sidewalk, so that anybody coming by would have had a problem in getting the right of way. One of these guys wore a felt hat adorned with various badges and pins and scalloped along the brim, and another had a big wide black motorcycle belt, dotted with silver studs and red reflectors, around his waist, but no cycle was in evidence.

Junior came along grinning, and he stopped to address the hillbilly in the window of the car.

"Hi, you shitface," he said genially. "How'd you like to have a new asshole, right between your eyes?" He pulled his sweater up and seized the butt of the pistol and began ever so slowly to withdraw the barrel from his waistband. Before the muzzle was clear the guy in the car hurled himself over to the wheel, started the engine with an explosion of unmuffled exhaust, and thunderously sped away.

Junior's back had been to the others, and therefore when he turned they were not prepared for what they saw. The pistol was out by now, and he held it straight down, against his right thigh, but it was as good as if it had been pointing at them. Their rapid exits, each in another direction, gave him a real laugh.

He considered going into the poolroom, for as it was, nobody inside could have known about his new power, because the windows were by town ordinance whitewashed on the interior so that underaged kids couldn't see the pool playing on their way home from school. But his ravenous hunger had first claim on him, and he went on to the lunchroom.

The lunch counter was essentially a one-man operation, if you didn't count the colored dishwasher, the owner, manager, and chef being a man named Curly McCoy, who had been gassed in the war and breathed heavily.

Curly was back of the counter when Junior entered, and the dishwasher, a tall, skinny man so lightly colored as to be almost yellow, was just bringing in a wire milk carrier full of clean dishes. There were two customers on the stools. One of them was eating a fried-fish sandwich on a bun, and on the plate beneath was a green-flecked yellow smear of tartar sauce. The other man, an old guy with no teeth, was dunking a doughnut in his coffee cup.

Junior stood back of a stool, and he said, "How they hanging, Curly?"

Curly didn't like that kind of talk, and answered, "Don't give me any lip, you runt. You want somepin t'eat, you just gimme your order."

"Hey, Curly," Junior said, raising his sweater just so the butt of the pistol could be seen.

Curly lost some of his florid color.

The old man withdrew his doughnut from the coffee, but it had been soaking too long and a third of the ring broke away and plopped soddenly back into the cup. Junior was really disgusted to see that.

He said, "You old dummy."

The other guy kept eating his fish sandwich, not looking up.

Curly recovered a little. "That thing ain't real, izzit, Junior? If it is, you better be careful. It could go off any time."

"You know it could," Junior said, grasping the butt but not yet pulling the pistol out. The man with the fish sandwich finally swallowed every crumb of it and was now sucking his fingertips clean.

Junior said, "Jesus," and made a face.

The guy turned his head quickly and brought it back, without really looking at Junior. He said, "You talking to me?"

Junior drew the gun at last, but held it along his thigh again, pointing at the floor. He asked, "What if I am?"

This guy had a tinge of gray in his sideburns and a long nose. He pursed his thin lips and said, "Listen, it's jake with me."

The old man fished the soggy piece of doughnut out of the coffee and sucked it from the spoon.

Junior turned to Curly in disgust and said, "How about some eats?"

"Sure thing," Curly said with animation. "Just have a stool, Junior. Coming right up!" He rubbed his hands on his dirty white apron and walked briskly along back of the counter to the swinging door to the kitchen, opened it, and went in.

Junior quickly understood that Curly wouldn't be coming back. On an impulse he stepped behind the cash register, hit some buttons at random, and the drawer flew out to the jangle of a bell. He helped himself to the bills therein: only a few were there, and most of them were ones.

When the money was in his pocket he stared defiantly at the man who had eaten the fish sandwich. He asked, "What are you looking at?"

"Just minding my own business, Ace," said the man.

Junior briefly considered taking this man's personal money, but he decided against it: he wasn't really a crook; also, you could never tell about a person who was so calm; he thought it was wise not to push him too far, because he wasn't sure he knew how to fire the gun if it had some kind of trick safety on it, and this guy looked like he could take it away from you and stick it up your ass. Besides, he was emptying the cash register merely to punish Curly for running out before feeding him.

He said, "So long, sucker," and left the luncheonette. When he got outside he saw both Curly and the colored dishwasher dart out of the side alleyway and run up the street. They were making an awful lot out of this incident, and Junior was amused.

He yelled, "Run, you yellow sons uh bitches!" He felt drunk though he hadn't had a drop.

He put his gun back in the waistband, pulling the sweater down, and swaggered along the street until he came to a tavern. The bar was about half full of customers, all men except for one heavyset young woman with strong features and lips heavily painted. Junior couldn't remember ever having seen any of these people before, though he ordinarily could recognize most of the persons he would pass on the Millville sidewalks on a normal day. He began to suspect he had crossed over to Hornbeck. It was funny how carrying a gun made you feel as if you were dreaming.

The bartender was a burly, low-browed man. Junior ordered a shot of whiskey.

The man scowled down at him. "You old enough?"

"Sure."

The bartender shook his head. "Hell you say." The man on the stool at Junior's right turned and smirked at him: he was an ugly devil with a wart beside his nose.

Junior pulled out the pistol. The bartender shrank a lot,

and he looked like he was trying to say something but couldn't find his voice.

Showing his money with the left hand, Junior said, "I ain't holding you up. I'm paying, see? Set 'em up all around."

The bartender began to line up shot glasses in front of him. The woman left her stool at the end of the bar and came slowly around to stand next to Junior and stare at the side of his face.

He finally got the nerve to look at her. She pressed right against him then, rolling her fat belly on him, her big breasts under his nose.

"Honey," she said, breathing whiskey fumes at him, "what you need is some uh this."

He had never felt a grown woman in this way before. She was a big fat slob, but he was mesmerized by her. He was grinning at her when in the corner of his eye he saw the bartender bring to shoulder level something that looked like a miniature baseball bat. Before Junior could dodge it, he was hit violently in the side of the head, and the lights went out.

Tony had not lied when he told Jack he would not leave until morning, but when Jack went to the bathroom, taking his book along, which meant he would stay in there for a long time, Tony changed his mind. When morning came he would probably have lost his nerve. What seemed possible now would appear crazy in the light of day: he could foresee that. He had never been a wild kid who gave in to impulses and sought quick thrills. It would be too easy for him to lose confidence. He would do well to make the most of what he had at the moment.

So he put on his green-and-white athletic jacket, with

the modest-sized high-school letter on the left breast (as opposed to the enormous middle-of-the-chest letter worn on sweaters) and the two final numerals of his year of graduation high on the right sleeve, and he added Jack's money to his own seven dollars, eighty-five cents, taken from an old rubber boot in the rear of the closet. If he waited for morning he could go to the Farmers National Bank of Hornbeck, where he maintained a savings account which currently held $17.37, the fruits of his summer job at the mill, but with his dad laid up, his mother might need that for the family, whereas he was able-bodied and would surely be able to get hired where he was going. Meanwhile, with Jack's contribution he had almost ten dollars on which to live for a couple of months if need be.

He went softly down the stairs and saw as he reached the living room that, as he had hoped, his mother had fallen asleep over her mending. She usually did that even when his dad was there and listening to the radio. He continued on through the kitchen and, quietly, out the back door, and then walked around front and proceeded via the back streets to Millville. When he had got near the block on which Eva lived, he grew cautious. He did not intend to be captured again by that lunatic of a cousin of the Bullards', who might still be on patrol. But Tony did not see him, or for that matter, anyone else on the sidewalk, and even inside the houses a lot of people had already turned off the lights and gone to bed. He feared that the same might be true of Eva, young as she was, and if so he would be at a loss as to how to proceed.

But when he reached the Bullard house he was relieved to see that most of the windows on both floors were lighted, as was the globe outside the front door, which signified that someone was out who was expected soon to come home. He hoped that that person might be Eva. He ran boldly between the concrete strips of driveway along the side of the house and, tripping on something in the dark, fell headlong, but luckily without making a sound.

He hurled himself up and continued to the back of the house, where the kitchen windows, being dark, told him nothing, but then a window was abruptly lighted on the second floor. Could that be Eva's? He went and felt the ground for something heavy enough to throw but too light to break the glass. A dog barked nearby, and soon, two back porches away, a light came on. Tony froze in position. A Scottie came out of that house, but all it did was lift its leg against a bush in the back yard, after which it was admitted again to its home and the light was extinguished.

But by now, when Tony went back to where he could look at Eva's supposed window, the room was dark! Nor could he find a single object, pebble or twig, to toss up against the glass. He now realized what a fool he had been to concoct the outlandish idea of confronting this young girl in the night and for the first time since rebuffing her two months earlier. He just stood there for a while, looking up at the darkened window and reflecting on how goofy he had been, he who had always been noted for his reasonable-mindedness.

Then the back door opened, in the dark, and Eva spoke down to him from the porch.

"What are you doing there?"

"It's me," said Tony.

"I know."

"Oh. I didn't want you thinking that I was a burglar or something."

"I didn't. I looked out when Skipper barked, and I saw you. There's enough light."

"Is that the name of that dog over there?"

"Yeah."

Tony had run out of things to say. If he had been close enough he might have tried to feel her breasts at this point.

Finally she said, "Well, I guess I ought to go in."

"Why?" He put this simple question as a kind of reflex, but it proved to be just the thing for breaking the ice.

She giggled and said, "I don't know. I'm here all by myself. My mother had to go over to Hornbeck, because my brother got in some kinda trouble over there. Was that something to do with your family again?"

"My family?" asked Tony. "Huh. I don't think so. I don't know anything about it, anyway."

Eva came down and sat on the second step from the bottom, and Tony joined her but kept a certain space between them.

She said, "Why'd you come over here tonight, anyway?"

"Because I was trying to write you a letter for a real long time."

"A *letter*?" Her voice had the rising note of pleasurable wonder.

"Do you like letters?"

"I guess so. I don't think I have ever got one."

He nodded. "I should have written you one, then. But I wasn't able to." He nodded several times again and looked down between his shoes. "Right now I'm going to get out of town. I'm thinking of heading for Canada. There are a lot of opportunities up that way. I wouldn't mind joining the Northwest Mounted Police. You know, the Mounties? There was a movie about them not so long ago. I don't know if they've got an eye test or not . . ."

"How far is that?"

"Canada? I'm not sure."

"Are you going to come back soon?"

Tony got the nerve to look her in the face. "Listen, you want to come along?"

She gasped. "To *Canada?*"

He couldn't tell whether she was pleased or simply amazed.

"Sure. We could get married."

Eva giggled. "You're really crazy, you know that?"

He joined her in laughter. "I guess you might say that. . . . Well, willya?"

Apparently she couldn't stop giggling, but she managed to say, "Well, I guess so. If you really want me to."

He said, "I would really like it, I'll say that."

"When are we going? Right now?"

"I guess we might as well," said Tony. "You know, before somebody tries to stop us?"

"Boy," Eva said, giggling, "will I ever get it, if we're caught! My family's supposed to be enemies of your family. I guess they'll think I lost my mind." She shook her head wonderingly. "Aren't we too young to get married?"

"We got to find a place where they won't ask us for a birth certificate," said Tony. "Then we can lie about our ages."

Eva's face was luminous in the dim light. He thought he could probably kiss her at this moment but decided it would be better taste to wait until they were married, else she might think he was a sex maniac and would not want to go with him.

CHAPTER

8

Nothing had gone right for Reverton that day, from the early morning, when he had to wait an unusual length of time for the use of the hall toilet in the hotel where he lived, hopping from one leg to the other, to the moment when he came back from eating to find that Junior was missing from the guard post.

Even the food had been a disappointment, though he usually ate anything homemade with enjoyment—you got that way in a lifetime of hash houses, lunchrooms, and diners—but Frieda had hardly anything left in the icebox or pantry, aside from some cold leftover peas, so she gave him a peanut-butter-and-jelly sandwich and a cup of Ovaltine. The raspberry jelly was full of tiny seeds, which instantly got under his upper plate and drove him nuts (all his teeth had either been knocked out in the bus accident or subsequently pulled by a dentist who was certainly a crook, though it could not be legally proved).

Rev was very uneasy to be in all-female company, being shy with all versions of that sex, and he had no more to say to Frieda than to the child Eva, who he noticed had, despite her tender age, all at once gotten an indecently protuberant bosom, and wondered whether that was another of the mistakes of Mother Nature, who made more than a few, or if this young girl had padded herself obscenely, under the influence of perverts who might next induce her to paint her lips scarlet and drink beer. It might not be seen as his business, but he had always believed both Bud and Frieda were too easy on their offspring. He had on occasion smelled cigarette breath coming from Junior, and he sensed that the boy took a carnal interest in girls, though he had never actually caught him at anything.

Yet he had let Junior keep his gun while he went in to eat! Even as he did it he had had a premonition that it was a foolish move. And a man in his position couldn't afford many: the bums were just waiting for him to make a mistake. He could expect no mercy if caught unarmed. Two of them would probably take each of his arms, and the others would line up to kick him in the belly, gouge out his eyes, and pull his hair out by the roots. Oh, they were a brave bunch when they had a helpless victim in their clutches. They'd pay a pretty penny to know that his holster was empty at the moment.

As he chewed the sandwich the peanut butter gave him as much trouble as the raspberry seeds, sticking to his dental plates and pulling them from a firm seat within his mouth. Had he tried to talk at such a moment, he would have produced a lot of clickety-clacking noises, shaming him before these female relatives, who like most women were no doubt just waiting to watch him show himself up. Once, as a boy on a Sunday visit to Bud's family, he had been too timid to ask where the bathroom was and both peed and crapped in his pants, and he could never forget how Bud's sisters had laughed and laughed. Bud himself had not joined them, which was why Rev had always liked him ever since, though he had become ever more aware throughout the years that his cousin's moral fiber had degenerated. Unfortunately this failing had become acute since the trouble began with the Beelers, and Bud had proved himself a complete weakling. To collapse at such a time and be put into the hospital! A soldier would have been shot for less. The elder Beeler had the mean little eyes of the resentful man: that type was capable of anything. The son was obviously a cunning, conniving type, and Rev wasn't fooled for a moment by the eyeglasses: turn your back on that kind of boy and get a knife in the spine. In the rough-and-tumble of life Reverton had learned to anticipate troublemakers. The place to be trained in what human beings were capable of was a toilet in a public building if you were the custodian who had to clean it up every nighttime. For years Rev had been one of the janitors at the county courthouse up in Wayland. He had been let go after the accident, which had incapacitated him for some months, and had since existed on the modest settlement he had been fool enough to accept from the bus company for agreeing not to sue for more, and though his needs were small, this had dwindled to virtually nothing because he had given a good deal of the sum to Bud for the purchase of the hardware store. He had assumed his cousin would quickly earn enough in profits not only to pay back the loan but to add a sizable dividend.

For reasons of pride, and to justify his carrying the pistol, Rev let the family think him a railroad dick. He did live in Hamburg, in a fleabag hotel near the railroad yard, but whenever he wasn't down in Millville at, formerly, his cousin's store and now the Bullard house, he was in the public library, doing research into various subjects that interested him: the extraction of gold from seawater,

Asiatic techniques for training the will, magnetism, and the Pope's secret plan to introduce into the non-Catholic areas of the world an army of secret agents whose mission it was to poison the public reservoirs.

It was unlikely that Junior had gone off with the gun of his own volition. Reverton knew him for a responsible youth. In fact, especially now that Bud had gone soft, Junior was the most reliable member of the family, and thus the one most likely to be the target of a cunning enemy.

Rev was suddenly more apprehensive than he had been in a long time. But that of course was just what They wanted, to debilitate their prey by moral means so that when they finally jumped him he would long since have been conquered by his own corruption. It was necessary that he keep his nerve, even though unarmed. He realized that the search for Junior might be useless if they had abducted the boy by car. But there was also a distinct possibility that instead they had lured him into a darkened back yard or vacant lot, disarmed him by some trickery probably involving indecent pictures—carnality might be Junior's Achilles heel—and beaten, stabbed, or shot him to death. Reverton would be saddled with the unpleasant job of informing the mother. "I'm sorry, Frieda, but this goes to show how we can't let down our guard even to eat a little supper."

The neighborhood seemed more quiet than it should have been: this was suspicious in itself. Rev carried a big flashlight he had come upon beside the back door and borrowed from Frieda, but did not turn it on, owing to the regular series of streetlamps along the route. He had gone several blocks north, to the last residential street, beyond which, after a little cluster of garage buildings having to do with car repair, the fields began, and having seen only a black-and-white cat, which ignored him, and a mongrel dog, which wagged its tail and would have followed him had he not pantomimed picking up a rock—Rev had nothing against a good pooch, but this was not the time— he had turned back when he heard the sound of a car door slamming. This issued from the auto body-shop buildings across the way, and yet the establishment was dark and obviously closed for business. What a perfect place to have taken Junior, whose battered, lifeless body but for this chance would not have been found until the next day.

Rev rapidly but silently approached the buildings. When he got to a point from which to survey the inner parking area, he saw the darkened car. He ran to it, turned the big flashlight onto the back seat, and forgetting he was not otherwise armed, put the evildoers under arrest.

Bernice and Ernie somehow got themselves disentangled and climbed out of the back seat. The flashlight kept going from one to the other, and before Bernice could get her eyes adjusted and see who was holding it, the glare would return to blind her. Also she had to pull up and/or adjust certain items of clothing. But she got this done before Ernie succeeded in doing the same for himself, and in spite of the lousy situation she was in, she almost snickered when the light left her at one point to show him with his pants at his ankles and his droopy BVD bottoms showing.

Their captor spoke no understandable words after his first furious statement, but was mumbling and muttering in a nasty way, so Bernice saw no possibility, at least at this time, of proposing to him the kind of deal which Ernie had described as being characteristic of Hornbeck's police chief, that is, helping himself to some of the fun.

But once he got his pants back on, Ernie surprised her by speaking up boldly. "Listen here, Officer," said he. "I don't criticize you for doing what you see as your duty, but the facts in the case is I have a perfect right to come here, as my otto is being repaired by the DeWeese brothers—you can check onnat—and I also happen to be a public servant myself, in my case a fireman, and all I ask is professional courtesy . . ."

But this reasonable comment only seemed to put the other man in a worse mood. "You shet your stinking mouth, you scum," he said. "You think you can come up here where innocent women and children are living and copulate like unto animals of the field, make a spectacle of yourself, hold up to mockery all the principles of God-fearing men, roll in slime and throw it in our face? I'd like to see you both kestrated."

He flashed his light on Bernice. "I mean you too, Missy. You are a slopbucket, for my money."

Bernice was stung by this. She said, "Lookit here, you ain't got no call to talk so nasty just because you wear a badge. What we was doing might not of been one hunderd percent on the upanup, but at least it's natural, and what I always say is, the human race can't get along without it, and it don't hurt anybody, and—"

"I tole you to shetcha filthy mouth!" he yelled, or really screamed, and a hand came out of the darkness and slapped her hard across the nose.

"Ow!" she howled, covering her face, and then immediately opening up to shout, "You lousy son of a bitch!"

And again Ernie surprised her. He said, "By God, you don't do that to any girl uh mine!" He waded in with both fists. The flashlight fell to the ground and went out. The cop, who turned out to be a littler fellow than she had thought, bent over in search of the light, and Bernice kicked him as hard as she could in the seat of the pants, and he went sprawling for a moment. But he quickly regained his feet.

"I'm gonna blow your guts out," he said, and he went into the kind of crouch you see in the movies when somebody's going for a pistol, and he clawed at his hip, but he didn't come up with a weapon. She could see him better now. Not only was he awfully little for a cop, but he wasn't wearing a uniform. It dawned on her that he might be one of those lovers' lane bandits you heard about sometimes, who preyed on people who had no place to go to do it but the back seat of a car, which from her point of view was even lousier than just plain highway robbery. And now she felt a wetness on her mouth, and she put her fingers there and discovered that her nose was bleeding from the slap.

She told Ernie, "This little rat ain't no cop! He's a dirty crook. Let's gettim!"

Ernie punched him hard in the side of the head, and he stupidly straightened up some, and Ernie then hit him so hard in the belly that his spine must have been curved by the blow, and while he was bent over from that, Bernice kicked him in the mouth with the full force of her right leg, and she was wearing a spike heel that probably wouldn't help his teeth much. Then Ernie knocked him down.

Bernice was still mad about her bloody nose, which was ruining her only good dress, and she looked around for some kind of weapon, but couldn't see much in the dark. She tripped on something: it was the big flashlight. She picked it up and raised it high over her head, with the intent to bring it down as hard as she could and crush his skull if possible, but Ernie stopped her.

"He's out." Ernie was breathing hard. "We don't wanna kill him."

"I sure do," said Bernice, with some labored panting of her own. "He's got it coming if a man ever did, the onry little skunk."

"Come on," Ernie said, gently but with strength taking

the flashlight from her. He dropped it on the ground next to the unconscious man.

Bernice would at least have stomped the rotten little bastard between the legs if Ernie had not led her to the car. She felt her face. It seemed as if the nose had stopped bleeding, but what a mess. It was just as well that the bulb in the ceiling light had long since been burned out and never replaced.

Ernie did not put on the headlights until he had quietly backed out from between the buildings and got rolling on the street. But when he saw her in the glow of the dashboard, he pulled to the curb.

"For God's sake, honey, you been hurt?"

Bernice was touched. She hadn't realized that Ernie was so nice a fellow. He got out a handkerchief that was clean enough, and he tenderly cleaned off her chin, and where the blood had dried he wet the cloth with his tongue and gently rubbed and dabbed. And finally he pulled his head back and took a general look.

"Wellsir, I guess that's the best we can do right now. But I'll get you home soon's I can." He pulled away from the curb.

Bernice felt better even than she had before the fight. She said, "You're a pretty swell guy, Ernie. I'm fit as a fiddle." She didn't add, "and ready for love," the rest of the line in the song, but figured he would get the idea.

"You're gonna be all right," he said, smiling not sexily but like a doctor. "We had a first-aid course at the Department. It looks like just a bloody nose to me and not broken. But I'd be glad to runya up to the hospital."

"I'm O.K.," said she, sliding across the seat to be near him and leaning her head against his shoulder. "It's still early. You know any other private places? That was kinda nice, back there, until we got so rudely interrupted."

"Gee, Bernice," said Ernie. "I never suspected you was such a good scout about everything." He put his hand on her thigh.

Bernice realized she was getting mighty fond of him. She said, "Leave it to Millville to have a nut like that wandering around the back streets. Don't tell me he was a real cop."

"Naw," Ernie said with a certain self-importance. "The tip-off came when he didn't extend any courtesy when I identified myself as a fireman. We was all over here from the Hornbeck Department just the other night when that hardware burned down. Heck, I was risking my life in his town. He would have acknowledged that if he had been a real officer. He might of been a new night watchman for the DeWeese brothers, but I tole him my car was right inside there—"

Bernice slid her hand up the inside of Ernie's upper arm and curled her fingers around his biceps, which he immediately tensed. "Forget about that monkey," she said. "We gave him more than he was looking for. We make a pretty good team, you know."

"By gosh, we do, don't we?" said Ernie, his hand growing warm on her thigh.

The bartender, whose name was Billy Schmitt, put away his blackjack and came around the other side of the bar and picked up the pistol Junior had dropped. He examined it, shrugged, and put it down in front of the nearest customer.

"How do you like that?" said he.

The man shook his head in disgust. "Little snotnose. He coulda scared us out of a year's growth."

Billy picked Junior off the floor and propped him on an empty stool. "Hey, Marie," he said to the plump woman who had distracted Junior by rubbing against him, "gimme that club soda uh yours."

She brought it over from where she had been sitting. Billy poured it, along with the ice cubes, onto Junior's head. The boy woke up slowly and looked at him through slanted eyes. His voice had a croaking sound. He said, "It was . . . just uh . . . joke, I swear."

"Sure, kid," said Billy, holding Junior's sweater front with one fist, which was almost as big as Junior's head. Billy weighed 248 pounds. "But what if I used the sawed-off twelve-gauge I keep back there, instead of the blackjack? You would of been hamburger meat, woontcha? Your guts would of been plastered all over them booths, ain't that right? That would of been a real funny joke, woont it? But you woont of been laughing, wouldja?"

"Huh-uh."

Billy put his hand to his ear. "Whadjoo say? Speak up."

"Naw."

Billy shook Junior with his big hand. "I'm hard of hearing, boy. You gotta sound off."

"No."

Billy patted Junior's cheeks roughly. He said, "You got a great sensa yumor. How long you think you could get away with pointing a starter's pistol at people?"

Junior frowned.

Billy said, "I guess you was aware that a gun like that only shoots blanks?"

Junior kept frowning.

"But," Billy whispered close to his ear, "if I was to stuff the barrel with rock salt and then put it up your asshole and pull the trigger, you woont be happy, I can tell you. That's what they call a Dutch enema, ever hear uh that?"

Junior shook his head.

Marie had gone back of the bar to get herself a refill of club soda. She grinned across at Junior.

She said, "Take it easy onna kid, Billy. We was all young oncet."

Billy shoved Junior away and poked a big finger at him. "You're gonna eat the next gun you point at me."

When Harvey Yelton arrived he put handcuffs on Junior.

Harvey said, "Who's coming, Billy or Marie?"

"I will," Marie said. "Billy's got to stay and pour."

Billy shouted, "Don't keep my old lady too long, Harvey. She's got work to do."

"He's a real slave driver," Marie told Harvey with a chuckle.

Contrary to what his enemies believed, Reverton had not been knocked out. He had instead been shrewdly playing possum, having soon realized that, unarmed and outnumbered, he would have no chance against these ruthless adversaries in hand-to-hand combat. Obviously both of them, including the woman, had been well trained in how to disable an opponent with as few precise, deadly blows as possible. Rev was not humiliated: there was nothing disgraceful about receiving damage from such a brawny female as that one. And the so-called fireman was a gangster pure and simple. They were a pair of real hoodlums, come out from the city. To take them on singlehandedly had been the work of a brave man.

When the car had driven away, Rev slowly sat up and spat his upper dental plate into his hand. One or more of the blows he took to the mouth had done something harmful to it. He was inclined to think that the principal cause of the damage was the spiked heel of the female's shoe. It was hard to see in the dark, but he could feel that some of the front teeth were missing. Groping about, he came upon the flashlight and switched it on, but it too had apparently been hurt in the fight and stayed dark, so he couldn't look among the ashes in the driveway for his missing choppers.

Getting to his feet was not easy. He had taken a lot of punishment from that goon squad. A lesser man might have cashed in his chips, but Reverton after a life of raw deals was a pretty tough cookie. What bothered him more than the physical pain, which could easily be found in any part of his body, was that the right knee of his trousers was badly torn. At least once he had plunged knees-first onto those sharp ashes. This was his only suit; in fact, these were his only pants. It was clear that his adversaries were diabolically clever professionals who knew exactly how to hurt a man in the worst way. What kind of respect could he inspire with a big hole in the knee of his trouserleg? It also occurred to him for the first time that it might well have been these people who had used Junior to get his pistol away. For example, why had Junior never tried to borrow it before? Why on just this night, when being armed would have made the difference between victory and defeat? Had Rev used the gun to back up his threat, that harlot would never have doubted his authenticity as a law-enforcement officer: it was at precisely that point that the tide turned against him.

That Junior could have been subverted was a terrible thought, being a blood relative, but the longer he entertained it, the more likely it seemed. Of course the woman, as usual, had been the instrument by which Junior had been manipulated; his skin problem indicated that he was a lustful youth who abused himself strenuously.

Rev removed his lower plate and dropped it into his pocket to join the damaged upper: with nothing to bite against, the bare gums were preferable. He started limping slowly, painfully, toward the street. He had not gotten far when a pair of automobile headlights were switched on, illuminating him alone in the darkness, and while he was squinting in the glare two men appeared, one on either side of him, and one carried a baseball bat and the other a hefty length of lead pipe.

One of them shouted, "Whatchoo doing here, you dirty old drunk?"

The other agreed, "Yessir, he's nothing but a filthy old drunk, Bobby."

Reverton hastened to say, "Maanuh milfantin theran—"

"He's so goddam loaded he can't even talk," said one of the men. "And look there where his face is bleeding. He fell down blind drunk and hurt himself."

One of them came around behind Rev and pushed him in the small of the back with the baseball bat. "Go on, you old boozer," he said. "We're the DeWeese boys, and if we ever catcha on our propitty again, we'll beatcha till you can't stand up."

Rev tried again to explain, but without his teeth he apparently couldn't talk so that they could comprehend him (unless they were part of the same conspiracy which had corrupted Junior and were only pretending to misunderstand for their own devious motives), so all his efforts got him were more violent pushes with the bat. And when they got him out to the sidewalk, one of them put a heavy shoe into the base of his back and gave him a shove that sent him reeling.

At this point the police car arrived, and Ray Dooley climbed out and said, "Whatsa trouble here?" He stared for a moment, and then he said, "Why, Reverton!" He looked at the DeWeese brothers. "You fellas do that to him?"

"We ain't touched him except to throw him off our propitty," said the one with the lead pipe. "He was falling down drunk when we got there. Bill Cox, who lives right over there, heard something funny going on over here, and he give us a call, so we come right on over."

Reverton, speaking as slowly and clearly as he could, tried to explain, but though Ray was more sympathetic than the DeWeeses, he didn't get far.

Finally Dooley said to the brothers, "This here's Bud Bullard's cousin. You know Bud, dontcha? Now it is my understanding that Rev don't drink." He was speaking as though Reverton were absent. "He's always been a little bit screwy, see. What I figure is he had some kinda fit and maybe wandered in here and fell down and hurt himself."

"He must of fell off the roof to get that banged up," said a DeWeese.

Ray nodded. "God knows what he'd do."

Rev was really burning, having to stand there and listen to these insulting statements. At last it occurred to him to put his teeth in his mouth and try to talk.

"I ain't nutss!" he protested when the dentures were in place. He could speak more clearly than without them, but the spaces where the missing front teeth had been caused an escape of air on the *s*'s. "They jumped me. There was two of 'em. But for me, they would of got to your autos and would of stole or stripped 'em to the hubs. I saved your bacon, and I don't expect no gratitude, but I'll thank you all"—he indignantly added Ray Dooley in this—"not to slander me right to my face, for pity sake."

The DeWeese with the piece of pipe was smirking openly. He said, "Damn me if that ain't some story. We dint see nobody else, did we, Bobby?"

" 'Course," said Ray, "they would of been gone by then, if what Rev says happened."

"Sssure! I run 'em out! I took a lot uh damage." Demonstratively he ran his hand up his bruised face and onto his bare head. "For God's sake! My hat!" he shouted, and he ran back between the garages and searched the ground, but being black the fedora was not easy to locate in the dark.

After a while Ray came in with the flashlight from the cruiser, and the hat was finally found, but it too had taken a beating and had been trampled into the ashes. Reverton poked it into shape, more or less, and brushed it with his forearm, but what it really would need was a professional cleaning and blocking, an expensive operation that might cost fifty cents or more.

He appealed to Ray in the matter of the DeWeese brothers, who were opening the doors of the nearer garage, and repeated, "I don't expect to be thanked, ssee, but—"

Ray said, "Just simmer down, Rev. We'll get this straightened out."

Reverton was plenty sore at Ray too, for calling him "screwy," but since Dooley was a police officer and carried a real gun he thought it better to conceal his resentment.

The DeWeeses came out to report that nothing was missing or had been damaged, including the cars on which they were working at present. Dooley asked about the other garage or shed, and they said that was empty anyway. Rev looked expectantly at them, but no apology was forthcoming. They climbed into their car, backed out, drove away.

Rev looked at Ray Dooley and bitterly shook his head.

Dooley said, "You look like you could use some first aid, Reverton. You been put through the ringer. Lemme runya down the station. We got a medical kit there, with iodine and shinplasters and all. Ordinarily it's in the car, but Clive left it in the toilet. He got hurt today himself: he run into a car door or something and cut his lip and got a black eye and all."

Reverton was touched by the offer. Except for the Bullard family, people usually weren't nice to him. That was probably because he had their number and they could see he knew they were no better than they should be, that is, rotten to the core.

"Appreshhhhiate it," he said, and then immediately worried whether that made him sound too soft.

The phone was ringing as they entered the station. Ray told Reverton to go on into the toilet, and answered the call. Rev looked in the mirror at his bloody, bruised face. The reason he had carried a gun was just so this kind of thing would not happen to him again. Being undersized, he had taken regular beatings from the larger boys in the orphanage, and when he got older, many's the time he would have been whipped by bigger men in hash houses, at streetcar stops, even in his place of business, the corridors and rest rooms of the county courthouse, had he not backed down. But after the bus accident he had armed himself. Anybody could possess a starter's pistol; you needed a permit to carry a real one. You didn't need to shoot to get respect. You didn't always even need to point it at anyone.

Ray Dooley appeared in the doorway and addressed Reverton's face in the mirror. "That was Frieda. She's got to get over to Hornbeck to the police station. Harvey Yelton's holding Junior for attempted armed robbery."

CHAPTER

Before going up to fetch Frieda in the cruiser, Ray had phoned Harvey Yelton to get the facts in the case, and after he had hung up, he said to Reverton, "The boy claims you gave him the gun."

Rev shrugged, and then he said defiantly, "Heck, it's just a sstarter'ss piztol that would shoot blankss, and it wassn't even loaded with *them*."

"That what you carry onna job?" Ray asked. "You wouldn't want them tough tramps to catch on." He rubbed the stubble on his chin. "Listen, I'm going to run Frieda over Hornbeck. Harvey Yelton, the chief over there, won't lemme cross the line in the Millville cruiser, so I'll drive up the Bullard house and leave it there and take Bud's automobile. Another thing: he says he won't let me come into town as a Millville police officer, on account of the bad blood between him and Clive. I says, 'You 'n' me don't have any quarrel, Harvey,' and he says he knowzzat, but I'm not the police chief uh Millville and old Clive is and he's got it in for him, so he won't let me come into town in uniform."

Ray unpinned the badge from the pleated breast pocket of the blue shirt. "I says, 'Well, my jacket's the regular leather civilian one I wear to work down the plant. If I keep it buttoned up and don't wear a police cap, izzat O.K.? My pants just come from my blue-serge suit. They don't have a stripe or anything.' 'O.K.,' says he, 'but you leave your gun behind and your badge too.' " Ray unbuckled his gun belt. "Just lucky Clive's under the weather. Harvey'd never let *him* in, and he'd be likely to throw the book at Junior. But seeing it's me, maybe I can get him to drop the charges against the boy. Harvey and me never had any trouble personally."

Reverton said sternly, "I'm the one who ought to go. I'm part of the family." He removed his battered fedora and brushed it with his forearm.

"Take my word for it, Rev, that wouldn't help," said Ray. "You stay here, and if any phone calls come in, you get in touch with me at the Hornbeck station. We got that police radio over there inna corner, and when Clive or me's in the station, we put it on. But it's too complicated to explain how to use it in a few minutes, and anyhow, anybody in town needs the police, they call onna phone." He went to a full-length locker near the door to the cell and put his gunbelt and badge on the shelf at the top, and covered them with the cap. He found a key in his pocket and turned the little lock. "I'll only be out of touch for a couple minutes while we're driving over there and then again when we come back." He sighed. "I just hope we can get Junior out. That family's got enough trouble, and it sure won't do Bud any good if the boy's in jail." Ray had known them all for years, and he regarded Bud as a square shooter.

When he reached the Bullard house, Frieda was waiting for him on the porch. He told her about the conditions imposed by the Hornbeck police chief, and he went inside and found the car keys. The automobile was in the garage at the back of the yard. They went there and got in, and Ray backed the car down the driveway. Then he drove the cruiser into the garage.

On the way to Hornbeck, Ray told Frieda about the weapon Junior had brandished.

Frieda shook her head sadly. "Reverton is a good-hearted soul. You got to feel sorry for that poor devil. I never liked the idea of him bringing that gun of his around here, but I didn't want to say anything and hurt his feelings. He's Bud's first cousin, you know, and he was an orphan."

"It's just a starter's pistol, I guess," said Ray, "and it just shoots blanks, but Harvey's taking it pretty seriously."

Frieda hung her head. She was not the type to complain, unlike Ray's own wife, who could get pretty loud over a lot smaller problems than this one.

Alongside the Hornbeck town hall there was room in the little official parking lot for Ray to pull the Bullard car in, but he strongly suspected that Yelton would be opposed to that, so he left the automobile at the curb, and he and Frieda went inside the police station.

The Hornbeck chief was sitting behind the desk, writing on a form with a fountain pen, and across from him was a fat young woman with messy bleached-blond hair.

"Hi, Harvey," said Ray.

Yelton took his time about looking up from the desk. When he did, he did not return Ray's smile or, for that matter, the greeting.

He said, "It's a waste of time for you to come over here tuhnight. I ain't gonna wake up our magistrate just for this punk kid. He's gonna be behind bars for a long time: he might as well get used to it."

"This here's the boy's mother, Harvey," said Ray. "He

ain't been in any kind of police trouble before. His dad's bidniss burnt down a night or two ago, and the poor fellow's inna hospital. If there'd be any way we could get around charging the boy, it would sure help these poor folks. Boy's dad is a real good friend of mine and one of the leading bidnissmen in Millville."

Yelton's grave expression did not change. He said, "This here young lady's co-owner of Hornbeck's leading bar 'n' grill. She anner husband run a respectable place, and this punk kid comes in and threatenza customers with a deadly weapon and—"

"Excuse me, Harvey, but ain't the weapon just a starter's pistol, which just shoots blanks?"

Harvey slowly shook his head and developed a grim grin. "Ray, you know as well as me you can fill the barrel of a blank pistol with rusty nails or broken glass or any of a numbera other things, and you put a blank cartridge inna chamber and you got a weapon that at close range will do as much damage as you want. Take a man's eye right out of his head."

"But there wasn't any of that stuff inna barrel of this gun, was there?"

Harvey looked mysterious and muttered, "That's under investigation."

The blonde had her broad back to them, but now she half-turned, with some difficulty, owing to her figure, and she said, "You shoulda seen that little twerp!"

"I doubt he meant any harm," said Frieda. "He's a good boy, but he's so worried about his poor dad."

"Well, he shoulda thoughta that first," said the blonde.

Frieda looked miserable and replied, "He's jist a youngster."

"Maybe that is so, Missus, but that don't change what he done."

Ray said to the chief, "Harvey, could his mother see the lad?"

Harvey took a breath and released it very slowly. He said, "In time. But first I wanna know about what kinda fambly you got." He was looking at Frieda. "You let young kids carry weapons, do yuh?"

"No sir, see, this here cousin of ours, he's a railroad detective—"

Harvey interrupted. "And carries a blank pistol? That's a lie and you know it. The weapon belongs to your boy. Suppose he poured gravel downa barrel? He could of put a hole in somebody's guts. If he put it inna person's ear on one side, he could shoot the brains out the other."

"But Harvey," said Ray, "there wasn't really anything in the barrel, was there?"

Yelton frowned with his thick eyebrows. He said, "This here is my police station, Dooley. You ain't in Millville now. You're in Hornbeck, and I run things over here, not your fat-slob boss Clive Shell."

"I sure know that, Harvey," said Ray. "You 'n' me never had any trouble between us. I just mean you are too fair a man to misrepresent the facts to the poor mother of some young kid who got himself in trouble."

Harvey found a key and opened the lower right-hand drawer in the desk. He reached in and pulled out a little .22 automatic, holding it by the barrel.

Ray looked at it and said, "That ain't a starter's pistol."

Harvey moved his heavy jaw. "I never said it was. I am just showing you what kinda weapons I've took away from kids. You could kill a man with this." He extended it toward Frieda, who shrank away. "I took it offn some kid who had it down the dump, shooting rats. Now the slug from one of these can travel a mile or more and kill or maim. Or suppose it was to hit the head of an engineer of an express train going to the city: he'd fall down on the controls, and the train'd keep going when it got to the terminal downtown and plow right into the building and kill everybody on board and a whole lot of innocent strangers who just happened to be there at the time. That's what a gun can do."

Frieda said, "Yessir. I know you are doing a fine job."

Harvey put the gun into the drawer and brought out a starter's pistol. It would not have fooled anybody who looked at it in a calm state of mind, expecting to see a gun that fired blanks, but Ray was aware that people tended to get nervous when somebody was carrying a gun, and it was anyway a good idea to work with the benefit of the doubt.

Harvey said, "I'm gonna confiscate this."

Ray nodded. "You're doing your duty, Harvey."

The blonde got out of her chair and turned to Frieda. She said, "Anybody knows me, knows I ain't got a mean bone in my body, Missus. I like kids, but being in bidness like me and Billy don't leave much time for having a fambly. . . . I don't wanna cause you no grief, but you oughta watch that kid of yours so he don't go wrong and grow up and be a bum or something worse."

"Yes, ma'am," said Frieda. "If you could just let him go this time . . ." She looked sorrowfully at the woman's feet.

Harvey said, "Well, it's up to Marie. If she wants to prefer charges . . ."

Marie said, "All right then, Missus, I'll tellya what: you get him to apologize tuh me, and I'll call it off. I ain't a nasty person, as anybody over here can tellya."

Harvey got up and went down the corridor. He could be heard unlocking the door of the cell. In a moment he was back, pushing Junior before him. The boy was wearing the same sullen look he had acquired a few years earlier. Some kids changed in their teens and some did not, and some who apparently changed were just pretending so as to act big for their friends. Ray thought it wise to take Junior seriously: Harvey might have been exaggerating in his remarks on guns, including blank pistols, but as a fellow police officer Ray agreed with him in general.

Harvey told Junior, "This lady might be willing to drop the charges againstcha if you apologize to her."

Junior remained silent. His mother approached him gingerly.

"Please, Junior . . ."

Ray had enough of this. He said, "Listen, Junior, if these folks want to, they can putcha in reform school for quite a while."

Junior turned his head somewhat to the side and mumbled.

"How's that?" Harvey Yelton cupped a hand at his ear.

Junior repeated the apology in a louder voice.

Harvey went ponderously behind his desk. He said, "Izzat good enough for you, Marie? Or you think he oughta come over after school for a couple weeks and clean out your rest rooms or whatnot?"

Marie shook her head. It had been a surprise to Ray to hear that she was a tavern owner; she looked like a whore.

She said, "Naw, that's O.K. I don't wanna be nasty. We run a real respectable place, and we hope to keep it that way. You just grow up first, sonny, and then you come over and see us. We don't bear no grudges." She gave Junior a great big smile. Ray could see now that she was a pretty nice person, and he thought he might drop in at the bar & grill, next time he was over in Hornbeck, and have a brew.

He said to Junior, who looked as though he would continue to maintain a sullen silence, "Why, that's real nice, don't you think, Junior? Now you just thank the lady."

Junior said, "Thanks."

"God bless you," said Frieda.

Harvey opened a tomato-soup-colored fountain pen and put the cap onto the butt. He handed it to Junior and then turned a piece of paper and slid it across the desk.

"You sign this receipt," he ordered sternly. Junior did so, and the chief reclaimed it. "That weapon of yours is hereby officially confiscated. Which means you don't get it back. Now, you are just lucky the lady decided to drop the charges, but don't think that means your slate is clean." He put a big finger in Junior's face. "You're banned from entering the town limits of Hornbeck for—how old're you now?"

It was Frieda who answered. "He just turned eighteen. Yes, sir."

Harvey glowered at Junior. He said, "I don't want to see you in my town for three years, see? Till you're twenty-one years of age. You're supposed to become a man then. We'll see about that. Meantime, if you come over here any sooner, I'll make you wish you was dead."

Ray was sorry to see that Junior did not look as though he found this threat impressive. He just stared at the Hornbeck chief for a while and then dropped his eyes.

"He won't," said Frieda. "You can count on that. I want tuh thank you, sir, you been real nice to us, and you too, ma'am. I'm real sorry we causedjany trouble. We won't be back."

Ray said so long to Marie and shook Harvey's hand for the favor to a fellow professional which he considered had been done here, and he, Frieda, and Junior went out.

As soon as the door closed behind them, Junior swung around and put his thumb to his nose and blew a raspberry at the station. Then he lowered his hand with the thumb still erect and the index finger extended, in which position it was a simulated pistol.

"Bah-ROOM," he said, pretending to shoot through the door.

Ray grabbed his arm and, pulling him aside, said in a lowered voice, "Lissenere, you little shitass, I come over here and used my influence to getcha loose because of your dad and mom, but by God you keep acting like a little smart aleck, and I'll kick your butt alla way back to Millville. And I hate to think what Clive would do to you if he knew. He'd figure you disgraced him in front of Harvey Yelton, and he hates his guts."

Junior nodded and said, "O.K.," but he didn't look like he was bluffed. Ray couldn't understand the kids of the present time. When he was a boy he would have crapped his pants if a cop gave him so much as a dirty look.

Frieda had already climbed into the back seat of the car, as if she were a prisoner.

"Why're you back there?" Ray asked.

"Junior always likes to ride up front," said she.

There you had the reason for the way he acted: he was spoiled rotten. What the boy needed most was to have his ass whipped.

"You gonna leave all them lights on?" Tony asked Eva as they were going down the driveway to the front sidewalk.

"Sure! Otherwise Mama will be suspicious when she comes back. This way she will probably think I already went to bed, and it'll be morning before she realizes I'm not there."

"Oh, yeah." Until now that way of looking at their going off together had not occurred to Tony. "What'll you think she'll do when she finds out?"

"Go crazy," said Eva, shrugging. "I don't know. Maybe call the cops."

He decided that pursuing this matter at the moment

could only be unpleasant. Once they reached Canada and
he joined the Mounted Police and got a red coat, shiny
boots, and a horse, no woman would object to his taking
care of her daughter. Besides which he had no intention of
doing anything illicit to Eva until they were married.

"Speaking of the cops," Eva said as they reached the
sidewalk, "I wonder what happened with my brother."

"Brother?"

"I told you he was arrested in Hornbeck." She had a
slight edge to her voice. "Junior 'n' I don't get along so
well. He stole some money I was saving up and bought a
pack of Chesterfield cigarettes and a bottle of grape wine.
I would have had him arrested myself if he hadn't been my
brother. Once a couple of years ago my cousin Clara? She
came here to see me and she was using the bathroom, and
Junior walked right in, and it wasn't a mistake, because he
just stood there watching her with a big grin on his face
while she was sitting on the you-know-what, and he wouldn't
leave till she said she would yell for my mother to come."

Tony had little interest in any of this. But neither did
he have any real plans as yet on how to get to Canada from
Millville.

He said, "It might of been simpler to wait till daylight,
but tomorrow morning there'll be plenty of people who
will want to stop us. I guess if we get over to the pike we
might hitch a ride from some truckdriver going north."
This was a good idea! He felt his assurance return.

"But that doesn't mean I would *really* like to send Junior
to jail," Eva went on. She was quite a talker, it seemed,
when she got started. "He *is* my only brother, after all,
though I guess Mama had a little baby boy before him,
but it died. It was only a couple days old, but they gave it
a name and buried him in the cemetery. It's really strange
to go there on Decoration Day and see his little gravestone

with his name, Willard Bullard, the brother I never knew. Sometimes I like to think of him growing up, and I bet he'd have been nicer to me than Junior ever was."

Tony said, "Listen, Eva, I think we better cut through these back streets, because you can't tell who might come along if we go down to Main, but I don't know so much about Millville beyond here."

Eva said, "Could we get a Coke 'n' chips or something first? I'm pretty hungry. We didn't get much for supper, just scrambled eggs, because my dad's in the hospital. He had a nervous breakdown, and he was acting *really strange*. Our store burned down. Some of our family think that your family did that. But I don't! Why would you set fire to our store and then come around to see me?" She giggled.

For an instant Tony wondered whether she was all there, but then he realized she was just young. "I don't know if there's any place to eat still open around here. It's getting pretty late. If we hitched a ride maybe we could stop at an all-night diner. The truckdrivers go to those diners and drink coffee to keep them awake."

"Oh, yeah," said Eva. "I saw that in a movie with, you know, that girl who wears that dark lipstick . . . Well, anyway, there's this fellow—"

"How far can we go on this street?" Tony asked. They were at the end of the block, going west, at the edge of, for him, unknown territory.

"Maybe Curly will still be open," Eva said. "Curly's Luncheonette? I don't know if you ever ate his chili. Some kids don't like it, but I do, a lot. It's on spaghetti?" She walked in a childish way, sometimes lagging behind, sometimes swinging out in front of Tony. She was wearing a sweater set in powder blue, and looked a little bit heavier than she had been in the summer, or maybe it was just the extra clothes. He still really liked the way she looked.

He said, "I just worry about who we might run into if we go down there."

"Oh, that's all right," said Eva. "I can go out if I do my homework, and I finished it earlier. Of course, I'm not supposed to stay out after ten, but Mama probably won't notice, with everything else going on."

Tony wondered whether he had heard her correctly. He thought he had explained clearly at the beginning: this wasn't just a date. What did she think he meant when he was talking about hitching a ride on a truck? Had she listened to anything he said? But it made no sense at this point to ignore her wishes.

"Are you serious?" he asked. "Are you really hungry?"

"Yeah, but I don't know for *what*. Maybe a chocolate soda . . . *I* know! Cider and doughnuts! It's that season again, ladies and gentlemen." She was imitating some radio announcer.

"The only thing is," said Tony, "they don't ever serve that *out*, do they? You got to buy the cider and the doughnuts, and have them at home, I think."

"The junior class runs a booth at the football games," Eva said, doing a little skip along the sidewalk. "They sell cider 'n' doughnuts and hotdogs and potato chips and stuff like that. Gee, I wish it was Friday night, and then we'd be at the game."

"Except that I'd be playing somewhere else, for Hornbeck," Tony pointed out. His depression was growing.

"Oh, yeah. Well then, you couldn't have any! So why don't you move to Millville? It's a much better town, anyway." She leered at him under a streetlamp. "We always say that all the dumbbells live in Hornbeck."

"Oh, yeah?" Tony didn't want to get into one of those stupid my-town's-better-than-yours games at this point.

"We say it's where you have to go to find all the dopes."

He had certainly begun to feel like one. He probably should have thought this whole thing out much more thoroughly. "Well, a person don't have much say in where he's born."

Eva came up to him. "I was just kidding, Tony. I wasn't trying to insult you."

What a terrific girl she really was. He returned to being crazy about her. She had such good manners and delicacy of feeling: he had never known anyone like that.

"Gosh, I know you were, Eva. But, see, I really do think Millville is the best place to live. You know why?"

"Huh-uh." She had a fragrant smell, not perfume, but something in the wool of her sweaters, maybe mothballs, an odor he had never previously cared for.

"Well, isn't that where you live?"

She lowered her face in a kind of embarrassed pleasure, and then looked up with an impish grin. "Are you getting gooey?"

"Huh?" Was that something dumb again?

"That was in another movie," said Eva. "This chorus girl met this guy who played the saxophone in some night-club? It was one of those places, uh, you know, Broadway or Paris or someplace like that, real sophisticated? Maybe you saw it? After all, the nearest movie theater's in Horn-beck, isn't it? Score one for your town!"

Tony realized that they were in the last block before reaching Main Street, just exactly where he had not wanted to end up, but Eva was proving somewhat difficult to manage, in a way he had not anticipated.

He said, "I go to the movies quite a bit, but I don't re-member them so well. My brother does, though. He reads a lot too. He's just a young kid, but he can talk on any subject." He remembered that Eva was even younger and wondered whether he should have said that about Jack.

"*My* brother got thrown out of that theater once," said Eva. "He brought along one of those things they call Bronx cheers, you know? You blow in them and the rubber thing makes an awful noise? Every time the boy would say something to the girl in a love scene, Junior would blow that thing."

Tony actually thought that was pretty funny, though he remembered seeing Junior at the hospital coffee shop and hadn't like his ratty looks much at that time. But he was glad to hear that his future brother-in-law had a sense of humor. He felt somewhat sensitive about Junior's having been arrested in Hornbeck, but then he himself, if spotted by that cop he had punched, was surely in danger of going to jail here in Millville.

He asked Eva, "Are you still hungry?"

Her voice had a note of aggrievement. "Well, since I haven't eaten anything, I don't know why I wouldn't be."

He asked stoically, "Where is this chili place?"

"Come on."

He hunched up in his jacket and tried to assume a different stride, so as not to be immediately recognizable, but he knew that his glasses would be a dead giveaway if any of his Millville enemies appeared.

But they reached Curly's without incident. The luncheonette was dark.

"Darn," said Eva, stamping her saddle oxford on the concrete. "My life is ruined."

Tony tried not to show how relieved he was. "That's too bad, but if we get out to the pike, it won't be too long before we catch a ride and then we can stop at one of them all-night—"

Eva socked him painlessly in the chest at this point, snickered, and ran up the side alleyway next to the luncheonette. There was a streetlamp at the intersection with the north-south alley, but darkness came again not far beyond. Tony was at once sexually excited by the chase, which apparently was to be a standard feature of his association with Eva, and unpleasantly anxious in being further frustrated in his attempt to get out of town. He was determined this time not to let her give him the slip even momentarily, and not far beyond the perimeter of the ring of light he seized her from behind. She immediately stopped and pressed back firmly against him, and when he began to move again, they walked as one, with his hands around her waist and her bottom against his thighs.

Just across the street from the top of the alley was the park where they had first met. Tony was now in such a state as to forsake all plans to go to Canada or anywhere else: he had lost his will altogether and was not his own man. His hands were clasped just below her weighty breasts, not touching them except in accidental grazings. His face was against her hair. Her aroma now seemed to be that of teaberry gum. They were marching in a synchronized way that would probably have looked clownish to an observer: Tony was strangely objective in this thought. There probably were cars that passed, but he didn't notice them at all as particulars.

In the park they reached a low retaining wall on the far slope beneath the concrete slab where the dances were held. The light was dim there; the trees screened that of the moon, and there were no lamps. They stopped simultaneously, without a thought on his part, and sat down side by side on the wall. Tony hadn't done much kissing aside from the party game Spin the Bottle, in which he was always worried about his glasses being in the way and what to do with his nose. At the conclusion of both his dates with Mary Catherine Lutz she had nervously stuck out her mitt, and he had shaken it gratefully.

While being occupied mentally with the matter of kissing he had put his hand up under Eva's skirt without thinking about it at all. In fact, he only finally took note of the action because of how agreeably she moved her knees apart.

When Curly and the colored dishwasher had seen Junior leave the luncheonette, they came back down the alley and returned to their duties, though the dishwasher, whose name was Homer Waters, was not too thrilled.

He said, "What if he be back?"

Curly thrust his chin forward and moved it slowly from side to side. "He won't. That's the Bullard kid. He had a few drinks, I bet, and he's feeling his oats, but he's all mouth, take it from me. I seen lots of that kind. I should of kicked his little ass, but I don't like to mess around when somebody's carrying a gun. Thing is, his dad's laid up, in the hospital. Poor devil lost his store inna fire the other night. I don't want to cause him any more trouble."

Homer said, "I don't foke with no guns *or* knaves. I hate that kine shat. I don't like to get hoit, and I don't wanna hoit nobody else." He wasn't any too crazy about working himself to death, either, but Curly knew you had to settle for either somebody who was regular and lazy or one who would work hard till payday and then get drunk and never show up for three days. Homer was professedly a teetotaler, and Curly had never seen any reason to doubt him.

They went in through the kitchen door. The same dishes had been stacked between the sinks all day, so far as Curly could see. He put a finger in the soapy water in the right-hand sink. It was cold as could be.

"I wish you'd get these cleared up," he told Homer. "It's

closing time." He went through the swinging door to the counter. The old man was gone and had neglected to leave any money, but Curly knew who he was and would get it out of him next time.

The fellow who had eaten the fish sandwich was sitting behind an empty coffee cup. He winked.

Curly said, "How about that? He's a kid from town." He told about Bud Bullard's bad luck.

The man shrugged and got up from his stool. He pulled a half-dollar from his pants pocket.

When Curly went to make change, he saw that the cash register was empty of folding money. "By God," he said forcefully. "Was *he* at this drawer?"

"Yeah." The man wore a salt-and-pepper suit and a gray tie and felt hat, and he had a five-o'clock shadow.

Junior hadn't touched the change. Curly found a nickel and a dime and gave them to the customer. He said, "I'm gonna have to think about this now. I was gonna let the other thing ride. Just walking around with a pistol, and nobody hurt. But he robbed me?"

"That was a starter's pistol," said the man. "Just shoots blanks."

Curly disregarded this information. He said, "I had only a few bucks, in ones. Rest of it's inna sack for the night deposit."

"Bank here in town?" asked the man.

"Yeah," Curly said. He was breathing harder than he had after his run. He was aware that people thought his shortness of breath was due to having been gassed in the war, but it was not. He didn't know what it was, and neither did the doctor, but he had never been near any gas. "That little son of a bee! I'll fix his wagon now, sick dad or not. You can't let somepin like this here go on."

"You got him dead to rights," said the man. "What time's bank open inna morning?"

"Eight A.M.," said Curly. "Little bastard think he can sashay in here and rob me blind . . ." He chewed his tongue.

"I'm here in connection with a bidniss oppitunity," said the customer, "and am looking for a good bank."

"Well, thizere one is real good," said Curly. "The vice-president eats here on occasion. You wanna go there, you say I sentcha. I'm Curly McCoy. Whole town knows me." He put his hand across the counter, and it was shaken.

"Smith," said the man. "Bill Smith."

"Please to meetcha."

"Sure."

"What line uh bidniss joo say you was in?"

Smith narrowed his eyes and said, flatly, "Bowling balls."

"Zat right? We got a poolhall up the street, but the nearest bowling alley is, oh, on out past—"

"You got a good police force here?" Smith asked. "Keep the crooks out?"

"Why sure," said Curly. He had his own criticisms of Millville, but would not mention them to a stranger. "Chief's a personal friend of mine, a fellow name of Clive Shell. He don't let the riffraff go too far, and he keeps the coloreds over where they belong. He's pretty tough on kids who get outa line, which is why I wasn't gonna say anything at first—"

"Just one guy onna force?" asked Smith. "What happens onniz day off? All hell break loose?" He had a lantern jaw when he grinned.

"Cousin's a part-time patrolman," Curly said. "We got a nice little, quiet little town here. But we could use something up and coming."

"I sure like what I seen of it," said Smith, grabbing a toothpick from the shotglassful next to the cash register—

just one, not a whole handful like some of the local customers helped themselves to.

Curly said, "That wouldn't be a whole plant that made bowling balls, would it?"

Smith put his head at a knowing angle and squinted. "Why, sure. You got some people who ain't afraid of work?"

"We could ahweez use a new bidniss," said Curly. "I wouldn't doubt what they'd givya a break onna taxes."

"Izzat right?" Smith's toothpick was at a jaunty angle in the corner of his mouth. "Been a real pleasure," said he, and went out the door.

Curly called the police from the phone booth at the rear of the luncheonette. While the bell was ringing at the other end, he probed at the top of the money-return slot to see if anybody had stuffed paper up there to trap refunded coins. He found some on occasion, but had never detected anybody in the act of putting the paper there. It was hard to manage some things in a one-man operation (not counting the dishwasher). Over the course of the year he would also lose a considerable number of spoons and forks, though not many knives; lots of salt shakers but hardly any peppers; and always some sugar containers and napkin holders: there were those who regarded it as classy to have such things on the home dining table. But this pilferage was probably no worse than anywhere else in the world, and he did not regard it as necessary to give Millville a black mark for it so far as Smith went.

The telephone rang so long without being answered that Curly figured Ray Dooley must be out of the station. Daytimes, if Clive wasn't there, the city clerk, in the office next door, could answer the police phone on an extension, and if it was an emergency, come over and call the cruiser on the station radio. But only Ray was on duty at night. If it was a real crisis, and the station was empty, you could go out on the street and look for the cruiser, or wake up Clive at home, or the fire chief, if he was more appropriate.

Curly was about to hang up when a not-quite-familiar voice came on the wire.

"I'm trying to call the police," Curly said.

"This here's the police station."

Curly asked, "You a new cop?"

The voice took on an unpleasant note. "You get fresh, you'll find out who I am quicker'n you want."

Curly had always been on first-rate terms with Clive Shell. Though the latter was not famous for his geniality, he had never shown anything else to Curly, who didn't charge him a cent for the considerable amounts of grub he put away at the luncheonette, and, furthermore, his presence tended to drive business away from Curly's to Tom's Restaurant, at the end of the block, though true enough, Curly made up for it when Clive went to Tom's, for not even normally law-abiding folks wanted to eat near a cop.

"Wellsir," Curly said, "you don't have to get on your high horse. This is—" He was speaking in a joking tone, assuming that when he had identified himself, the other fellow would have a laugh and return the favor, for everybody in town knew Curly and vice versa. But he was interrupted by a scream of hatred.

"You goddam dirty yella dogs! I'll git you and all your tribe! You'll eat dirt afore I'm through with you, and *you'll like it.*"

Curly hung up. It was obvious that he had gotten a wrong number. Or else one of the cops had arrested a maniac, who had broken out of the cell and answered the phone. He might have tried again, or even walked on up to the station, because he really believed only the first of the alternatives, but the resistance to his original plan to report Junior's crimes was sufficient to give him second thoughts. Even to tell Ray Dooley might embarrass the Bullards and add to their troubles. Junior would be around town, and when Curly saw him next time, he'd get those five bucks back or make Millville a living hell for that little piss-willy.

Sitting with Eva on the concrete wall in the Millville park, Tony, without prior intent, proceeded to feel her up in a way that turned out to be systematic. He ran his hand up her smooth, sturdy thigh, down into the valley where it joined its partner, deep down to where there was a double layer of fabric in the vee of her underpants, where it was a lot warmer, and then up to the coolness of her belly. She did not resist this exploration. In fact, she facilitated it by moving her limbs, but she did nothing else. She was his to do with as he pleased, it seemed, would provide her body but nothing further. She was so quiet that he could not even hear her breathing. He was certain that he could go right up to the waistband of her pants with both hands, and she would lift her bottom so that he could pull them right off. This power, hitherto unknown, was not simple to accept. How could you just go ahead and exercise it without being prepared for the consequent responsibility? In short, *what was he supposed to do then?*

He came out of her skirt and went up under her sweater. There was the top of a slip there and, beneath that, a brassiere: a device the back-strap and fastening clips of which he had usually felt when waltzing with partners at the high-school dance classes, though on occasion he had drawn little freshman girls with the bird-chests of children. Yet here was Eva, only fourteen, with these jugs that were so large as to seem insensitive. He pursued them now through the obstacles. This time there was not much that could be done by her to ease his way—not unless she took a hand, which of course was unlikely, since she was not a whore.

So he labored under her sweater, and eventually came to the point at which to go farther he might have torn some item of her clothing, unless he actually removed the cardigan and then the sweater underneath that, and then went on to work on the straps up at the shoulders. But aside from the matter of decency—they were in a public park, where anyone might come by at any time—the night was too cool to expose to the air the entire upper body of a young girl. She might end up with pneumonia, and how could he ever explain that?

At last he gave it up, came out, and pulled the sweater neatly down at her waist. At this point she seemed to sigh, but so softly that he might well have only imagined it. Her legs were still apart, with the hem of the plaid skirt over her knees. Her feet were swinging, in their saddle oxfords and white anklets, and the heels bounced away from each impact with the wall. Her round face was expressionless; in this kind of darkness her eyes looked smaller than in the light. All at once it occurred to him that Eva was too young to have any personality, so that while she was so pretty and physically perfect in every way, there was nothing else about her that was interesting.

It would have been easy to panic at this point; he had after all promised to marry her and furthermore to take her to Canada, a place which he didn't even know how to reach, let alone get a job in. In addition, it was a foreign land, and perhaps not even a very scrupulous one, if it claimed to own the Niagara Falls. They might draft him into their army and then get into a war with some nice little country like Holland. And now that he was in this pessimistic state of mind he remembered that in the movies about the Northwest Mounted Police they were always drinking toasts to the Queen, as they did in the ones about India, with which they were intermixed in his memory, whereas he was a one-hundred-percent red-blooded American who did not bow down to foreign monarchs.

Now Eva sighed loudly and complained, "Gosh, am I *hungry*."

This was a beautiful excuse for him to get out of his immediate predicament. He said eagerly, "Well, we better get something to eat before we go anywhere else. I'm real hungry myself. Ain't there anyplace open in Millville?"

Eva groaned. "It's so *late*." She added peevishly, "Why didn't you come over earlier?"

He saw an opportunity here to get into a quarrel that might free him of her completely, but was too softhearted to use it. "I was busy," he said. "But I guess you're right. It probably wasn't the best time, but a person can't always control these things. . . . Say, maybe we *should* wait till tomorrow."

Eva jumped nimbly down from the wall. "Are you getting cold feet or something?"

She had a way of keeping him off balance. He had heard that about women, but until now it had been merely theoretical, applying to grown men.

"Not me! I was thinking about *you*."

"Then get me something to eat," she wailed. "I'm *starving*." She walked away from him. She was just a selfish, small-minded little girl, obviously incapable of doing any of the things that a wife should do for a man. She didn't even seem to know that it was the female who was supposed to take care of the food. But he also understood that he was cutting an inferior figure, losing the authority with which he had begun. Relative to her, at least, he should be a man of the world, and yet— But then, inspired by desperation, he got the first practical idea he had had all evening, perhaps the best since the beginning of this romance.

He caught up with Eva. "There's a bakery in Millville, ain't there?"

But now she was turning against him. "Why do you always say 'ain't'?" she asked. "Don't your teachers in Hornbeck tell you it is ignorant?"

Tony stiffened. "I don't like to talk like a girl. Somebody might think I was a pansy."

Eva put up her chin in a snippy way. "Well, you don't have to talk like some stupid person to be a he-man." She proceeded to mention a movie star or two who spoke like gentlemen while also being tough as nails.

Tony realized that the situation was in danger of deteriorating beyond recovery unless he showed heroic patience at this point. "You're talking like some *teacher*," he complained, but not bitterly, and he went on, "They work all night in bakeries, and usually you can go there and they'll sell you doughnuts they just made, while they're still hot."

Eva was transformed. "Really?" She went up on the tips of her toes. He had never seen her this excited. "I didn't know that. I hope you're right." But until he was proved otherwise, he was climbing in her estimation. She was at her best when in good spirits, and for the moment anyway he was not bored. He had learned the truth that nothing in the world can provide as much simple joy as the presence of a pretty girl who is anticipating some pleasure that is within one's power to provide.

The Millville bakery was just beyond the bank. That the bakers were at work was not in doubt: the yeasty aromas could be smelled for a block. The shop was closed, of course, and they went around back, through the alleyway, and saw that the wooden door was thrown open, with only the screen door in place. Tony opened the latter and stepped inside. The ovens made it really hot in there; no wonder the door was open. The several bakers wore T-shirts and overseas caps in white, and their hairy forearms were prominent as they manhandled lumps and hunks and ropes of dough on a long floury table.

"Hey whatcha want?" the nearest man shouted, not letting up on the dough he was shaping. He had light curly hair.

"You got fresh doughnuts?"

"More 'n' you can eat and den some," the baker yelled jovially, and he went to a high rack with many shallow shelves and before choosing one asked, "Blain or bowdered or yeast or chelly or crullers regular or French?"

Through the screen door Tony asked Eva what she wanted, and when she said she didn't know, he turned to the baker and said expansively, "Mix 'em: a dozen all mixed."

It was a pleasure just to stand there and watch the man deftly fill the order from tray after sliding tray, plucking up, inside one of those little squares of baker's paper, two of each type of doughnut and depositing them, speedily but gently, inside the big white paper bag, which here and there soon showed almost transparent areas of absorbed grease.

When Tony paid for the doughnuts the baker made change from the pocket of his white canvas pants. The other men had continued to work briskly all this while, going back and forth to the big ovens at the far end of the room. The one who had waited on Tony went back to the loaf of bread he was braiding.

Tony was reluctant to leave this hot, aromatic place. He opened the screen door and handed the bag out to Eva, who immediately plunged her arm into it.

He came back and spoke to the baker. "How do you get started in this line of work?"

"Baker? Bractice. Onna chob. You wanna be baker, kid? Hard work, I can tellya. Nights ain't choorown. You go to bed when dey're all getting up."

"But you like it?"

"I'm just a dumb Dutchman," said the baker. "I don't know no better. You wanna chob, kid? Helping out in the shop on Saddy? You want it, you get here early, else we'll get somebody else. Kid we had got hired at the oil station. Just don't expect to get rich quick."

Tony stared in amazement. "This coming Sairdy? I'll be here real early."

"O.K., kid. What's your name?"

"Tony."

The baker laughed. "Whadduh yuh, some Dago?"

"Huh-uh."

The baker laughed again. "It's all the same to me. You come on Saddy."

Outside, Tony caught up with Eva, who was slowly walking out to the street, chewing away. She held a fragment of doughnut too small to identify as to type.

"Hey," Tony said, "know what?" His glasses had fogged up in the cool night air, and he got out the piece of toilet paper he carried for the purpose and cleaned them as he talked. "I just got offered a job there."

"No kidding," said Eva. Having swallowed the rest of the doughnut in hand, she went into the bag and brought out a French cruller. "Gee, this one's cold. The others were not exactly hot, but they were warm anyway. Boy, what a good idea. How'd joo know about it? I never did, and I live here." With one bite she took away almost half of the cruller.

"We always do that over in Hornbeck."

"Huh."

He put his glasses on and held out his hand. "Can I have one?"

"Uh." She surrendered the bag, which had a nice warm feel to it as well as that delicious aroma.

He said, "I guess if I work there I can get a cut rate on everything, breads and cakes and all." The prospect of a steady supply of doughnuts might serve to console her in case she had really set her heart on going to Canada.

They were under a streetlamp in front of the bake shop. She was watching him grope in the bag. "What are you looking for, jelly? There aren't any more."

"You already ate them *both*?"

She whined, "Well, they're my favorite kind."

"You eat so fast, you'll get a stomachache, for God's sake," said he. He assumed he had had a jelly doughnut coming, since it was all his idea and he had paid for the bag.

"Well . . ."

What a baby she was! What was he doing here? He found a plain doughnut, his own least favorite. It tasted of nothing but grease. She took the bag back.

"Listen, Eva," he said. "Maybe we oughta wait a while before running away. I mean, you're pretty young, you know."

"O.K." She now was eating the other French cruller. Apparently she had no concept of fairness. You might have thought she was an only child. He pitied her poor brother if she acted like this at home.

"You don't mind?"

Her mouth full, she answered after a delay. "Naw. I always did think it was just something you were saying."

That was pretty insulting, but it was probably better than if she were kicking and screaming about his broken promise.

"Oh," said he, "I was plenty serious, but I got to thinking about your age, and my dad's in the hospital, and all."

"So's my father!" Eva said competitively. "Are you just saying that because of my father?"

This kid stuff burned him up. "No," he said in a mocking tone, his mouth screwed up, "I didn't say that because of your father. I didn't even know about your father, for God's sake."

"I'll thank you not to curse at me," she said. "That might make you a big shot in Hornbeck, but it doesn't go over in this town, and that's where you are right now, and don't forget it. Also, I distinctly remember telling you all about my father being sick in the hospital because of what your family did to him." Her face twisted up, and she began to cry.

As soon as he saw the tears Tony felt like scum, and he said, "I'm sorry, Eva. Don't cry. Have the regular crullers. Or listen, I'll go back and get some jelly doughnuts or anything you want. . . . Come on, I didn't mean it. Honestly. And my family didn't do anything to your dad. It's probably all some kinda"—a sudden inspiration supplied him with a high-toned phrase he had heard somewhere, no doubt from Jack—"it's probably a comedy of errors."

"Well, I don't know if it's anything to laugh about!" She continued to cry. "I think you're the meanest person I ever met, and no wonder, considering what an awful family you come from."

"Now wait a minute! That ain't right—"

"There you go saying 'ain't' again. You are the most ignorant person I ever did—"

"Aw, go to hell." Tony astonished himself: this was not premeditated. He was sicker of her than he had realized.

Eva stared at him for a moment, but she had stopped crying. She finally said, "Boy oh boy," shook her head, brought a powdered doughnut out of the bag, and, eating, walked away in the direction of her home.

He let her go. He had an instinctive feeling that an apology would not be well received at this point. Besides, he was getting some satisfaction from his new-found freedom.

The house was dark when Tony got home. He went near the garage and took a quiet pee so that he wouldn't have to use the bathroom, then entered through the kitchen door. He climbed the stairs quietly and reached his room in the dark, without bumping into anything. He had lived in this house all his life. Without putting on a light he got into his pajamas and climbed into bed. He would have gone to sleep right away had not Jack spoken up from the other bed.

"I thought you took off."

"I thought about it," Tony replied, in a low voice: the doors to all of the rooms were usually kept open, unless someone was sick. "Mom say anything?"

"Huh-uh," Jack said. "I told her you went to bed early, in case you didn't want it known."

"Yeah, I wouldn't have, so thanks. . . . Listen, I'll give you your money back in the morning."

"No hurry," said Jack. "Hey, Tone, it's like the old days, huh?"

Tony said, "I decided to get a job around here. . . ." He remembered that Jack was just a kid. "Listen, it's getting pretty late. You better go to sleep."

Reverton was awakened by the sound of the telephone, coming from out front. He climbed off the bunk, left the cell, and limped up the short hallway barefoot and in his union suit, but before he got there the bell stopped ringing and he heard Ray Dooley pick up the instrument and talk. Rev was near the lavatory at this point. He went in, and having lowered the trapdoor in his underwear, sat down on the throne and began to grunt.

Daylight was coming through the etched-glass window above him. He proved to be constipated, and before long he rose and returned to the cell. He felt the effects of the punishment he had taken the night before: he was sore all over and half-lame. He was getting into his clothes when Ray came to the doorway.

"Oh, you're up. Clive just give me a call. He says he's got quite a shiner from that there door he walked into yesterday, and he don't think it looks good for the chief of police to be seen like 'at, and he wants me to stay on duty. Ordinarily I'd be going to work right now onna first shift down the mill."

Before going to sleep the night before, Rev had put his teeth into a tin cup full of water, on the floor beneath the bunk. There wasn't any chair or table in the cell; the cup had hung from the wooden peg that now held his coat and hat. He put on those items and returned the teeth to his mouth.

After a yawn Ray continued, "I been up all day 'n' night. I need to get me some sleep, before I pass out. I'd be obliged if you could stay around for a while and answer the phone if it rings. Just gimme a holler if somepin serious might happen, but not if just somebody's goddam mutt just run off, get it?"

Bad as he felt, Rev did not forget his pride. "Wellssir," he said, "I might ssee my way clear to doing you a favor. I mysself ain't due on duty up the railroad yard till ssafternoon."

Ray had filled him in the night before on the monkeyshines of Junior and the confiscation, in Hornbeck, of the starter's pistol. So he was permanently unarmed now, and his only clothing was an eyesore. He took his battered black hat off the wall-peg and put it on his head, and he went up to the police office.

He sat down in the chair back of the desk. This was some compensation for the punishment he had taken, but unfortunately the desktop was clean except for a double pen set in a chamfered block of stained and oiled walnut. Burned into the wood, between the two rat-tailed pens mounted aslant, was a legend: *Young People's Club, Abyssinian Baptist Church.*

He would have liked to examine some official police documents, but he was too scrupulous a man to open any desk drawers or those in the filing cabinet nearby. But on the wall above the latter was a bulletin board, with papers of various kinds thumbtacked to it. He had just gone there and was reading a note that said, in block printing, CLEEN THAT TOILET! when the door opened behind him.

Rev whirled around, forgetting he was in the police station and expecting to be jumped, but it was just some old man who shuffled on runover shoes. He didn't look as if he had sufficient strength or energy to be a dangerous criminal, but Rev thought it wise to speak sternly.

"You got bidniss here?"

The man nodded. "Custodian," said he. "You a new one?"

"Don't you worry about what *I* am," Reverton said. The man began to shuffle toward him. Rev put out a hand. "Where you think you're going?"

The old man shrugged. He was wearing overalls, a shirt with a frayed collar, and a scrawny four-in-hand necktie. He said, "He genly leaves a word for me." Having taken an eternity to raise his arm, he indicated the billboard.

"Uh-huh." Rev was pleased to figure that out speedily. "Here ya go," said he, and he went to the note, put a finger on it, and moved his head back far enough so that it came into focus. "Ssays to clean the toilet out real good."

The janitor turned and shuffled away.

Rev remembered he had not eaten since the evening before, and then his supper had been only peanut butter and jelly, after which he had been beaten to a pulp by those trash. He still had not given up on Junior, and believed he could give guidance to the boy if permitted. He had got this far in life himself only with the aid of a few principles formulated in young manhood, the first of which was, *Don't let anybody get away with anything without calling him on it.* Others were: *Always respect the weaker sex and people older than yourself. Be neatly dressed at all times. Never tell anyone else, including relatives, much*

*about your private affairs. Avoid being foulmouthed unless
provoked beyond your capacity for forbearance. Worship
the Lord, but never trust a preacher any farther than you
can throw him.*

He had at least a cup of coffee coming! He went down
the corridor, passing the washroom, where the old janitor,
back to the hall, was feebly sprinkling scouring powder on
a wet cloth. Rev looked into the cell. He wanted to ask
Ray how he could get a cup of coffee, but the part-time cop
was already in deep sleep, his mouth open, and breathing
heavily. His police cap and gunbelt hung from the peg on
the wall.

Then the phone rang up in the office, and Rev hastened
back to answer it. The caller's voice was so excited that
the words could not be distinguished. Rev wondered
whether this was another hoax.

"This here'ss the police 'tation," said he. "I don't know
what you want, but you better ssay it quick."

The caller panted for an instant, and then said, in a
breaking voice, "Bank's being held up!"

Reverton was strangely calmed by this information. He
said, "All right. I'm coming. Just don't you worry."

He hung up the phone and went down the corridor again
and into the cell, where he took Ray's cap from the peg
and exchanged it, on his head, for the black fedora, and
then he lifted off the gunbelt, which was a lot heavier than
he expected, what with the weapon, the loops full of
cartridges, the handcuffs, and the clip that held a clump
of keys, and he put it around his waist, underneath the
suit coat but over the tails of his vest, and fastened the
buckle, which he slid up as far as it would go. It was still
loose, for Ray had quite a gut on him, whereas Rev was a
slender man. Also, the cap was too large to be worn in the

proper position and would slip to cover his eyes unless he kept it pushed way back. He knew that might make him look stupid to some, but he was carrying a real gun now.

As he was passing the washroom the janitor, who was wiping the mirror, saw him in the glass and said, "You got to go, I'll step out for a minute."

Rev held on to the belt, so that it wouldn't slide down too far, and kept moving. The police car was pulled up into the slot just outside the door, and the key was in the ignition. He hadn't driven in a while: it took him longer than it should have to find reverse and back out. He stalled the engine once and had to start up again, but at least he didn't flood it. Once he reached the street, he gave it the gas.

Unfortunately he did not know how to activate the siren and he had no time now to look for the button or switch, and at the end of the block was a light that turned red before he got there, and the traffic came across to block his path. Blowing the horn and waving the police cap out the window, however, he forced his way between a Mack truck and a faded-maroon Chevy, turned, nearly collided with a Ford coupe coming from the west, then floored it for the final run to the bank.

Everything looked normal from in front of the building. He wondered whether someone could still be trying to make a fool of him: the smart aleck who had tried to hoax him the night before had perhaps come up with a more ingenious scheme to trick him into drawing the gun and rushing into a bank in which nothing was going on but the ordinary business of the morning.

He therefore left the car at a dignified pace, holding the belt with his right hand while with his left he made sure that the police cap was secure on the back of his head. He had reached the base of the three concrete steps just as a respectable-looking gent, carrying a shopping bag, emerged from the bank.

Well, there you had it: you would hardly see a businessman calmly coming out if some crook was inside.

But just to be on the safe side, Rev was about to ask if everything was on the up-and-up in there when the gentleman reached under the salt-and-pepper suit coat, brought out a snub-nosed revolver, and fired it twice. The police cap flew off, and Rev fell onto the cold concrete steps. He stayed there for a while, and knew that blood was leaving him.

But, by God, he had taken enough punishment from these scum! He struggled to his knees, on the lowest step, and tried to get the pistol out of its holster, but the strap was fastened, and pulling it loose was not easy, and his vest was soaked with blood, but he got the weapon free and he raised it, turning toward the street. The bank robber was walking down the sidewalk as big as you please, as if he owned the whole town. Holding the pistol in both hands, Rev pressed the trigger. Nothing happened. He lowered it and looked for the safety, but his close-up vision, none too good at best, was swimming now. He probed and poked and finally pulled the hammer back till it caught, and lifted the barrel and began to fire.

The first slug broke the glass of a streetlamp high above the departing criminal, and the man turned, his own weapon quickly in hand, but he missed Reverton, his bullet striking the step alongside and whining off in ricochet.

The heavy gun was wavering in Reverton's failing grip; his second shot was so low and wide of the target that it struck the middle of the street, and the third shattered the rear window of a parked car in the next block. The robber's second slug hit Reverton in the left arm. Rev dropped one hand from the gun. He was getting hurt badly, no mistake, and it wasn't right. But you could count on the trash of the world to kick you when you were down. He raised the pistol with all his remaining strength, and his fourth shot caught the son of a bitch right in the face, just below the right eye, which disappeared. He had no more strength. He dropped the gun and heard it clatter down to the sidewalk, and that was the last he knew.

Bernice's three minutes ran out, and she didn't have any more change, and therefore was cut off before she could repeat that she and Ernie were over the state line at a place called Varnerville, where you could get a marriage license and have the ceremony performed within a very short time.

"I guess she was pretty excited when she heard?" Ernie said when Bernice came out of the phone booth to join him at the lunchroom counter where he sat drinking coffee.

She shook her head. "She never did pay me much mind. I mean, I done quite a few things in life. You might think she'd be interested, but not her."

Ernie drained his cup, holding it up for a while, probably to get the undissolved sugar in the bottom. "Trouble with my mom is, she's always been *too* interested in what I done. I don't know as I have the nerve to tell her about us yet. I just wish there was some of that bottle left." He looked at the clock on the wall. "It's still too early to buy any more."

They both could feel the effects of what they had drunk the night before, when they had drained the bottle of Rock & Rye in the course of marathon back-seat lovemaking which was no less strenuous for the frustrations of the earlier evening. Ernie had driven out in the country and parked in a cow pasture. They finally went to sleep, intermingled, and stayed in that condition until being awakened by the mooing of cattle. Ernie had backed out onto the unpaved road and driven to the highway and across the state line.

"My gosh," Bernice had said, "we're getting pretty far from home, Ern."

"You only live oncet," said he.

She regretted not having made his acquaintance earlier. He was a guy who liked his fun without turning nasty. That was rare in her experience.

She started to ask again why they had passed each other up until now, but remembered suddenly that she was older than he. He had been two years behind her in school. She hoped he wasn't going to remember the same thing and brood about it, begin to think of her as an old grandma or something. Heck, why should it matter? But the fact was she was worried it might.

"There's supposed to be a place over here where they have the best foot-long hotdogs you ever tasted," Ernie said.

"For *breakfast?*" Bernice screeched. "Boy, Ernie!" But she really was impressed by his originality.

"Why sure," said he. "Anen some coconut-cream pie for dessert! I wanna celebrate."

"Oh, yeah?"

He grinned while keeping his eyes on the road. "I don't want to say anything out of line, Bernice, but you are quite a woman."

She slid over to him and snuggled against his side. "Well, I ain't got any complaints, either."

He chuckled. "Is that right?"

"I wouldn't wantcha to have any doubts."

"Bernice, uh . . . I'm gonna tell you something. I was pretty drunk last night." He took a quick peek at her. "No, I mean it. I wouldn't of had nerve to astcha out if I wasn't."

"Why, you were a perfect gentleman, if that's what's worrying you," said Bernice.

Ernie turned sober. "Listen, what I wanna tellya is: I never done it with a nice girl before."

Bernice wiggled happily against his side and said nothing.

He continued. "You probly think I'm kidding, but it's the God's honest truth. All's I ever had, to be truthful, I paid for. You might not know it, but there's a house up outside of Hamburg."

"I wouldn't know." She sensed that Ernie would prefer her to be ignorant in such matters.

"I guess some would criticize a person for that, but what I say is it's the greatest protection for womanhood, from one point of view, on account of it cuts down on rapes. . . . Listen, Bernice, I'm sure trying to figure out a way to tell you what I want to without hurting your feelings by talking dirty, but it ain't easy."

She made a false sigh. "Well, I couldn't get outa hearing an awful lot of things down the city that shouldn't be said in front of a lady. That's life, I guess. Go ahead, Ernie. You're a nice fellow. I doubt I'll be mad at you."

Ernie swallowed. "All right, then, don't blame me!" He made a fake flinch and looked admiringly at her. "Bernice, I wantcha to know you're a lot better than any whore I ever screwed."

She scowled briefly, but she knew he meant well and in fact she was really flattered, so with just a bit of reluctance, because she didn't want him to think she was some floozy in front of whom anything could be said, she told him, "Well, Ernie, I'll take that as a compliment." She slipped her fingers around his biceps and squeezed it affectionately. "I just hope you don't think I make a practice of letting people take liberties in the back seata cars. We might not of gone out together before, but we have known each other all our lives, and I always considered you a close friend."

"You did? By gosh, I wish I had known that. You know, Bernice, I might as well tell you, well, the fact is . . . I sometimes can't even do it. I have a few drinks and I get the idea, and I go up there to that place in Hamburg and get as far as right in bed, if you'll pardon the expression, with one of them girls there—and I can't get any further if you know what I mean."

Bernice squeezed him harder. "Lemma tellya something, Ernie. I don't know this by experience, you understand, but I am like a sister to certain guys sometimes, maybe because I really do have a couple brothers I am real close to. But fellows feel they can talk to me and I won't criticize 'em. Well, listen here, a lot of them have the same complaint as you, and some are real big strapping guys, real man's-man types, see. But gee, you must not have that trouble much, Ern." She snickered. "A billy goat like you?"

Ernie laughed in delight. "That's all your doing, Bernice! By George, I never felt so good in my whole life as now." All at once he braked in the middle of the road, but it was still an empty highway, out in the sticks and early in the morning, with no other vehicles in sight.

"How about it, babe?" he asked, taking both her hands in his. His were callused, as she had noted the night before. "You wanna get hitched?"

She answered quietly, her blood rising. "I wouldn't kid about something like that, Ernie."

"I ain't kidding. I'm almost twenty-four and not getting any younger. I thought I'd wait till my mom died, but heck, that might not happen for years yet. She's real healthy—uh, thank the Lord. But life could be nice with a good woman like yourself, Bernice. Might as well live in Mom's house till her time comes, 'cause it's rent-free. I got my own room: you could move right in."

Bernice felt that the night's experience just went to prove

that something nice might happen at any time, no matter how black things looked. This had actually worked out better than if she had got anywhere with Harvey Yelton, who after all was already married and as old as her father. Whereas Ernie could be considered a pretty good catch by any standard. He was not exactly a big tycoon, but he had a regular job pumping gas at the Flying Red Horse on state route 35, and his mother's house was only a few blocks from Bernice's parents'. Ernie's mother sat on a porch glider every evening in summertime. She was thought to be a sour kind of person, but what the devil, Bernice could get along with anybody if necessary.

Ernie was still looking at her. He said, "Come on, how about it?" He winked. "Winter's coming in a couple months. Be real nice to snuggle up in bed on them cold nights. Trouble is, when would we do any sleeping?" He cackled merrily.

Bernice decided not to mention their difference in age. He must be aware of that himself, since they had known each other for so many years.

She said, "If you have to have an answer right this minute, Ernie, it'd have to be yes."

He gave her a big kiss. When she finally pulled away to catch her breath, his hand stayed up under her skirt.

"By George," she said, looking into his lap, "I bet you're ready to do it right here in the middle of the road."

They climbed into the back, and the car stayed where it was until some old farmer came along with a tractor and made Ernie pull over onto the shoulder. Later on they drove to the nearest town that had a courthouse, and until it opened they were drinking coffee in a lunchroom.

But after a while Ernie had fallen into a less than enthusiastic mood. He said again that he was scared to spring the news on his mother and that maybe when they got back

to Hornbeck he would have to proceed by degrees, first
pretending to have just a date with Bernice for the movies,
and then walk her back past where his mother would be
sitting on the porch glider, which she continued to use
until the weather turned really cold.

"At that rate it'll take quite a while, won't it?" asked
Bernice, who was beginning to get a little concerned that
he was having second thoughts. "Might be Christmas, for
golly sakes."

Ernie said, "Well, the house does belong to her, you
know, and I think she was figuring on me staying single
for the rest of her life."

Bernice decided to call his hand. She got off the diner
stool and she said, "It's been real nice knowing you, Ernie."

"Hey, come on, Bernice."

"You some kinda Indin-giver? You talk about being
married, and then when you get whatcha want, you take
it back?"

"Now just sit down," said Ernie, glancing with embarrassment at the other patrons in the nearby booths. "I
don't mean we shouldn't get married right now. I just
mean I'll break it slow to my mom. Meantime, if you don't
mind staying at your own house? It ain't so far away."

"Oh." Bernice was mollified. Her pregnancy would be
covered: that was always her main worry.

Jack's mother returned to the kitchen from the dining
room, where she had been talking on the phone with
Bernice. When it rang she had taken the skillet from the
burner and turned off the gas. She now reversed that
process and began to fry eggs again.

"Oh, gosh," she said in a moment. "These are pretty
far gone. They sure look like they're cooked through."

Jack whined. He hated it when the yolks were not molten

but crumbled into yellow dust at the touch of a fork. There was one means by which to pull this from utter disaster, according to his friend Dickie Herkimer: you mashed the yolks and whites together along with lots of catchup, and you spread the resulting mixture on a piece of buttered toast and then salted it heavily. Dickie had a solution for every problem, but the only trouble with this one was that Jack loathed catchup.

"Well," said his mother, placing on the table before him a plate bearing two eggs and a quantity of fried potatoes, "you're just going to have to make do, Jack. We can't afford to throw these away, and if I keep 'em warm for Tony they'll just get harder and tougher."

Jack grimaced at the plate. "Don't we have any bacon or sausage or anything?"

"No we don't," his mother said positively. "Your dad's in the hospital, remember? And he can't earn a living on the flat of his back. You oughta thank your lucky stars you get good fresh eggs to eat, with all the starving people in China."

"What about toast?"

"Oh, my! I forgot." She rushed to the shelf of the kitchen cabinet, where the toaster, at the end of a long cord stretching from a baseboard socket, was smoking. She opened the little door on each side and removed the contents. "Not too burnt to be saved!" She took the toast to the sink and scraped each piece on both sides, then came to the table and seized the bowl that held the blob of country butter, which was supplied by the same farmer who came to the house once a week with the fresh eggs. Jack hated this hick stuff and yearned for the civilized product that was cut into smooth sticks and wrapped in translucent paper: this junk came in waxed paper which, after it was refolded a few times, was crisscrossed with white lines and looked soiled. His mother started to smear the scraped toast, but Jack stopped her.

"That makes it worse!" He took the toast from her, and began to put jelly on it, apple jelly, the most tasteless kind, but there wasn't any other flavor in the house. He was ready to be bolder in his complaints about food in the absence of his father, with whom such objections did not sit well, but then it occurred to him that he would be acting like a punk in view of the family's troubles. "I'm just kidding," he lied, trying to ignore the diseased look of the burned and scraped bread. "It's O.K."

"That was Bernice," his mother said, pouring him a glass of milk. "I guess it's all right to tell. She never asked me to keep it under my hat. She's getting married. They went over the state line."

This was amazing news to Jack. He dropped his toast on top of the eggs. "Married? Who to?"

"Ernie Krum."

"*Ernie Krum!* My God Almighty."

"Well, do you have to curse, Jack?"

"I'm sorry . . . but he's a real moron, Ma. *You* know that."

"I don't know anything of the kind, Jack, and neither do you. And if you did, it would be a good idea not to mention it if he's gonna be your brother-in-law."

"Ernie Krum? He happens to be the most stupid guy in Hornbeck. You know, he's on the fire department, but when he was burning some paint off his garage with a blow-torch he set it on fire, and he goes and gets the garden hose, but by that time it's outa control and the whole department has to be called out?"

"Well, if I was you," said his mother, tidying up around the sink, "I wouldn't dwell on it."

"Oh, *gee!*" said Jack. He was really humiliated by the thought of being related to Ernie. "Can't you stop her, Ma?"

His mother said, "Why, of course not. And I wouldn't if I could. It's high time Bernice settled down. She's not getting any younger. She's had her fling, but life isn't all beer and skittles. She can make a mighty fine housewife if she puts her nose to the grindstone, and Ernie is a real nice boy. He used to come around and sell magazines when he was a kid. He was always a real little gentleman and would tip the baseball cap he always wore in those days. He was cute as a button."

In indignation Jack suddenly remembered, "He's *younger* than Bernice!"

"Oh, but just a year or so. That don't matter at all." She walked into the dining room and in a moment could be heard calling up the stairs, "Tony!" When she came back she said, "Is your brother O.K.? Not like him to be last for breakfast."

"He claims he's got a job." Jack wondered whether he had done the right thing, but he couldn't recall Tony's having sworn him to secrecy.

"He's got another think coming," their mother said firmly. "That boy's going to finish high school, or else."

Jack toyed with his eggs. He was still thinking about Bernice. God, it was really lousy that she was getting married to Ernie Krum. He felt he could never live that down. He shrank to think of what Dickie Herkimer would have to say. And not only was Ernie younger than Bernice, he was also probably shorter. He was a little bowlegged runt of a guy. If they had a baby it might be stunted or something. This was a catastrophe.

Tony appeared and quietly took his place at the table.

Their mother said, "Your eggs are coming up." She began to crack them into the skillet: Tony always had at least four, even when there was meat in accompaniment. "I hear you're supposed to have a job?"

"Sairdies," said Tony.

She said to Jack, "Durn it, why dint you tell me that?"

Jack shrugged and told Tony, "Bernice is getting married to that goof Ernie Krum."

"Jack!" their mother protested. "Don't you cut me off like that! And I don't wantchoo go around talking like that about Ernie. Do you hear me?"

Jack lapsed into sullen silence and began to mess up the food on his plate so that it would look as if he had eaten more than he had, but this was unsuccessful and ended up in creating a seemingly greater quantity than that with which he had begun.

Tony drank some milk. "Ernie's not so bad," he said. "I think he works out with weights, you know. I seen him with his shirt off once in a while, washing his car, and he's got good lats: they come from body-building. Like the trapezius, you know?" He indicated the muscles between the neck and the shouldercap; presumably he was flexing his own, but they didn't show that much with a shirt on. However, Jack had seen them often enough, and the rest of Tony's terrific build, but the truth was that he was out of patience at the moment with all this stuff and thought it basically pretty dumb—great as it might be. He would rather have been taking a steamboat cruise in tropical waters, outwitting professional cardsharps in nightly games and winning a king's ransom, the thinnest of gold cigarette cases (with its own built-in lighter) in one tuxedo pocket and a tiny but deadly pearl-handled automatic in another; in the cast of characters, a raven-haired beauty with a cruel red mouth and a squat, greasy, pockmarked hoodlum, whose boss has fair hair and eyes pale as window-glass and devastating cunning but no conscience whatever—

"Jack!" His mother had just served Tony. "I want you to eat some of that good food you are smearing all over the place. Do you hear me?"

He groaned an assent and began to fork up a series of the tiniest morsels possible. These did actually have a different taste from that of larger pieces, strange as it might seem, in addition to which the process had a somewhat comic quality to it. At least his mother thought so. She laughed and said, "What a nut you are!" He could usually get on her good side by doing something crazy.

The telephone rang again. She went into the dining room. Jack didn't like to listen to only her end of a conversation, because it was invariably boring, so he said to Tony, "What kinda jobja get?"

"Bakery." His brother's eggs were just right, Jack noticed: sunny-side-up. Tony broke one yoke with the corner of a piece of toast, and then he soaked the toast in it, just as Jack would have done if able.

"All the free pie you can eat?" Jack asked. "You get paid besides?"

"Sure," Tony said, chewing. "But it's not the one in Hornbeck. It's over in Millville."

Again Jack was astounded. "*Millville?* For God's sake, you're a wanted man over there!"

Tony winced while swallowing, and then he snorted. "You know, I forgot all about that? You think that cop'll recognize me again?"

The secret of the man of action apparently lay in not being conscious of very much. Though certainly a dreamer, Jack himself was always thinking of consequences when it came to practical affairs. He wouldn't have punched a cop even if he were physically able to, because before doing it he would be restrained by the thought of retribution. Could Tony be called courageous or stupid, or were they the same thing?

The hum of his mother's voice had stopped coming from the next room, and she had hung up the telephone but did not immediately return to the kitchen. It suddenly occurred to Jack that before she got back he might quietly dispose of the remaining food on his plate by some other means than eating it, but the idea came too late. He got no farther than pushing back his chair.

Their mother was in the doorway. She had a special look, not necessarily sad, not even shocked; it was serious, of course, but then, except when he was clowning around, she was usually serious, like most other adults. But this was a look of another dimension.

Tony had been wolfing down his breakfast, most of which was already gone, but it was he who first responded to their mother's strange appearance in the doorway. Jack remembered that later, and once again he revised his innermost opinion of his brother, who was certainly not an insensitive person. Perhaps each of us has only a limited amount of feeling, and Tony reserved his supply for that which mattered most.

"What's wrong, Mom?"

"It's your father," she said. "Last night he took a turn for the worst."

Tony dropped his fork and went to her. "Better come and sit down," said he. He led her through the dining room into the living room, Jack coming along behind.

It was unprecedented that anyone would use the front room at this time of day. Tony saw their mother to the couch. She sat down, but reluctantly.

"I have to—"

"Not for a minute or two," Tony said. "You just sit there."

Jack was scared, but he managed to say, "Well, if he can get worse, he can get better too, you know, Ma."

Tony frowned at him behind the glasses. "Shut up, Jack."

It was rare for him to talk this way to his brother, and Jack wondered whether indignation would be in order: he had just tried to be comforting.

But Tony was still staring at him. Finally Tony said, "He's gone, don't you see?"

But Jack really didn't until his mother began to cry.

CHAPTER

11

Frieda dreaded having to tell Bud about what happened to Reverton, to add to the troubles that had laid him low, but Dr. Swan assured her that it would be impossible to keep this news under their hats when it was the talk of not just the' whole town but the southern part of the state and would maybe go much farther, for the editor of the weekly *Millville Blade*, sensing the appeal such a story would have, had been in communication with one of the national press services.

So Frieda accompanied the doctor to the Merryvale Hospital and went in to see her husband alone. She waited in the little lounge assigned to visitors to the mental ward. After a while Bud came out, attended by a brawny, cheerful nurse. He looked sane enough though pale and tired.

The big nurse said jovially, "Here's your hubby, dear," and to Bud, "Now you be nice." And she went away.

Bud was wearing the pajamas and robe Frieda had brought on her first visit. The spinach-green robe had seen too much service, and in fact she had long since planned to replace it at the next Xmas, but that would be too late for now.

She asked after his state of health.

"Ohhh," he sighed. Obviously he was vague about it.

She decided to get right to the point. "It's your cousin, Bud, see . . ."

His previously lackluster eyes brightened. "Rev?" he said. "Yeah, I would sure like to see ole Rev. It's O.K. for him to come here. But you know I don't wanna see any of the others. The fuss they'd make!"

Frieda shook her head. "Bud, see, Rev . . ." Deciding to strike the nail on the head did not necessarily mean you would hit it. "See, they held up the bank, and—"

Bud got a strange look. He said, in a voice that began very softly, "I used to think Reverton was a crank of some kind, but it's coming true, isn't it? First they burn the store, then they loot what's left, and now the bank." He stared suspiciously around the little waiting room, where they sat alone.

"No, Bud," Frieda said quickly, "that's not what I'm trying to tellya. It was just one robber. He was a man named Reno Fox. He was wanted by a good many states and also the guvmint. Clive Shell and also the post office had a Wanted notice on him. Your cousin Reverton shot him dead, and they recovered all the money. The bank's gonna pay Rev a real nice reward, because this Fox cleaned out the vault. He waited for the time lock to open first thing this morning. Turns out he ate a fish samwich at Curly's last night just before he closed up. Junior stopped in there to drink a bottle of pop and he saw this crook, sitting at the counter big as you please, says he looked like he could be as mean as they come, but he was nice as pie to Junior, which is why Junie never reported him or anything. Now what happened 'smorning is that Rev was just going into the bank when this Reno Fox was leaving with his bagful of stolen money. Being as how he's a detective by profession, I guess Reverton recognized him from the Wanted posters, since he ordered him to halt, and they both drew their pistols and Rev shot him dead. They say it was like the Wild West."

"My God," said Bud. "My God Almighty. He finally got his chance. Good for Rev! But he's one lucky man, not to get shot himself by some professional crook like that."

Frieda lowered her chin as far as it would go. "Thing is, he did get shot."

"Rev?"

"He's still hanging on," said Frieda. "But Doc Swan says he isn't long for this world."

This marked the end of Bud's nervous breakdown. He was ready to leave the nut ward in his robe and pajamas, but Frieda went out into the corridor and brought in Dr. Swan, who cleared things with the nurse while Bud was putting on the street clothes his wife had brought him.

Reverton was in the emergency room, where he had been brought a few hours earlier, directly from the bloody steps of the bank. Various tubes were connected to him, and in attendance were people dressed in white.

His eyes were open when Bud reached the bed. Bud roused himself to say, "This is a fine kettle of fish, Rev! Whatchoo doing here anyway? Why, you look fit as a fiddle."

Rev had never much been one for jollity. His voice was so feeble that Bud had to lean way over to hear the words.

"I got a reward coming. I want Junior to have it."

Bud was trying to keep up his nerve. "Why, I think you can put it to mighty good use yourself, Rev," said he.

Reverton had a funny smell to him, a mixture of medicaments and, probably, death. His voice became ever so slightly stronger now. "I want Junior to have that money. . . . Don't you worry none: I got a little inssurance policy to get buried on. . . . You see Junior getss the reward. Tell him . . ." His voice failed.

"Sure, Rev, I sure will," said Bud into his ear. "Now you get yourself some rest." He was about to leave when he remembered that thus far he had not said what he wanted his cousin to hear before dying. But he had a superstitious feeling that if he didn't say it, Rev would not die. It was an awful choice to make, because Reverton might expire anyway, and then Bud would have to live the rest of his own life with the knowledge that he had not said it in time, and the fact was that though Bud went to church regularly and certainly called himself a Christian, he didn't for a minute believe in an afterlife of any kind. Therefore it was important how a man was thought of while he was alive, or anyway for a while after his death, though eventually just about everybody was forgotten, when it came to that. But nobody else in the family so far as he knew had ever shot it out with a crook on the steps of a bank.

He bent down to Reverton's ear again, but before he could say a word his cousin spoke. "Tell Junior . . ." The voice failed again, but suddenly it returned strongly, at normal volume: "To buy himsself a real gun."

A nurse and a doctor came to the bed on opposing sides. They said nothing to Bud, but suggested by their movements that he was in the way.

He stepped aside but asked, "If I could just tell him one more thing?"

They were bending over the patient. In a long moment the doctor straightened up and said to Bud, "It's too late now."

Ordinarily at such a juncture Bud would have turned regretfully and made a sad exit, but now he silently forced the doctor to give him access to his cousin's body.

He didn't care whether he was overheard or not. "So long, Rev. You were one swell guy, for my money. Listen . . ." A greater grief than he had been conscious of suddenly enveloped him. He had to use all his strength to add, "Listen. The whole family's real proud of you." He found Reverton's hand, which was unusually small and finely made, like a woman's, though you could never have told him that. He shook it once, then put it back.

He thought he would break down when he got outside the room, but in fact he did not. He told Frieda, "He's gone. I got there just in time. You know, everybody but me always thought he was a mighty queer duck, and God knows he wasn't your ordinary run-of-the-mill, but I liked Rev. I always had a soft spot for him, and on his side he would of put his hand inna fire for me. You recall how he give me a good deal of his settlement money from that accident, for the store. Well, the last thing he said before passing away was he wanted me to have this reward money he's got coming, to get the business started again. Ain't that somepin?"

He stayed O.K. until they went to Reverton's rooming house, in search of the insurance policy mentioned by the deceased. While going through his cousin's few pathetic effects, he found an old snapshot which had undoubtedly been taken by his own mother, with the big box camera, showing little Rev in cloth cap and knickers, on a Sunday visit from the orphanage. The knickers had in fact been worn by Bud himself for several years before being passed down.

Bud was sitting on the edge of the narrow bed. He lowered the photo and began to weep in almost silent gasps.

But after a while he got up and joined Frieda at the grimy window from which she was looking onto the nearby railroad yard.

Harvey Yelton led the funeral procession for Dolf Beeler, but he pulled aside at the gate of the cemetery and did not enter. He was an old friend of Dolf's and had been even more intimate with Bobby many years before, but when he could, he avoided all actual funeral ceremonies no matter for whom, except of course those for his sainted mother. (His father had been a dirty drunkard who disappeared one day when Harvey was six.) It was around back, on the other side of the cemetery, that he regularly apprehended violators of the ordinances protecting public decency. The damnable fact was that no matter how faithfully you patrolled Lovers' Lane you could still find used rubbers and empty liquor bottles there next morning. These were obviously the work of no-goods who did not have to get up in the morning and earn an honest living with the rest of the human race, but could just drink and fuck their nights away, and Lord help them if they came around earlier, but he had to sleep sometime.

He had turned the cruiser around and was about to head back to the station when he saw a boy come to the cemetery entrance and look furtively within. He recognized him as a kid named Dickie Herkimer. He knew most of the local lads and could spot potential troublemakers among them, but Dickie was a clean-cut live wire who would make a good businessman when he grew up, a go-getter real-estate agent or a used-car dealer.

"Hi there, Dickie," he said through the open window. The morning was sunny and warm for October, though the leaves on the cemetery trees had pretty well all turned color. Assuming that Dickie probably wanted to go to Dolf

Beeler's gravesite—he being a friend of Jack's and a responsible young fellow—Harvey said, pointing, "It's on in
there to the left, around back of the Mumphrey crypt."
This monument was a landmark in the Hornbeck cemetery,
being the largest and the most elaborate, with stone angels
and so on, the Mumphreys, whose line was now extinct,
having been the prosperous but childless coal dealers of a
generation past.

But the Herkimer kid stayed where he was, grinning
foolishly.

Harvey beckoned the boy over to the window of the
cruiser. "Dickie," he said, "you look kinda peakèd. You
O.K.?" Harvey had a police officer's sixth sense with regard
to people, especially youths.

Dickie was grinning ever more wildly, and then all of a
sudden the grin burst into a big sob, and tears coursed down
his face, on which the skin was clear except for a developing
boil on the chin.

Harvey reached over and opened the passenger's door,
and Dickie came around and climbed into the cruiser. He
rubbed his eyes on both sweater sleeves.

He stared desperately at the chief and said, "I'm turning
myself in."

Harvey put the car in gear and began to move slowly
along the street. He asked, mostly tongue-in-cheek, "What
am I supposed to charge you with?"

Dickie sniveled for a while, and then he began to sob
again. Harvey got a certain pleasure from the tears of
young girls, but male crybabies gave him the willies. He
had thought better of Dickie. He felt like slapping him silly.

He said, threateningly, "You gonna tell me?"

The boy was sharp enough to know when he was going
too far. He breathed deeply and said, "Murder, probably."

Harvey grunted in his kind of laughter. "Who'd you kill?"

"Mr. Beeler."

The chief braked at a stop sign. While at the halt he looked at Dickie. "Gun or knife?" He started rolling again. "You ain't pulling my leg, are you, Dickie? Or dint you know Dolf died of heart trouble?"

"I think what I did," said Dickie, "was what gave him the heart attack."

"Whajoo do?"

"Blew up his automobile," Dickie said. He sniveled for a while. "I had some cannon crackers saved from the Fourth, when I got sick and couldn't shoot off all my fireworks, and I tied the fuses of a whole lot of 'em together, and I put 'em under the hood—"

"Oh you did, didja?" Harvey wouldn't give the little fart the satisfaction of seeing him surprised.

Dickie said, "I guess I thought it would be funny. See, Jack told me they had been having 'sargument with some family over Millville. I figured *they'd* probably get the blame. I thought it would be a neat joke, I guess." He was staring anxiously at Harvey.

The chief drove several blocks in a silence that he expected Dickie to find unbearable. At last he said, "Wellsir, you ain't telling me anything I dint pretty much know already, Dickie. I just been so busy I didn't get around to picking you up on it. Then I was worried about what would happen when your dad heard about it. He might just whip you to death before we could ship you out to the reformatory." From the corner of his eye he could see Dickie begin to quiver. He turned and pointed right in his face. "You start to bawl again, I'll take out your front teeth, you goddam smart-aleck little shit-ass. I don't know what you punk kids think you're doing, but by God you won't do any more of it in my town. I'm gonna declare a curfew at sunset and run you all off the streets. And that definitely includes Halloween and the week before. Going around in masks for handouts is all finished in Hornbeck, and anybody who does any damage—I mean, so much as throws a handful of corn on somebody's front porch—he won't ever know what hit 'im. You hear me?"

Dickie said, "Yezzir."

"Now, about this here damage you done to the late Dolf Beeler's auto. He's dead and gone, so you can't make resitooshun to the man whose propitty the car was. Now if Bobby Beeler didn't have two strapping sons, I'd send you over to cut the grass for her and run down the store and other errands, but as it is, you'd just get inna way, and Tony would probly end up kicking your butt for you, so I tell you what you do: you come down the police station every Sairdy till Christmas and make yourself useful, warshing windas and mopping the floor and all. You can simonize the cruiser."

"Yezzir."

Harvey stopped at the next corner. "Just keep your nose clean, Dickie, cuz I alweez got my eye on you." Dickie did nothing: he seemed pretty thick. "Go on," Harvey said. "Make yourself scarce."

After the kid got out, the chief drove slowly past Hornbeck's bank, something he had been doing frequently since the events of two days before over in Millville, when that part-time cop had shot it out with a bank robber. If the latter was part of a gang, Hornbeck might well be next on the list, and if so Harvey had no intention of getting out of the cruiser and trading shots on the sidewalk: clipped to the back of the front seat was an automatic twelve-gauge shotgun. The first crook he saw, he would start blasting from the window while driving one-handed at high speed.

At least it hadn't been Clive Shell who made the kill. Harvey had called up Ray Dooley to get the score, for

Dooley owed him one since he let off that little Millville punk with the starter's pistol. Ray said the fellow was by profession a railroad detective and had been deputized to fill in while Clive was sick.

"You birds ain't ever gonna kill yourself with hard work, that's for sure," said Harvey. It was always a sore point with him that Shell even had the part-time services of Ray.

"Heck, Harvey," said Ray, "we got a bigger town than yours, and you ain't got no colored district."

"Shit, you don't ever go into Jigtown unless they call you special!"

Ray couldn't deny that, having told him more than once that experience had proved that if you just let the coloreds stew in their own juice, a lot of otherwise painful situations would never come up, so he changed the subject and told Harvey, "This thing sure shows the sense in keeping up to date on who's wanted, don't it? You can't ever tell who'll blow into town."

Harvey's practice in the past had been to glance briefly at each circular as it came in and then clip it with the others and drop the thick sheaf back into the drawer, in an assumption that Hornbeck's little bank would hardly be attractive to a professional. But he had changed now. He could only pray that no practical joker ever turned in a false alarm about a bank robbery, for he intended to arrive on the scene behind a spray of hot lead.

Junior's crotch itched him like crazy during the Reverend Amburgy's remarks on the late Reverton Kirby, and he tried to bring relief by doing a slow grind on the pew seat, but to no avail, and when he bumped against Eva, she whined and gave him an elbow. He began to think he had picked up a dose of crabs, but since he had still had no intimate contact with a living female, they must have come from someplace else: maybe the toilet in the Hornbeck police station, the dirtiest crapper he had ever seen, and he would not have used it had his sudden realization that he was arrested not given him instant diarrhea.

His father and five adult male relatives served as pallbearers for Reverton. Junior was humiliated by his father's request that he walk alongside in an honorary role because the coffin was too heavy for him to tote even a sixth of its weight, but owing to the recent escapade he felt he was skating on thin ice, and he therefore complied, while making another secret entry on his shitlist.

As he watched the bronze box being lowered into the grave he could not help thinking of that little ditty that went: *Your eyes fall in/ Your teeth fall out/ The worms crawl over/ Your nose and mouth.* Dying was a lousy thing, and he intended to avoid it, for its inevitability seemed only theoretical to him. How did they know that you couldn't live forever? Had anybody ever tried it?

After Reverton had been tamped down in the grave, all the relatives returned to the Bullard house and began to stuff themselves on the food prepared by Junior's mother and various females related to the family by blood or marriage. The dining-room table was covered with loaded platters, but few held anything that Junior liked, and by the time he reached the macaroni 'n' cheese (having been forced by his father to let the guests go first) all the brown crust was gone from the casserole, with only the lower contents left, which looked like fat maggots. Then, at dessert time, his portion of Jello contained no fruit beyond one maraschino cherry half and a withered white grape, not to mention that the dollop of whipped cream had returned most of the way to the liquid state.

For some reason, among all the assembled relatives there was not one single male kid of his own age. A good many of these fat old biddies were childless, if not old maids, and most children who did exist were so much older than Junior that they seemed of the generation of uncles, except for his cousin Clara, who was about the same age as Eva and originally not very good-looking. He had got her in the corner of the cellar once when he was younger and showed her his dong and she told on him, and in revenge he thereafter terrorized her in various ways, sometimes furtively, as when the girls would go to the public swimming pool with their bathing suits on underneath their clothes and Junior would sneak into Eva's room and smear mustard in Clara's underpants; and sometimes openly, as on the famous occasion when he barged into the bathroom and jeered at her while she sat on the throne.

Now, however, in some magical way, Clara had turned overnight into one of the prettiest girls he had ever seen in his life, with long lustrous brown hair, oversized eyes, no skin trouble, high firm neat breastworks, and long legs above fantastically small ankles (the last-named being a feature he had only recently begun to look for). He could only too easily have fallen for her had he not had that unfortunate past to overcome, and for her at least it was at the moment unforgettable. "Hi, monkey," she said on encountering him at the funeral home. "Did the organ grinder give you a day off?" He was forced to answer in kind—"Wanna pick my fleas?"—but for the first time his heart was not in it.

Clara and Eva had gone to the latter's room after eating. Junior was hoping their cousin would stay overnight: he thought he might be able to pierce a spyhole into the bathroom ceiling from the crawl space overhead, to which he had access from his attic quarters. If he kept it close to the base of the ceiling light, it would go undetected. However, some further thought disclosed to him the strong possibility that from such a perspective he might well see only the

top of her head and her titty-tips, and not the pubic brush
if she sat in the orthodox position in the tub, facing the
faucets. He wouldn't see much if she sat on the toilet, for
she was unlikely to do that while naked—unless of course
she *went* before taking a bath. Junior himself liked to piss
while bathing, but only in a shower, not a tub, where you
would have to sit in it.

But what he would have liked to do most of all was to get
hold of another gun, a real one this time, and go over again
to that tavern in Hornbeck and make that big fat Marie
play with his peter, and if the bartender so much as raised
the blackjack, blast him right between the eyes. But first
he wanted to stop at Curly's and have a couple of hotdogs
with sweet relish on them, and a piece of blueberry pie,
and a bottle of chocolate pop, and—

His father drew him aside. "Junior, I wanna tellya Cousin
Reverton, God rest his soul, thought the world of you. Your
name was on his lips when he died. How about that?"

Junior nodded. "That's nice."

His father frowned slightly. "Well, I'd say it's more than
just nice. I'd say it ought to be an inspiration to you to
wanna make something of yourself in life."

Junior smiled as feebly as he possibly could.

His father said, "I don't know if you can unnerstand
that Rev was a lot more than you could see. I mean, he
wore that one suit of his so much it could of walked by
itself, and then he was just a skinny measly kinda little
guy physically speaking, and you know, he began to go
bald when he was about your age, I believe, and always
wore that hat all the time for many years. And I don't know
as you ever observed his funny way of walking? Which I do
believe was due to one leg being shorter'n the other from
birth, and uh course the injuries from that accident sure
didn't help. You might of looked at him and thought he

wasn't much, and by George, he *wouldn't* of been on the outside alone, but by gosh, *inside* he was quite a man. That little guy can teach a lesson to us all. Going up against *Reno Fox*, for golly sakes, wanted all over the country from coast to coast, and it's our Rev gets him. I betcha that'll get in the big city papers, believe you me."

"Wellsir," said Junior, "I myself stood right next to Reno just the night before down Curly's, and he never said beans." He had already related this incident many times. "He seemed like a real nice guy."

His old man's face grew hard: he glanced around at the jabbering, gluttonizing relatives, and then he turned back to Junior. He said, "Yeah, Curly finally got in touch today. He told me what you was doing in there: helping yourself to the cash register when he was back inna kitchen. He told me you owe him five dollars."

Junior took in some quick air and with all the indignation he could muster he said, "Me? Reno Fox the master criminal is right in front of that register, and Curly accuses *me*?"

His father smiled grimly. "Reno Fox is preparing to risk his life at the bank for thousands, and he would filch five dollars from a lunch-counter till? That don't make sense, Junior. Now, I tell you what Curly says. He's a real nice man, that Curly. Curly says he knows that with all my troubles presently I don't have any extra five-spots laying around. So he says, 'I tell you what, my colored dishwasher has run off, probly got himself some white lightning rotgut and is laying drunk in some alley in Jigtown,' and Curly says, 'I'm fed up with him. *Junior* can work off that five bucks by doing a little dishwashing after school.' I says I thought that was the perfect solution. You start tomorra."

Junior said, "The hell I do."

His father slapped him so fast he didn't see it coming and so hard he was knocked against the frame of the doorway to the living room. Not one of the relatives seemed to notice this. For an instant he thought he would strike back, but his father was still slightly larger than he and probably the dirtiest of fighters, who would knock his son to the floor and kick and trample him, and if the victim continued to resist, all those fat uncles would jump on him and smear him into the floorboards. He could expect no mercy in this family.

"And then," his old man went on as though nothing had happened, "in your free time I expeckcha be down the store, where we're gonna be seeing what we can recover and maybe get rid of in a fire sale, and then I'm going to rebuild with the help of that reward money left me by Cousin Rev, and I don't think the bank will refuse me a loan since it was their own bacon he saved the other day by laying down his own life. And by the way, his pitcher goes in the window of the new store when it's built." He smiled at the son he had just hit in the face with all his strength. "I hope you're gonna take more interest in the new store than you did in the last, Junior, for I'll tell you this"—he leaned confidentially close—"all of that'll be yours one day, son."

Junior recoiled from his father's sentiments and bad breath. The aftereffects of the slap had now arrived in full force. He slunk upstairs to the bathroom and inspected himself in the mirror. It looked as if he had painted his face to be a Halloween Indian, with the purple and yellow of the acne and the reddened patch left behind by the blow. His nose also was home to a tribe of brand-new blackheads. While he went to work on them with the tips of whichever fingernails he could find that had not been chewed blunt, he realized he would have to get out of this house, and since the town was so small, out of it as well, and he couldn't go to Hornbeck, being forbidden to do so by law.

After he took a leak with the toilet seat down, shooting through the aperture, Junior went into his parents' bedroom, where the outer clothing of his relatives had been put onto the bed. Not all the women had taken their purses downstairs, and he ransacked those that were here, collecting six dollars and thirty-two cents. This was his entire fortune, for he never saved a penny of the dime-per-hour he had been paid for his after-school and Saturday service at the hardware store, and someone at the Hornbeck tavern had rifled his pockets while he was unconscious after being coldcocked by the bartender, and had helped themselves to the money taken from Curly's cash register. The world was full of crooks.

En route to the back staircase, Junior passed Eva's closed door. He briefly considered luring her to open it with a promise of some treat and then sending her away on a wild-goose chase, so that he could rape the newly attractive Clara in her absence, but he knew this as an impossible fantasy while he was concocting it. For some reason his nerve did not extend to grown girls, but he was sure it would in the future if he could only escape from Millville and into the great world outside.

At the foot of the stairs he peeped around to see if his mother was in the kitchen. She was not, and he slipped past the stove and out the back door, shutting it quietly. As usual he cut through the Durkeys' property. No flowers were in bloom at the moment, the season being fall, but Old Man Durkey had nothing better to do with himself than hang around outside, endlessly sprucing up his back yard, raking up every leaf as soon as it fell, painting his screens for next year, and so on.

There he was now, just coming out of his garage. His eyes widened when he saw Junior.

"Say, Junior, that was your cousin Reverton down the

bank? Many's the time I seen him right over your house.
And I'm proud to say I chewed the fat with him on occasion. He was quite a man."

Junior stepped around the corner of the garage so that
he would be out of sight from his own house. He said,
"Yezzir, that's right. But you know, I myself run inta that
bank robber down Curly's night before the robbery. He had
them little mean eyes set right together, and a real low
brow like a nape's, you know? I knew right away he was on
the wrong side of the law, but I dint have any way of proving
it, and I tried to get Curly to tell the cops, but he wouldn't
do it, and I wouldn't be supprised if he was in on it."

"I can't afford to eat out," said Durkey, who was all bent
over and whose bald head was covered with brown spots,
"so I never go down Curly's. I been in Tom's a time or two,
though. I like to get the old woman outa the kitchen on
her birthday, so might take her to Tom's for what they
call the blue-plate special." He wrinkled his nose. "But it
ain't much good: ham croquettes, you know, low on the
ham and big on the croquette, string beans . . ." His voice
faded. He was getting too old for his own good, and should
probably be put out of his misery. Junior intended to knock
himself off before he ever got that old and became an object
of scorn.

"You didn't miss much if you ain't been to Curly's,"
Junior told him. "He's dirty as a pig, and he's got some
black African coon for a cook who spits in the food. I hear
he's gonna be closed up by the health authorities."

"They all should be," Durkey said with some heat. "All
of 'em." He seemed to be getting weak-minded.

Junior left the neighborhood and walked west until he
got near the district where dark-skinned people abounded,
and he made a wide detour to the south: he had always
heard that boogie girls had hot asses and would give it

away for free to anybody who asked, white or black, but he didn't want to risk having his guts cut out by some big buck's razor at this stage of the game.

When he reached the highway he went above the intersection a block or two and began to show his thumb to the cars that passed. This proved to be totally useless for a good half hour. Most drivers didn't even seem to see him. He was beginning to get discouraged in this venture and to consider going home. If he could only watch his mouth and be patient, there might come a time when Curly would trust him—and have more than a few dollar bills in the register while his back was turned. The same might be true of his father, at the new hardware store. Meanwhile he could make it up with Clara, and maybe joke around and get into a mock-wrestling match on a bed when everybody else was downstairs and feel her tits and maybe even get his hand up inside her pants as if by accident, in the heat of the game, and, rolling around, before she knew it, his pecker would be right up her giggy and she would be moaning, "Oh, oh, oh, please don't, please . . . don't . . . stop!" He remembered this bit of erotic dialogue from one of those little cartoon fuckbooks, shown him by that cousin of Howard Bing's, that smart-aleck kid from Hornbeck named Dickie Herkimer, who thought he was a big shot because he had this book and a brand-new rubber in its original folder, like a matchbook. Junior would have had to trim his ass if he was forced to spend much time with him.

Just as he was about to turn away from the road now, a little green coupe stopped opposite him, the door was flung open merrily, and a middle-aged guy looked out and said, with a grin, "Hi there! Hop in!"

Junior did so hastily. This guy was wearing a suit and tie and a felt hat. He looked pretty successful.

He asked, putting the car in gear, "Where you headed for?"

"Just about anyplace." No sooner than he'd said it, Junior realized it hadn't been a wise statement. The man could well be with the Authorities.

"By gosh," said his benefactor, "you met just the right fellow. I got my customers outa the way for today, and I was just thinking I'd have me some fun." His hand, on which there was a big ring with a red stone in it, closed over Junior's kneecap. "But what I always say is, you can't have much fun alone. Don't you agree?" His hand was moving slowly but surely up the inside of Junior's thigh. Nothing like this had ever happened to Junior before, yet he knew exactly what it was, and he was ready for it.

"Let's have a nice picnic in the state park," said the salesman, and it wasn't long before he turned into the entrance of the place in reference.

But when he found a remote place to park and turned to deal with Junior, the latter slid against the door and said, "Gee, I guess I oughta be getting home, though I'm gonna be in dutch when I get there."

The salesman's pink, hairless hand pursued him. "You mean, for doing naughty things? But how will they know?"

"Naw," said Junior. "I lost some money I was holding for my dad."

The salesman got a funny look. He reclaimed his hand. "How much?"

"Five bucks."

The salesman now acquired a definitely peevish expression. He deliberately lifted his rump and took a wallet from his back pocket. He said, "All right. But for that kinda money I want what I want."

This turned out to be something Junior had not expected or even known that anybody really did, despite all the jokes on the subject. It also was so painful that it brought tears to his eyes, but he stuck it out like the trooper he was.

CHAPTER
12

Bobby Beeler had made a little shrine to Dolf on an end table in the living room: a hand-colored portrait photo of him taken in the days when he had held office at his lodge, five years or more ago, which seemed to have been the period of his life in which he was happiest, was flanked by two vases full of flowers. But when the blossoms from the funeral floral pieces had withered, it looked as if the vases would stay empty, at least until the following spring, because only rich people could have afforded to buy the hothouse products of the Hornbeck florist in the ordinary course of events.

But Bernice said, "I sure hate the look of empty vases, Mama. They got some real nice-looking artificial flowers downtown at Gobel's. They ain't cheap, but gee they never die." She sat at the kitchen table, drinking beer from the bottle's mouth and puffing on a cigarette. Bobby had assumed that smoking was a newly acquired habit, but Bernice assured her that she had enjoyed it for years but did not indulge when on visits home so as not to disturb her late father. She had also lately taken to drinking beer in mid-morning.

Bobby had just lugged in a big wicker-basketful of sun-dried clothing from the lines in the back yard. She now put up the ironing board and began to sprinkle the garments that needed dampening.

Bernice said, "Maybe I'll go down there 'safternoon and pick up some of them. Japanese cherry blossoms are nice. They make it look like spring all year, and you can't hardly tell 'em from the real thing. A couple dollars' worth'd do it, I bet."

"A couple dollars!" said Bobby. "That'd feed us the better part of a week." She dipped her fingers in the soup bowl that held the water and flicked them at a shirt of Jack's that lay in that peculiar rumple of sun-dried clothes, which was altogether different from that of clothing rumpled by wear or, again, neglect. Bobby was a real journeyman in the craft of keeping house. She rolled up the shirt and began to flick water on another. "I'm sure Dad would understand, up there." She looked at the ceiling. Though she wasn't really sure he would hear her words as such, she knew that wherever he might be, he was aware of her: you couldn't dismiss all those years of marriage merely by dying.

"We have to watch our pennies now, Bernice. That insurance won't take care of much more than the mortgage for a year or two." She had made the same statement morning, day, and night ever since the funeral, and though both the boys had taken it to heart (though neither was ever extravagant in the old days), and Tony now had that Saturday job—Bernice gave no evidence of having been affected by it in the least. Not a day went by without her suggesting some new expenditure.

"Well, I sure wish I could help," Bernice said. "But with this one on the way"—she patted her stomach, which thus far was perfectly flat—"I got my work cut out for me. I got to build up my strength." She had apparently retained some smoke inhaled earlier, for it all came out now, in pale blue, from her nose and mouth.

"Then you better not go downtown," said her mother, "and have to dodge those trolleycars and fire trucks and police cars and swallow a lot of fumes. They always make me sick to my stomach."

"You sure got a hick's idea of the city," Bernice said, and then lifted the bottle and poured some of its contents down her throat. Bobby wondered where she had picked up this unladylike style. "You don't notice stuff like 'at when you're used to the big town," Bernice went on, having swallowed and burped. She polished off the rest of the bottle and got to her feet. "Maybe I'll just go down and do some winda-shopping. Better'n sitting around here all day. And Ernie can't make it for lunch today. His mother wants him home. He's gotta fix something." She sighed sulkily.

"Well," said Bobby, "it's sure your personal business, Bernice, but I believe Miz Krum will have to find out some-day. Whatcha gonna do when the baby comes?"

"Oh, Ernie's gonna tell her any day now. He's working her up to it by degrees." Bernice lifted her shoulders and let them fall. "Well, I guess I'll take a bath, anyway." She was still in her pajamas, under a satin dressing gown some-what the worse for wear. She shuffled to the dining-room doorway in her runover mules, then turned back. "Maybe he could come over for supper, though. He gets out some-times to go down the firehouse for a stag evening, you know, to play cards and have a few brews. Maybe he would come over here for supper for a change. . . . Say, Mama, coont you make something else for a change but a casserole? Some nice baked ham, maybe? Or fried chicken?"

Bobby sighed deeply. "Bernice, I just wish you would think about—"

Her daughter threw up her hands and howled, "O.K., O.K."

When Bobby had finished dampening all the clothes, it was a quarter after eleven, and she had no food on hand for the boys when they came home from school for lunch, so she took off the apron she wore even when doing clean housework, fetched her purse, and went down the street to Wessel's little corner grocery. Bernice was still in the tub, she knew, because every now and again she could hear the faucet running as her daughter warmed up the water. Luckily she had the wash all done early, for there wouldn't have been enough hot water for the machine had Bernice been soaking at the same time. A new hot-water tank had been on the list of improvements Dolf made from time to time and shared with her as they undressed for bed. For some reason, that was his favorite time for discussing such subjects. That had never seemed at all odd when he was alive, but now she saw that some people might have found it so. He had got around to realizing few of the projects he had mentioned over the years, and maybe that was just as well, for look what had happened when at long last he was ready to strip the paint from that old dresser which she suspected might be, underneath it all, solid walnut. As a result, the last few days of his life had been unhappy ones, and it was a really unfortunate coincidence that his death came at that moment rather than at one of the many times when he had been satisfied with his lot.

At Wessel's, Bobby bought a couple of cans of soup— Tony would put away one all by himself—a pound and a half of baloney, a big hunk of rat-trap cheese, and a loaf of unwrapped rye bread with a nice shiny crust.

Wessel, a short, bald-headed man with a brushy gray mustache, wrapped these items in brown paper and put them in a bag. He pushed it across the counter.

"Say, Bobby," said he, not meeting her eyes, "with all your troubles and all, I didn't want to to mention it, but, uh, your bill is running real high, uh, and I was wondering if . . ." He cleared his throat. "See, maybe I should of . . . well, the fact is, Bernice is charging quite a bit of beer and cigarettes and potato chips, salted peanuts—?"

Bobby had lifted the bag. Now she lowered it to the scarred but polished counter. "She's been putting the beer on the tab?"

"That's right," said Wessel. "I first just thought it was O.K. You know, it seems like yesterday you used to send her down here when she was just a kid, to pick up something you forgot, sweet pickles or mustard or—"

"That was a long time back," Bobby said. If she thought about those days she would cry all over him. "I'm sorry, Alf. I never knew. You better not do that any more. And if you're getting worried about the bill, I'll take care of it 'safternoon, if that's O.K.?"

"Aw, listen, Bobby," said Wessel, with his sad eyes, "I didn't mention it for that reason. I just thought you ought to know. You pay me when you can. I ain't in no hurry."

Bobby realized she was going to have to come to a showdown with her daughter, and when she got home she left the groceries in the kitchen and wearily climbed the stairs to the second floor.

But Bernice had gone, leaving a wet towel on the bathroom floor, a soap-ring inside the tub, a smeared mirror, and, in her bedroom, dirty clothes all over the place.

Bobby went downstairs. Passing through the dining

room, she saw on the sideboard something that had escaped her notice when she went by in the other direction: a piece of paper, propped against the base of a glass candlestick, a stiff piece of paper, firm enough to withstand the air currents put in motion by the movement of a woman as large as she. The sheet was imprinted with lines and at the upper righthand corner projected a tab that showed the letters XYZ. This was more of Bernice's work. For her notepaper she had torn out the last page of the telephone-address book that Bobby had used for years. True, it was the least-used.

The penciled note was neatly written. Maybe she had taken that page so that she could follow its lines.

> Momma the bath brought IT on finnaly! See I was late and thought You Know What, which accounts for Ernie & all. Who I never even dated before, my Gosh. Well! I don't see anny sense in waiting around here all day every day for that momma's boy to show up, so have decided to go back to the city anyways it'll be one less mouth to feed now poor Daddys gone. As I am temporly out of funds I hope you don't mind I took the silver cream & sugar (which you never use) and will hock it till I get on my feet again. Think I can get an anulment since we weren't intimate. Yr loving d,
>
> Bernice

Chief Clive Shell finally returned to the Millville police station on Saturday morning. His eye still showed some discoloration from the shiner. Ray Dooley secretly wondered whether Shell's wife, a battle-ax named Mamie, had given it to him. Ray himself was pretty bitter, having had to stay away from his job at the plant, for which absence he would be docked, losing money, for the factory paid more than the police, and every time he tried to settle down to catch a nap, somebody would claim to have seen a mad dog foaming at the mouth, or a guy would want him to come and ticket a neighbor's car that was blocking the driveway. And then the one important event, the only major money-crime ever attempted in Millville, so far as anyone could recall, had occurred while he was getting the only sound sleep he had had, and was dealt with by a person (furthermore pretty much of a nut) who had no official connection with the police, and in fact none whatsoever, as it turned out, with the railroad, as Ray discovered when he tried to report Reverton Kirby's death to them. At first he could find nobody at the Hamburg yard who had ever heard of him, but finally somebody came on the phone and said, "I believe there's some little gent of that name lives onna top floor of the Roundhouse Hotel. He don't look exactly like a bum, but so far as I know he don't do no work of any description." This information Ray thought better of sharing with Clive Shell, who was mad enough without it.

"By God, Ray, if you wasn't married to my sister, I don't know! God Almighty, you was sleeping at the switch during the only bank robbery in the history of Millville?"

"Thing is, Clive, how the devil could I know when it was going to take place?" He had explained ten or twelve times that Reverton had been instructed to wake him in an emergency, but Clive rejected that excuse, nor did he look kindly on Ray's expedition into Hornbeck to rescue Junior Bullard. He suspected Harvey Yelton would score it as a personal triumph. Nor, though he liked Bud well enough, did he think his son worth saving.

"Mark my words, that little pup will be going to the pen sooner or later," said Clive. "If anybody finds dog shit smeared on their porch steps at Halloween or a dirty Kotex in the mailbox, it'll be the work of Junior Bullard. You know that. He's the nastiest kid in town. He always has been. He's got some kinda grudge against the human race. You remember last summer when somebody busted in the chemistry lab at the high school and stole some acid and poured it all over the classroom next door?"

"There wasn't any real proof it was Junior, though," said Ray, though he personally had no doubts. "I just feel sorry for Bud 'n' Frieda, is all. Especially the other night, with Bud laid up and the fire and all."

"You can cover up just so much," Clive said sanctimoniously, and then he grinned in malice. "You know what I'd do if I was able: I'd throw the little bastard over the Hornbeck line and let Yelton deal with him permanent. You know, what do they call it, exile, like the Russians with Siberia."

Ray wasn't any too sure about this reference. Clive once in a while read a city newspaper—as Ray's wife, the chief's own sister, said, "if he found one somebody threw away"— and he was inclined to show off what he read there, while being in reality the most ignorant man Ray had ever known.

Nevertheless Ray laughed diplomatically. It would be to his advantage if Clive got distracted by his hatred of Yelton. "Yep, Harvey wouldn't thankya for that."

Clive's big nose twitched. "He'd prefer the little Bullard girl. Little kids is what he likes, you know. In any other town he'd be arrested as a sex fiend. How'd you like him patrolling a schoolyard where your little daughter was playing jacks?"

Ray really felt guilty in being a part of this character assassination, and anyway he hoped to get away before the bank robbery came back as the conversational subject, so he moved toward the door, saying, "I guess I'll be—"

Clive said, "Just a minute. Joo check the Wanted circular for any rewards offered for this Reno Fox? You know, Kirby was what you call *in facto* a deputy police officer of this department. Remember to say that if anyone asks. Which means any and all rewards are payable to the Millville Police Department."

"Of course you don't mean the one the bank is paying?" asked Ray. "Bud Bullard's getting that one as Reverton's next-of-kin."

"I be damn," said Clive, striking his desk with two extended fingers. "I'm gonna look into that."

Ray said quickly, "I think public opinion'd be on the other side, Clive. You know, your term comes up for renewal next spring."

Shell made a disgruntled face. "You're a real crapehanger, ain't you. And it's all your fault this ever come up inna first place. A police officer don't sleep on the job! Which means he ain't ever caught, anyhow." He pushed his chair back and stood up. "You been here all week, you can stay a little while more, while I go down the bakery and get myself a sweet roll or somepin. I missed breakfast this morning. The little lady's under the weather."

Ray was desperate to get home. "Whyn't I run down inna cruiser and get it for you?"

Clive grimaced. "Because I wanna pick it out myself. I like them carmel rolls with the nuts on 'em, but that Dutchman don't always have them fresh but maybe a day or two old, and he'll try to put them over on you. I might take an apple turnover instead—unless all of them are stale too." He smirked proudly. "He wouldn't let anybody else bite into something and then turn it down."

Ray was always being surprised by new ways in which Clive managed to throw his weight around.

* * *

On Tony's arrival at the bakery the Dutchman gave him a white apron and overseas cap, just like those he himself wore. After sweeping out the shop, Tony cleared from the showcases all the pastry which his employer pronounced too stale to sell at the regular price. Some of this was placed on a table in the corner. No sign or label was posted, because the status of the day-old goods was presumably self-evident to the customers. Then some of the stalest cake and bread was taken in back to be transformed into crumbs, for certain uses on the premises (for example, crumb-cake) or to be bagged and sold at retail. Finally, the Dutchman made a selection to be given to a maiden lady who was coming around from the old folks' home, which was situated in the unincorporated area south of Millville. He assured Tony that these products could be revived by being sprinkled with water and run through a warm oven. It was a revelation to Tony that the public good could be served in a bakery.

After the cases were emptied, he washed them with soapy water and then in clear and dried them with clean rags. Then he and the baker filled all the shelves therein with loaves, rolls, cakes, muffins, cupcakes, cookies, and other items in various sizes and textures and flavors.

Just before eight the Dutchman's wife came down from upstairs, where they lived, and opened the shop for business. She was a rosy-cheeked woman, and she wore an apron so white it almost hurt your eyes to look at it. Her hair was pinned up under a round white cap.

Her husband introduced Tony, but not vice versa, and as yet Tony had not even learned the baker's own name, so he just called her "Ma'am." She instructed him to make sure his hands were clean at all times, and that if something fell to the floor he was to clean it up immediately with dust brush and pan, and if it landed icing-down he was to fetch a wet sponge, and after anything of this kind he must wash his hands. And of course if he went to "wash his hands," he must wash his hands thereafter: he immediately understood this to mean if he went *to the toilet*.

The Dutchman at last concluded his own tasks and went upstairs to sleep till the middle of the afternoon. The other bakers were already gone when Tony got there at seven. It was an unusual profession, but a very interesting, clean, and fragrant one, and Tony was looking forward to following it for the rest of his life.

Customers began to arrive, and while the Dutchman's wife got first choice of them, whenever more than one was on hand Tony stepped in and filled the orders and even accepted the money, though if change was needed he waited for the woman to make it at the cash register. But soon enough, during the occasional lull, she began to give him lessons in the operation of that machine and predicted that before long he would be proficient at it.

Not long after ten the Dutchman's wife said she had to run upstairs to her kitchen to check on the pot roast she had put to simmer, and if any customer came in meanwhile with whom Tony needed help, she would be back in a minute.

She lingered for a moment and smiled maternally upon him. "You're a real good worker. I bet your folks are proud of you." She didn't have a special accent and seemed a real American.

"My dad passed away the other day. I hope it ain't too long before I can work full-time. We could use the money."

"I'm real sorry to hear that, Tony." The baker's wife shook her head in sympathy. She looked as if she might have hugged him to her thick bosom if she had known

him only a little better. "You got a tough row to hoe. I
don't know, I think he's got everybody he can use right
now back in the bakery, and I can handle it out here. We
ain't getting rich on this business. But gee, I sure will ask
him for you, I really will." She turned toward the door that
led upstairs, but then turned back. "Listen, if nobody
comes in while I'm gone, you help yourself to a doughnut
or cupcake or something nice. Just put it down where they
can't see it if a customer comes in, because it don't look
good. And if you lick the icing off your fingers, be sure
and wash your hands." Her broad back went through the
door.

Tony's mother had made him a larger breakfast than
usual for his first day on the new job, rolled oats, flapjacks,
and so on, and after being on the premises for several hours
he did not find the aroma of the baked goods as seductive
as it had been on his arrival, but he believed he was hardly
in a position to pass up an offer of free food. He looked
down through the glass tops of the cases. Doughnuts were
not attractive to him, the memory of Eva Bullard being
too recent: he had avoided thinking of what he would do
if she ever came into the shop while he was on duty. He
was no brooder over past unpleasantnesses and no worrier
about personal problems that might or might not be on
the horizon. The way it had worked out, with the death
of his father, he wouldn't have been able to give Eva the
attention she deserved, anyway, and he suspected that she
was too young, along with being of the wrong sex, to understand what it meant to be the man of the family.

There was a little scalloped-edge tart that looked good,
with a filling that seemed to be of cherry jam. A row of
these was nearest the front glass, just beyond a rank of
similar pastries filled with pineapple. But first came a high

lemon-meringue pie, which he might well graze with his forearm in reaching way out to the tart. He removed the pie and placed it on the flat top of the case, alongside a tray of blueberry muffins displayed there.

He had bent again and was reaching for the cherry tart when the front door opened, disqualifying him temporarily from having the treat. When he straightened up he was looking at the cop he had punched the week before. The eye still showed the yellowish remains of the bruise.

The funny but fortunate thing, however, was that the policeman seemed to have made no identification of *him*. In fact he was ignoring Tony altogether in favor of the baked goods in the case before them.

"Them turnovers look mighty good 'smorning." The cop bent and pointed. "Apple or cherry?"

As it happened, Tony didn't know. "It's my first day here," he said. "I better wait till she comes back down."

"Don't matter all that much, I guess," said the cop. "Either one's' good, but I like to know what I'm putting my teeth into." He began to beat a rhythm against the glass with the point of his index finger. "Sure looks like a leetle bitta red juice is leaking from that there one. You can't see it from in back. Come around here and take a look."

Tony did as asked: he went around the counter, and just as he was bending over to look into the case, the cop seized his right wrist, yanked it painfully up into the small of his back, and crowed, his mouth at Tony's ear, "Gotcha, you stinker!" He forced the arm higher. "On your knees, you little mutt."

But to have obeyed the command would have been to hurt his arm even more, for the cop continued to exert an upward pressure on it. Therefore Tony spun on his feet, turning toward his enemy, and as he did so he picked up the lemon meringue pie with his left hand and smashed it, over his shoulder, into the policeman's face.

Eyes and nose covered with goo, the cop fell back and let him go. Tony was out of apron and cap before he reached the door, and he dropped them behind him. Too bad: there went a beautiful career! He raced through the back alleys and side streets until he had put many blocks between him and the scene of his latest crime, and before long he was back in good old Hornbeck, which he realized he had been a fool ever to leave.

Harvey Yelton was on routine patrol in the cruiser when he saw just the fellow he had had on his mind the last couple of days. He pulled up in the gutter, opened the right-hand window, leaned across, and said, "Hey, Tony. Get in."

This invitation, even when given benevolently, made any civilian nervous, and Harvey, even when benevolent, didn't mind: respect for the power of the law could never be too great.

When Tony got himself seated, Harvey said, "I'm real sorry about your dad. You know, him and me went through school together—well, as far as either of us ever went, I mean. I never made it to high school. He might of, I don't remember."

"Huh-uh," said Tony, shaking his head.

"Well, he was sure a swell guy. Know what we used to call 'im? Beeler the Peeler. 'Cause he got a real bad sunburn oncet and his hide come off in sheets. That's why we gave him the name. . . . Not to change the subject, but I been thinking, I'm not getting any younger my own self. We could all go any minute, you know. It just ain't right for me not to have a relief man of some kind on this job. By God, the Council'll find money for every other thing, painting the mayor's office, buying themselves new chairs, putting up Welcome to Hornbeck signs on all the roads into town, but they don't gimme a part-time patrolman. I ain't gonna take it any more. Over in Millville that fat slob's not only got Ray Dooley, but when the bank was robbed other day, there was even some other guy on duty. Fact is, he's the man got himself killed." Harvey turned and looked out his own window for a moment, and then he came back to Tony.

"Your mom said you was going to be eighteen soon."

"Next month."

"You wanna work for me? Come on after school for a couple hours, and then maybe some of the weekend?" Tony seemed dumfounded. Harvey said, "I don't know what they would pay. They might try to take it out of my salary, but they'll shit too."

Tony finally said, "This is some surprise."

Harvey winced. He said, "You know, me and the missus never had any kids of our own. Her health was always too delicate, see. So I ain't got any of my own flesh and blood to pass anything on to. I mean, what I learned on this job year in and out for the last twenny. This here's the place to find out about people, boy. It's a lot better'n a college education."

"Yes, sir," said Tony. "You think you could tell my mom it would be O.K. for me to quit school right now?"

"Women are funny, you know," said Harvey. "They'll generally try to keep you all tied up in something that ain't practical, particularly if it's supposed to improve your mind or character, like church or school and so on. Did you ever hear of one who wanted you to fight or go hunting or play poker or anything? Women always wanna *keep you from* doing the things you want to do." He sighed. "But maybe God made 'em that way to see us boys don't go all to hell in a handbasket. Sure I'll talk to her." He put out his hand. "Deal?"

Tony blinked behind his glasses. "Yeah, I sure would like to be a policeman." He shook on it with Harvey.

Harvey always had had a special feeling for Tony, whether or not he was his real dad.

On several of the nights following the death of his father, Jack had been having those dreams which give you the second chance that reality does not allow. In the dreams his dad was still alive but threatening to die if Jack did not change his ways and begin to do more things his father approved of, like giving up reading and daydreaming and taking up sports. So he would get himself a football uniform, helmet, and shoes, and be jogging along on his way to his dad's bedside—then he would wake up, and nothing was changed.

He hadn't ever been much interested in his living father, but he realized that what he had always had in the back of his mind was eventually getting to know him better when he, Jack, was somewhat older and more settled. There was no longer any possibility of this. He certainly did not think that his father had been given two heart attacks in succession by reason of anything *he* had done. On the other hand, he did have a certain suspicion that his father's life might have been prolonged had he been more satisfactory as a son.

Without explaining why he was doing it, Jack had therefore asked his brother if in Tony's opinion he could make the football team if he trained all year under Tony's supervision and went out the following fall.

Tony shook his head. "You're awful light, Jack."

"I was thinking of something like quarterback. They're small guys usually, aren't they?"

"Only because the linemen are bigger, I guess," Tony said. "They're not all that little, and I never seen any as light as you. I wouldn't want to see you hurt. How could you be a foreign correspondent if your hands got too broke up to pound a typewriter?"

No doubt Tony meant well, but one had to make certain decisions oneself in this world of ours, and when his brother wasn't around to discourage him Jack went out to the garage with the intention of beginning secretly to work out with Tony's weights until he was a mountain of muscle.

He started with the dumbbells as currently set up, which turned out to be forty pounds each, and he was unable to lift either one and in fact could hardly budge one at a time using both hands. He found the little wrench and reduced each dumbbell to but a five-pound disc on each end, but ten pounds per hand was still too heavy for him, and he could not find any lighter weights among Tony's supply.

He decided that it was impractical to try to be what he wasn't: he might only, as Tony suggested, ruin himself for what he really could do, and then his father would have scarcely been pleased to see him play football badly. If on the other hand he became a famous foreign correspondent he would bring glory to the name of Beeler and make a lot of money with which to support his mother, and for that matter help out Bernice and Tony too if need be.

The other decision he made was (even though, with Bernice's latest departure, he had regained his room) not to wait endlessly each night for Mary Catherine Lutz to undress. The last time he had done that, it turned out that she never appeared at all, having either gone to bed at an unusually early hour or spent the night away from home. He had stayed on his vigil till almost half-past twelve. He had been making a fool of himself. He never saw much anyway: nothing bare at all, just her in her slip, after which she would go into a closet and then come out in pajamas in which you couldn't see the difference between her and a boy.

But since that had been his entire life's sex life, he tried to think of something more decent, more dignified, with which to replace it. He was also lonely in general, for Dickie Herkimer seemed to have faded out and as yet no candidates had appeared for the role of best friend. Perhaps he was simply getting older: more hair was growing in his armpits and around his private parts, and he believed that his voice was getting deeper, though it was still not the rich bass he was hoping to acquire.

He had not forgotten about the young people's group at the Millville church, to which the fat preacher had invited him and at which he had hoped to meet the clear-faced girl with the big breasts, but enjoying oneself was hardly the thing to do when your father had just died. Nor for several weeks did he follow his inveterate practice, instituted as far back as the seventh grade, of attending the Sunday afternoon matinee at the Hornbeck movie house. He had every intention of going through the remainder of his life without any pleasure, and so to atone for all the times he had displeased his father, and at mealtimes he made every effort to eat heartily.

But finally the Sunday dinner came when his mother said, "You polish off your gingerbread and then why don't you go to the picture show this afternoon? We've got to get back to normal around here."

"Aw," Jack said, "we can't afford it."

"We can afford fifteen cents."

They were in the dining room, just as in the days when his father was alive. Tony sat across from him, wearing, as he usually did these days even when he wasn't on duty, his royal-blue epauleted policeman's shirt, with a navy necktie.

With this he wore the regular pants from his civilian blue-serge suit. He could not afford to buy a real policeman's coat yet, so for outdoor duty he wore a sweater underneath the shirt and Harvey Yelton's extra cap, for they had the same head size. Tony was what was called a provisional patrolman, and his pay was ten dollars per week.

Tony now reached into his pocket and produced a nickel, which he handed across the table to his brother. "Get yourself some candy afterwards."

Jack realized that to turn it down would not be in good form, but he was not entirely happy with the change he had begun to see in his brother, who since becoming a cop was also getting to be something of a stuffed shirt. For example he now proceeded to echo their mother.

"I hope you're not gonna leave all that gingerbread."

Jack said, "Maybe I could put it away for later." He had used up all his appetite, and then some, in swallowing the meatloaf, mashed potatoes, lima beans, and stewed tomatoes.

Tony beckoned to him and said briskly, "O.K."

"What?"

Tony said impatiently, "You want me to eat it or not?"

"Oh." He seemed to think Jack should be a mind-reader. Jack handed the gingerbread over.

Their mother said, "Bring me my pocketbook. It's on the kitchen cabinet." Jack did as told, and she went inside it, got out her change purse, and found fifteen cents for him. "Better get going if you want to make the picture on time."

He glanced at the clock on the sideboard. "You're sure it's all right?"

"You mean, can we afford it?" She nodded. "We'll be doing a little better now, Jack. There's Tony with his job, and then I rented out the back room."

For a moment Jack had the crazy idea that an extra room had been discovered in the house. But then he asked, "You mean my room?"

She avoided his eyes. "Well, it really was Bernice's, wasn't it? Whenever she came home she always got it. And then Tony says you always like to be back in there with him."

So this was news only to the younger son! Not only did Tony already know about it, but it might have been his own idea.

Jack was about to leave when Tony said, self-importantly, "I might seeya down the theeyater later on. I might drop around there. I don't need a ticket, you know. They're glad to have you if you're in uniform: it has a good effect. Harvey told me the kids been getting rambunctious on Sundays, lately."

"Maybe I'll see you then," Jack said, hoping the prediction would not come true. He would consider it pretty embarrassing to be seen in such a place with a policeman brother, not long after Halloween had been banned from Hornbeck.

As it happened, if Tony did appear at the theater, Jack failed to see him. Nor did he spot anyone else to whom he was or had been a close friend, though he recognized the Hornbeck kids who were as old as he or older. The movie was a really good one, being about the British in India and having almost all male characters and very little of a love story. It concluded with a tremendous charge by thousands of swarthy mounted men, assaulting a handful of English soldiers standing calmly in a square formation. The latter held their own for a while but were gradually falling away despite having downed enemies too numerous to count. Undoubtedly the white men would have been wiped out had not the British cavalry arrived, pennons flying, through a hitherto secret pass in the mountains.

Jack was always transformed by a picture that so held his attention, and whenever he afterward emerged from the theater onto the main street of downtown Hornbeck he invariably felt somewhat dizzy for a few moments and then pretty depressed.

The day was becoming cooler as the wind picked up. He lifted the collar of his jacket and fastened the top button. It was not the weather for pith helmets and khaki tunics. He was debating whether to spend Tony's nickel at the nearby candy store, which was jammed at the moment, or to return the money to his brother and so gain a moral victory of a kind, when he saw Her, the girl from the hospital coffee shop. For God's sake, he had never expected that. And at first he had no idea of how to go about meeting her or what to say, but walking behind her vigorous stride for a block or two—she was alone, like him—it eventually occurred to him that the obvious would be appropriate.

Therefore he quickened his pace until he was even with her on the sidewalk, and he said, "Hi. I saw you at the hospital a couple of weeks ago, I think. In the coffee shop?"

He noticed the blue of her eyes as they grew smaller in a smile. "It probably was, because my father was there. But he's better now."

"Mine died."

She looked carefully at him. "You serious?"

"Yeah."

"Huh. It must be lousy not to have a father."

He realized that the statement was well intentioned. "Yeah. . . . Do you go to those young people's things at your church?"

She raised her eyebrows. "How'd you know about that? I've been once or twice, but I was embarrassed whenever my brother showed up. I hate to be anywhere he is."

"Oh yeah?" It seemed they already had something in common.

"He always gets in trouble, is why," said she. "But he's run away from home now, so it would be O.K. I guess. If he shows up again, my dad swears he will beat him up and then have him thrown in jail. I might go to the young people's with my cousin."

Jack didn't like the sound of that. "How old's he?"

"*She.* She's almost fifteen. She's really good-looking. She's got this long dark curly hair."

"I guess that's nice," said Jack. "But I prefer a lighter color. Not exactly blond, you know, but kinda—"

She looked at the pavement, her cheek coloring slightly. "Like mine?"

"More or less."

"You've got quite a line," said she.

"What's that mean?"

"That you'd say anything to a girl."

He frowned. "I would just say what I thought."

"Well," said she, "I happen to be going steady with someone quite a bit older."

Jack stopped walking. They had almost reached the Millville line. He said, "It was nice knowing you." He had turned when she spoke.

"I was only kidding."

He came back. "Or are you kidding now?"

"Take a guess."

This was awfully silly, and he wouldn't have been able to admit it to another soul, but he found her the most attractive person he had ever met in his life. He accompanied her on into Millville, and they exchanged good-natured wisecracks all the way to her house, where, on the front sidewalk, she suddenly punched him in the stomach. Then she ran up the driveway and disappeared around the corner of the garage.

Having followed, he discovered that the structure backed up against the chicken-wire fence of the neighbor in the rear. She therefore must have gone inside through the pedestrian door. He opened that door and stepped inside. No car was there, but a shallow pool of black oil lay in the middle of the floor. She was standing very rigidly in a corner, her spine pressed into the joint between the rough, unpainted wooden walls. He was careful to avoid the oil as he came to her.

He put his hands at her waist. She brought hers to cover his. She closed her eyes and breathed deeply, then opened them to display an impudent glint.

"Boy," she said, "you just think you can get away with anything, don't you?" She lifted his hands and put them on her breasts, the first he had ever felt. She said, "You've got all the nerve in the world."

He could hardly breathe.

She asked, smiling as if across a great distance, "What's your name, anyhow?"

He told her.

She howled, "Oh, no!" But she didn't take his hands away.

"What's yours?"

"Eva."

"Eva what?"

"You'll find out soon enough when my parents come home!" She brought her face so close to his that they seemed to be breathing the same air. She had very sweet breath. She said, "My dad will probably murder you. But I don't expect them back till suppertime."

"Well, what *is* your name?"

She grinned, her face still close to his. "Bullard!"

He stepped back. "I'll be darn."

"A real coincidence, huh?" Eva stepped forward, to close the distance he had made between them.

Jack asked, "Are we supposed to hate each other?"

"I don't *know*." This was a kind of squeal. She was grinning more than ever.

"What's the joke?"

"It's only that I used to go out with your brother. . . . What's the matter? Don't you believe me?"

He began to back slowly away. "I think I better be going."

She made a provocative expression, almost but not quite sticking out her tongue at him. "Are you scared he will be jealous or something?"

"Tony? Naw . . . He's a cop now, you know. He doesn't have any time for . . ." So it was this girl to whom Jack had unwittingly almost written that letter. He decided it would be bad taste to reveal to her that Tony had lately been talking about getting engaged to Mary Catherine Lutz.

Eva stopped stalking him. She stayed where she was and asked, "What's wrong with you, then?"

He tried to think up a good answer, for himself as well as for her, but the best he could come up with was, "I guess I don't want to get in any trouble that would jeopardize my profession."

"*Profession?* You're just a kid."

"Yeah, well . . ." He had backed all the way to the open doorway now. "Maybe I'll see you at the movies next Sunday?" That would be on his own ground, in Hornbeck. He stepped backwards over the threshold.

She followed him to the doorway, her hands joined behind her back. Her breasts looked fantastic. She answered, "Not if I see you first."

Yet he did look for Eva at the movies on subsequent Sundays, but when he finally spotted her again she was accompanied by a Millville boy. Jack suspected he had made a mistake that day in the garage, and he still regretted it, as men do, many years later, though by then he was filing dispatches from the other side of the world.